All Her Little Lies

All Her Little Lies

Becca Day

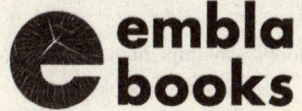

First published in Great Britain in 2022 by

Bonnier Books UK Limited
4th Floor, Victoria House, Bloomsbury Square, London, WC1B 4DA
Owned by Bonnier Books
Sveavägen 56, Stockholm, Sweden

Copyright © Becca Day, 2022

All rights reserved.
No part of this publication may be reproduced, stored or transmitted in any form or by any means, electronic, mechanical, photocopying or otherwise, without the prior written permission of the publisher.

The right of Becca Day to be identified as Author of this work has been asserted by them in accordance with the Copyright, Designs and Patents Act 1988

This is a work of fiction. Names, places, events and incidents are either the products of the author's imagination or used fictitiously. Any resemblance to actual persons, living or dead, is purely coincidental.

A CIP catalogue record for this book is available from the British Library.

ISBN: 9781471415456

This book is typeset using Atomik ePublisher

Printed and bound in Great Britain by Clays Ltd, Elcograf S.p.A.

Embla Books is an imprint of Bonnier Books UK
www.bonnierbooks.co.uk

For Élise and Evie

PROLOGUE

ALEX

It sounds like I'm underwater. There is a rushing in my ears and the distinct sense of them needing to pop. I suck in a breath and realise I'm not underwater; I'm wading out of a deep sleep, my senses slowly returning to me. The high-pitched screech of pigs echoes through the barn. That's the only way I can tell where I am, that and the sharp bite of manure. But I can't see anything yet. My eyes are still firmly clamped shut, and no matter how hard I struggle to open them, I can't quite manage it.

I let out a groan as I lift a weak hand to my head. Dried blood flakes away onto my fingers. Suddenly, it all comes rushing back to me. My eyes snap open and I jolt into consciousness with a gasp. My sight is still blurred from the impact to my head. Dark spots dance across my vision any time I try to focus. I try to ignore the throbbing at the back of my skull, instead concentrating on what else I can feel. My back propped up against one of the barn walls, my legs stretched out before me, and something else. Something cutting into the skin of my ankles and wrists.

I'm tied up.

The realisation sends my blood running cold, my pulse racing.

'Help!' My scream returns to me again and again, bouncing off the wooden walls and, beyond that, the vast empty fields surrounding us. I know what's out there. Nothing. We are alone here. No one for miles and miles.

Fear surging through me, I instinctively squirm against my restraints and a soft click sounds as the cable ties tighten a notch. I freeze, press myself back into the wall, try to centre myself and slow my erratic breathing. I need to stay calm. Panicking will only make things worse.

Stay calm, Alex. Stay calm. The mantra replays over and over in my mind, but I'm not sure how much good it's doing. I can feel my blood pressure rising, an incessant thumping in my ears as if I've been dunked into a swimming pool. I'm already struggling to see; the last thing I need is to lose my hearing too.

I swallow hard and my ears pop. With it comes the return of the footsteps, slower now, edging towards me. My back arches, as if by pushing hard enough I might be able to burst through the barn wall and escape that way, but of course I have nowhere to go. I blink rapidly. The black spots are still there, but I can see beyond them now. I can see the figure looming over me, the outline of the rifle they're gripping.

'You don't want to do this,' I say, and immediately chastise myself for how terrified I sound, how severely my voice is trembling. I mustn't let on how scared I am. It'll be seen as a weakness. 'If you kill me, they'll know it was you. You know that, right?'

My breath catches in my throat as I wait for a response. This is my only play. My one chance to survive this.

CHAPTER ONE

ALEX

The Day of the Murder

'This is nice.' I swirl my red wine around my glass before placing the rim to my lips and taking a sip. 'It's been ages since we last hung out.'

Cynthia glances down at her lap and I feel a twinge of awkwardness, like I've said something wrong. My face burns. It really has been ages. Ever since Cynthia's mum passed and left the farm to her, things have been weird between us. I suppose we're still trying to figure out this new employer–employee relationship that's been thrust upon us. Cynthia isn't used to bossing me around. If anything, it's always been the reverse.

She must sense the unease in the air as much as I do, because she gives herself a little shake and tops up her own glass before offering the bottle to me.

'I know, I'm so sorry, Alex. It's just been mental, you know.'

I nod and pour the last few droplets of wine into my glass. I don't really know, but I can imagine. My job as farm manager is fairly simple. Get up, tend to the animals, make sure everyone knows if they're on crops or livestock duty, rinse and repeat. The paperwork side of the farm has always eluded me. I suppose I'm not particularly business-minded, not like Cynthia.

A shiver runs through me as a breeze picks up, and I shuffle closer to the firepit. The crackling and the woody smell evoke memories of simpler times. We used to spend most evenings huddled around it during our teenage years. It was our place to share the woes of annoying parents, to rate boys and scoff biscuits stolen from the high kitchen cupboard. It seems simultaneously like only yesterday and an eternity ago. The flicker illuminates the exterior of the farmhouse in such a picturesque way, like something out of an oil painting, highlighting the crevices of the old brick and plunging the surrounding fields into darkness. The only sign of life around us is the song of crickets amongst the grass and the lights from my house over on the far end of the farm.

Jase is working late again, so Daniel must have got home from his shift at the pub without my noticing. I stupidly feel rather guilty about sitting out here socialising while Daniel is home alone, even though, at nineteen, he's basically an adult now and more than capable of being on his own for a few hours. Jase has told me time and time again that I need to stop being such a worrier when it comes to our son, but that's easy for him to say. The accident never affected Jase in the way it did me.

My fingers twitch and I brush my hand over the scarred skin on my forearm, forcing my eyes away from the house and back to Cynthia. The fire illuminates her as well, her long lashes casting stripy shadows across her cheeks and her blonde hair shimmering. She looks so much like her daughter.

'How's Hannah coming along with her uni choice?'

Cynthia stiffens. This has been a sore subject for a while now. 'She's still not made a decision. She wants to take a gap year but she's not even travelling or planning on doing anything useful with her time. I think she's been a little distracted lately.'

'Distracted how?'

There's a pause while Cynthia pulls her cardigan tighter around herself and swigs the remainder of her wine.

'Oh, you know,' she says eventually. 'The never-ending problems of a teenage girl. Still, at least she's actually considering university. More than I can say about her brother.'

She purses her lips, bends down and balances her empty wine glass on the uneven ground. I consider offering to go and grab another bottle from my place but decide it's probably best not to. She's restricted herself to just the two glasses; ever the responsible mother. I, meanwhile, have made no such promise, but it's probably wise for Cynthia to stop drinking before she ventures past tipsy. I can always tell she's getting there from her body language, the way she starts retreating in on herself, just like she used to when we were underage teenagers sneaking cans of cider behind the pig barn. Once she gets past tipsy she always becomes sad Cynthia, mulling over things and moping about how underwhelming she finds her life.

She never wanted to own the farm. She wanted to be a designer, fashion or interiors perhaps. Farming was always my thing, my dream ever since I took the job as poo sweeper aged sixteen. She got plunged into it when her mum got ill, and now I think she only stays out of a sense of obligation. I think she knows there's some resentment on my part that I wasn't left in charge, especially after all my years of service, but blood runs thicker than water. I know that.

'Bradley still not decided what he wants to do?' I ask.

She doesn't try to hide her smirk. 'He'll be working at the Co-op for the rest of his life, guarantee it.'

'Mmm, that's boys for you. Daniel's just as bad. I had hoped he might pick up some good habits from Hannah, but it's as if having an overachieving girlfriend has given him a chance to slack off even more!'

I let out a laugh but trail off as I realise I'm the only one laughing. Cynthia's face is pulled into a scowl, her eyes fixed on the fire, the flames reflected in her glassy eyes.

'What's the matter?'

Her eyes flick back up to me and she shakes her head. 'Nothing. It's nothing.'

'Cynth, it's me. What's wrong?'

I wince, the words sounding strange on my tongue. Had this been a year ago, six months ago even, I wouldn't have thought anything of it. When you've been friends as long as we have, telling each other everything that's going on in our lives is a given. But our friendship has changed over these past few months, distorted, as if by becoming Cynthia's employee I've become a different person, the good times and memories erased.

Cynthia fiddles with a loose thread on the sleeve of her cardigan. 'Daniel has just been ... very intense with Hannah lately.'

I blink, taken aback. 'What do you mean?'

'You know what, forget it. Do you fancy any crisps? I'll go and grab some from the house. Thai sweet chilli OK?'

'Hang on.' I stand in unison with Cynthia. 'You can't say something like that and not explain.'

My mind is swimming. Of all the things I thought might be bothering Cynthia, my son certainly wasn't it. Daniel's been dating Hannah for over a year now and they've been happy. Classic teenage sweethearts. I've even made a few jokes to Jase in the past that we should learn a thing or two from them. He's been so busy at work these past few months we barely see each other, and when he does get home he's too tired for anything in the bedroom that doesn't involve snoring. I never thought I'd be jealous of my teenage son's romance.

Cynthia shuffles from foot to foot, her expression pained. 'I don't want things to be weird between us.'

I have to stop myself from saying, *Weirder than they already are?* and just stare expectantly at her instead.

'Hannah told me he's been making her feel a little uncomfortable recently. Talk of moving in together, asking her to choose a university close by. Apparently he even mentioned kids once.'

'He's just enthusiastic about their relationship. You know what teenagers are like. So eager to grow up.'

'But Hannah isn't ready for that kind of commitment,' she says. 'She's still figuring out what she wants from life. She doesn't want to be thinking about settling down and having kids.'

Anger bubbles in the pit of my stomach, my protective streak surfacing. 'She doesn't? Or you don't?'

'What's that supposed to mean?'

'I mean this sounds an awful lot like you pressuring her to go to uni rather than Daniel pressuring her to be in a committed relationship. Every time I see them together Hannah seems fine.'

We fall silent and our eyes lock onto each other. My heartbeat thuds in my ears as I wait to see who will speak first. It never occurred to me when Hannah and Daniel started dating that it might cause issues for Cynthia and me if they were to ever break up. But then again, I didn't think her becoming my boss would cause issues for us either. I thought we were stronger than that, after all these years.

Cynthia sighs, a few strands of hair falling over her eyes. 'Look, I'm not trying to be a bitch. I'm worried about Daniel, if anything.'

'What on earth are you talking about?'

'Come on, Alex. You know exactly what I mean.'

I swallow hard. How dare she. How dare she throw it all back into my face like that. It's been four years and she knows how much of a trigger it is for me.

For a long while neither of us speaks, but I think she knows she's crossed a line. Eventually, I clear my throat, trying my hardest to push back the tears that are threatening to stream down my cheeks in ugly, snotty sobs.

'I should probably get back,' I say, placing my own glass down on the ground and turning my back on Cynthia.

'Alex, please don't. Don't go! Alex!' Her calls circle the farmland, disappearing into the night, as I start trudging down the dirt path. Part of me desperately wants to look back, to see if she's still there watching me walk away, but I don't.

It's a fair old walk from the farmhouse to my home; twenty minutes at a casual stroll, probably about fifteen with my angry strides. Ordinarily, I'd have taken the truck, but it's such a lovely night, one of those crisp summer nights where you can still feel the heat of the day sitting in the air, that I'd chosen to go by foot instead. Now, as I pass through the gate and lock it behind me, I'm regretting my choice. I just want to be home, to be with Daniel. Aside from anything, it's rather spooky walking alone at night with only the moon and the stars to light my way, even though I know these fields like the back of my hand.

I quicken my pace, my temper dissipating with each step. I'll need to apologise to her for storming off tomorrow. If not for our friendship, for my job. I don't think she'd ever go so far as to dismiss me, certainly not over something as trivial as our kids going through a rough patch, but I can't be too careful. She's become unpredictable as of late. The stress is getting to her.

Before I've even reached my front door, I hear it. The high-beamed ceiling of the converted barn that serves as our home tends to amplify sounds – a door being shut with a little too much force can be reminiscent of an angry clap of thunder – but this is unmistakable. Smashing glass.

In an instant I'm through the front door, following the sounds of destruction up the stairs and into Daniel's room. The sight knocks the breath out of me. His desk chair is upside down on the wrong side of the room, the bits and bobs that usually sit gathering dust on his shelves are strewn across the carpet, and the handmade photo frame that Hannah gave him for their six-month anniversary lies shattered to smithereens at his feet.

'What . . . what . . . ?' My brain doesn't seem to want to connect with my mouth. It's been so long, nearly two years, since he last did something like this, I'm not even sure I've fully registered what I'm seeing.

Daniel doesn't speak, just stares at the frame, at the photo underneath the shards of glass. It's one of my favourite photos of him and Hannah, taken the day they visited the London Dungeons. Daniel looks bloody terrified and Hannah is laughing wildly at him, but they'd always talk about that day as one of their best memories together.

Daniel is shaking, his hands tightening into fists.

'Daniel? What happened?'

No reply.

'Please talk to me, darling.'

Finally, his eyes move from the photo to meet mine, the subtle movement causing the tears brimming at his eyelids to splash down his cheeks. Nothing more needs to be said. I take a step towards him and he a step towards me, and then we pull each other into a hug. He's taller than me now, a strapping nineteen-year-old boy, so he has to stoop down to rest his forehead on my shoulder. He still needs his mummy though.

I stroke his hair and we go through the motions.

'Five things you can see,' I say.

He resists at first, his muscles tensing beneath my embrace, but eventually takes a shaky breath and says, 'My bed, my desk, pot of pens, the window, the wheat field outside.'

'Good.' I give him a squeeze. 'Four things you can feel.'

'My feet on the floor, my heart beating, your warmth, your hair tickling my nose.'

'Three things you can hear.'

'Your breathing. The boiler. The pigs outside.'

'Two things you can smell.'

'The smoke from the firepit on your clothes. Your silly diffusers.'

I chuckle. He's always hated the floral scents I dot around the house. He refers to them as 'sneeze sticks'.

'One thing you can taste.'

He pauses, thinking. 'Metallic.'

We stay like this for some time, and eventually the sobs ease off.

'Do you want to talk about what happened?' I say, and he moves away from me and shakes his head.

'No, no. Hannah's a bitch, let's just leave it at that.'

I wince but don't push the matter. I wish he'd talk to me more. He internalises things. He always has done since he was small, but it's become even more of an issue these past few years, and it scares the life out of me.

'You look nice today,' he ventures, trying to change the subject. 'That top suits you. The one you wore yesterday made you look fat.'

Heat floods my cheeks and I look away from him. I don't think I'll ever get used to comments like that. I give myself a little shake and paste a smile onto my face. 'Have you eaten? Want some leftovers?'

'Mum, will you just piss off and leave me alone!'

His words slice through me and I flinch, but I chew on the side of my cheek to stop myself from retorting.

The remorse shows almost instantly on his face.

'Sorry, I didn't mean that. I'm fine, Mum, really. I'm sorry about the mess. I'll get it all cleaned up. You go and put your feet up.'

He nods at me, his way of trying to convince me that I really am OK to leave him, but something tells me I should stay. Then Jase's words repeat in my head: *You'll end up pushing him away if you cling on too hard.* I know, I know, he's right, so I suck in a breath and bury the worries, the anxieties, right to the back of my brain, lock them in a little box and leave the room.

Downstairs, my body is restless. I pace, sit down, stand up, go to look out of the window. The surrounding fields stare back at me, bleak, empty. No sign of headlights. I hate it when Jase is on lates. He works at the hospital, so his shifts vary constantly. Sometimes he isn't home until three or four in the morning, and even though he tells me his work schedule ahead of time, I can never remember when he's due home, so I never know whether to wait up for him or not. I really should get us a calendar and write it all down, or utilise the one on my phone like Daniel keeps on suggesting.

My foot taps on the glossy floorboards beneath me and my fingers twist round each other. I need something to distract myself, to stop me from going back upstairs and crawling into bed with Daniel like I used to after he'd had a nightmare. Giving myself a little shake, I move to settle myself in the armchair and pull out my latest cross-stitch; it's a tree, but the leaves are splashes of multicoloured paint, like a watercolour. This is my anxiety cure. It gives my hands something to do, gives my brain something to concentrate on. One of my favourite things to do is sit in this chair, the fireplace letting off a cosy warmth beside me, and slide the needle in, out, in, out. Repetitive. Mindless.

I jump awake with a start. The fire is still blazing beside me, the windows are still black. I haven't been asleep for long. Bleary-eyed, I check the time on my phone – 11.40 p.m. I arch my back, allowing the air between each vertebra to pop and click, then heave myself up from the armchair and make my way upstairs. Daniel's door is still ajar, but his light is off. He must be asleep. I peek round the corner, but my eyes are still adjusting to the dark and I can't see anything. Pursing my lips, I flick the landing lamp on, light flooding through the crack in the door and highlighting his bed. He's not there.

'Daniel?'

I check each room, slow and methodical at first, then quickening my pace as the sense of dread grows. It's always there, lurking in the pit of my stomach. Usually I can squash it down, pretend it isn't there, but as I push open the last door of our house, I already know it's won. I pull out my phone and press number one on the speed dial, listen to the drone of the ringtone and the automated voicemail message. Daniel isn't here.

I take a few long, deep breaths and reason with myself. He's probably gone for a walk to clear his head. Nothing to worry about. We live in a small, friendly village. Even at this late hour, it's not like he'll be wandering down city alleyways or running into drunk arseholes who fancy stealing his shoes. Daniel will be fine. Except that's exactly what I thought that night.

The front door bangs against the barn wall as I fling it open and the cold of the night hits me, winding me. I scan the fields, still empty, asleep, but the farmhouse's lights are on. The fresh air is enough to sober me up and clear my head. Hannah. Maybe he's gone to see Hannah, to talk out whatever's going on in their relationship.

My hands shake as I fiddle with the keys to my truck and I nearly drop them, but eventually I'm clambering into the driver's seat and powering down the dirt road, sending a cloud of dust billowing up behind me.

'Cynthia?' I call as I press my finger to the doorbell. Its trill sounds from inside the house, oddly piercing against the quiet of the night. When there's no response, after a few seconds I try again, then again and again.

My hands are so cold, my fingerprint doesn't work on my phone, and I curse as I tap out the code to unlock it. Part of me hopes I'll see a missed call from Daniel, that he's tried to call me back and in my fluster I haven't heard it, or maybe I accidentally put it on silent again. He's told me off for that so many times. But there's nothing, no missed calls, no messages.

I scroll to Cynthia's name and hit call. At first, I think she's not going to answer either, but eventually the ringing is replaced by a crackling noise. She's driving.

'Hello?'

'Cynthia, it's me.'

'Hello? Alex? Sorry, I can't hear you. I'm on the motorway.'

My chest tightens. *Don't lose your rag. Don't lose your rag.*

I raise my voice. 'Cynthia, I'm looking for Daniel. Has he been at yours?'

'What? Daniel? I don't think so. I'm not sure.'

I frown, noting the tension in her voice. 'What's the matter?'

'Nothing. Nothing. Sorry, I'm picking Bradley up from a club. Didn't think to take money for a cab obviously.'

'OK. What about Mark? Would he—'

Before I can even finish my sentence, she says, 'Mark's still on his work trip. Look, I'm sorry, Alex. I'm going to have to go. You know how much I hate coming out to rescue him like this. Always the same bloody story.'

I press my fingers to my forehead. I don't need to hear about her disappointment with her son, not today, not right now.

'OK, don't worry. Bye.'

I end the call before she can start telling me the latest Bradley misdemeanour story. I don't know where to turn now. Daniel doesn't have many friends. Hannah has been his whole life for the last year and a half.

I'm about to return to my truck and start aimlessly searching the nearby roads, when a low creak sounds, making me jump. I turn back to the house and frown. The front door is ajar, pushed open ever so slightly by the breeze of the night. Brushing an ashy tendril from my eyes, I take a step closer.

'Hannah?'

She's probably gone to sleep and just forgotten to lock up properly. I wouldn't put it past Daniel to sleep through incessant doorbell rings, but a sense of duty has me pushing the door further open and peeking inside. I've known the girl since she was a black and white blob on a scan photo, I owe it to her and her mother to make sure she's OK.

'Hannah?' I call again. 'Are you there?'

Another thought – perhaps Daniel is with Hannah after all. Maybe they've made up after their row, gone out together, left the lights on in their teenage obliviousness and forgotten to check the door was closed properly.

I pull out my phone again, this time scrolling to Hannah's number. The dialling tone sounds for a couple of seconds and then some poppy autotuned song starts reverberating around the house. Her phone is here, so where is Hannah?

I follow the tune, down the hallway, past the rickety old staircase, into the living area, and suddenly I feel like I've been hit by an explosion shock wave, punched backwards, right in the gut. My legs buckle beneath me and I grip onto the back of the sofa for support. I stare, take in the sight before me, and scream.

CHAPTER TWO

ALEX

The Day of the Murder

She's lying on her front, blonde hair splayed messily around her head. But patches of her hair, over on the right side, are matted red, and from those patches a puddle has formed, reflecting the overhead lights on its crimson surface. Her head is turned to the side, unnaturally so, and I'm overcome with the desire to tilt it down so that she's lying in a more comfortable position. Her face is partially covered with bloodied hair, but her eyes and mouth are still visible. Eyes wide with shock, yet empty, soulless. Mouth hanging open, as if she had tried to scream.

I stumble forwards, hunch over her and place a trembling hand in front of her mouth, waiting and praying for a hint of breath, even though I can see in her eyes that she's already gone. From my caved-over position, I attempt to straighten myself, but doing so results in a wave of nausea and I clap my hand to my mouth, run to the downstairs bathroom and hunch over the toilet. Vomit splashes off the bowl. I collapse to the cold, tiled floor, clinging on to the toilet seat, retching interspersed with loud, ugly sobs. I don't know what to do. Nothing about this makes sense. She can't be dead. Not Hannah. Not the little girl I've watched grow up, who came to me when she was twelve and asked me about starting her period, who I caught with a boy when she was fifteen and who made me promise not to tell her mum.

I sit and cry until the skin around my eyes grows red raw, then shakily pull myself up and edge back to the living room. Part of me thinks I'll see her sitting on the sofa and that this has all been some horrid dream, some anxiety-fuelled figment of my imagination. But no. There she is, alone, lifeless.

My eyes move to the floor next to her. A vase, Cynthia's mum's porcelain vase with the intricate blue and white pattern, lies shattered beside her head. I hadn't noticed it the first time I looked at her, was too caught up in the horror scene before me, but now I see the red staining the shards. It's as if someone has smashed her over the head with it.

I swallow and take another step closer, inspecting Hannah's body. My stomach tightens as I notice the telltale signs. The bruising along her neck. The specks of blood dotting the whites of her empty eyes. She was strangled. This was murder.

Bile rises in my throat again as I fumble with my phone. My fingerprint still doesn't work, and this time I can't even get the code right. I try four times before it eventually unlocks and, trembling, I tap in 999. My finger hovers over the call button, my mind racing.

Hannah is lying before me, murdered. Someone clearly attacked her. Probably an argument that got out of hand.

God, that word. Murder. You hear about it on the news, but you never, ever think it'll be on your doorstep. What even happens when someone is murdered? There'll be an enquiry, of course there will. A whole investigation. They'll look at the various suspects. It could have been anyone . . . anyone who was on this farm tonight: the mother, the brother, the workers on the farm, the boyfriend.

My blood seems to freeze.

It's always the boyfriend.

Daniel wasn't home. He has no alibi. The last I saw him he was trashing his room and calling Hannah a bitch. I have no idea where he went or what he did. My heart rate quickens as I picture Daniel being dragged away in handcuffs, visualise his name in the papers: 'Local Boy Murders Oxbridge-Bound Girlfriend'. Visiting him in prison. Not being allowed to touch him, hug him, smell his hair. And what then? Would that be his life? Would he ever recover? I don't think he could cope with prison, not Daniel. Not after everything he's been through.

Trembling, I erase the numbers from my phone and instead call Daniel again. Time seems to have slowed right down and the droning of each ring pierces my skull, a dull ache behind my eye sockets. I whisper a silent prayer under my breath. *Please answer. Please answer. Please answer.* But I can already tell it's going to go to voicemail before the message plays. My grip tightens on my phone as I listen to it and wait for the beep.

'Daniel...' My voice comes out a croak, as if the evening's events have stripped my vocal cords bare. I swallow hard, try to think of the best way to word this. I can't say anything incriminating. I don't know exactly what will happen next, but if anyone gets hold of this message, the last thing I want is for it to be used as evidence against my own son. After a slow, steadying breath I simply say, 'Please call me, darling. Let me know you're OK.'

I hang up the call and sit for a few moments, completely still, numb. I try to tell myself this wasn't Daniel. He's not capable of this, not really. He has his issues, yes. His emotions get the better of him. He argued with Hannah. But he wouldn't have killed her. Not my boy. I almost start to believe it, but then the events of that night nearly four years ago start replaying in my head. Terrifying snapshots, images on a loop that I've tried so hard to keep locked away in that little box at the back of my mind. And I can't be sure.

My heart decides for me. It's as if my brain switches off entirely and I'm no longer in control of my actions. I'm a third party watching from the corner of the room. I run to the kitchen and pull out a black bin liner and Cynthia's box of cleaning supplies. I have to be as quick as I can. The nearest club is a good forty minutes away, so at the very least I've got an hour until Cynthia and Bradley get home, but what if Jase gets home early and comes over here to find me?

Returning to the living room, I pull on a pair of washing-up gloves and drop the bigger shards of vase into the bag, then use the dustpan and brush to sweep up any of the smaller fragments. Blood stains the bristles of the brush. I drop that into the bag too and leave it on the floor beside Hannah. Cynthia might notice they're missing, but I'll have to risk it. Besides, by the time I'm through, I imagine it wouldn't take a genius to figure out that someone cleaned up the crime scene. I falter momentarily as I allow the gravity of what I'm doing to sink in, but quickly push any doubts aside. There's no time for second-guessing.

Next, I create a list in my head of everywhere I've been since I arrived this evening, everything I've touched. The sofa – I leant on it when I first spotted Hannah. That's easily explained. I've been in this house almost every day for the past twenty years. My fingerprints are bound to be on the furniture. But the bathroom – I was sick into the toilet. I pull the bleach out from the cleaning box and take it to the downstairs loo, where I proceed to flush the vomit away and drown the bowl in bleach. I scrub the enamel until my hand aches, then wipe the surrounding surfaces with more bleach in case any splashes leapt out from the bowl.

The kitchen cupboard. I'll need to clean that. The whole place will stink of disinfectant and the police will check the cleaning cupboard for fingerprints. I soak a cloth in yet more bleach and wipe it along the handle, the door frame, the edge of the counter. Is there anything I've forgotten? No. That's it. That's everything I've touched. There's no CCTV or anything on the farm, so there's just one more bit of evidence to deal with. The worst bit. The bit I'm not sure I can go through with.

As I approach Hannah's body again my gut clenches and a wave of light-headedness hits me. I force it away, urge myself to focus. I don't know how much time I've got until Cynthia gets back with Bradley, and everything needs to be done. There cannot be a trace of my having been here. Hannah, poor sweet young Hannah, is dead. But my boy is alive. I can't help Hannah, but I can help him.

I try not to look at her as I slide my hands under her body. She's heavy, heavier than I had anticipated, and I have to put her back down at first and reconsider the best way to carry her. In the end, I opt for a sort of fireman's lift, draping her top half over my shoulder and gripping on to her arms and legs. Years of hard labour on the farm mean my legs are toned and strong. I push myself to standing, Hannah's body lying limp over my frame, and trudge towards the front door.

There aren't a huge number of options available to me. I could put her in my truck, drive her to a faraway field and place her there, ensuring I clean off any trace of DNA. I could head to the lake just south of the farm, drop some stones into her pockets and let her sink to the depths. But the easiest option is staring right at me. I don't want to. I can't.

My stomach is churning and I feel like I'm going to be sick again. Hannah is gradually growing heavier, and now that I'm outside I feel as if she's pushing me down into the damp mud beneath my feet. I can't breathe. I don't want to do this. But it's the only way. It's close enough that I wouldn't have to put her in the truck and risk having to clean that too. The pig barn.

CHAPTER THREE

HANNAH

The Day of the Murder – 7.20 p.m.

I check the time on my phone for the sixth time in four minutes. I need to leave soon if I'm to have any hope of getting there on time. He understands, of course. He knows how difficult it is for me sometimes to get out, especially recently. Mum seems to have been taking even more of an interest in me lately. Perhaps because the deadline for uni applications is fast approaching, or maybe because she's given up on Bradley doing anything worthwhile with his life. Whatever the reason is, it sucks. But I always find a way. I might be a little late sometimes, but I always get there eventually.

It keeps me sane. If it wasn't for meeting him, for being with him, I think I might just go crazy. I can't stand living here anymore. The pressure to do well, to meet expectations, is crushing me. Not to mention the stink of the place. I'm fed up of walking into my classroom smelling like poo. But when I'm with him it all disappears. Besides, it's even more important than ever that I see him tonight.

One quick glance in the mirror to make sure my make-up is still in place, and I'm off. As I pad down the stairs and edge towards the back door, anticipation bubbles inside me. A mixture of nerves and excitement. This isn't like the other times. This is a particularly special day, one which I've spent the past twenty-four hours playing out in my head. I can't wait to see him.

CHAPTER FOUR

STEFANI

Two Days After the Murder

DS Stefani Warner waits on the doorstep of the farmhouse, an acute sense of unease settling over her. She shouldn't be here. Not really. When the phone call had come in to the station yesterday from a frantic Cynthia Carmichael informing them that her daughter had gone out the night before and never returned home, her chief had made it quite clear that this was not considered a missing persons case yet. Hannah is too old – at eighteen, she's considered an adult in the law's eyes – and she's not been gone for long enough. But Stefani's own daughter goes to school with Hannah. Though it's not strictly professional, she can't help but feel an obligation to at least check it out. Of course, she's out of uniform, technically off duty, but she's never really fully off duty. Her high blood pressure reminds her of that every day.

When the door is eventually opened, it isn't Cynthia who stands before her, but a boy who bears a striking resemblance to Hannah; the same blond hair and pinky pale complexion, but with dark circles under his eyes. This, Stefani assumes, is the twin brother, Bradley. Though they're both in the sixth form, she hasn't yet met Bradley, though she's heard about him a couple of times. He's a quiet boy, keeps himself to himself. Though he looks like Hannah, it would seem his personality is the polar opposite. She supposes that is often the way with twins.

'Hi, I'm Stefani Warner,' she ventures when he doesn't say anything. 'I'm a police officer. Your mother called, said your sister left the house two nights ago and never came back.'

Bradley doesn't say anything, just nods and steps to one side, opening the door further by way of invitation to come in. Stefani does so, stepping over the threshold of the farmhouse and taking in the interior of the old building. It's rather like something out of a storybook. Classic English cottage vibes. China plates with floral designs hang on the walls, frilly rugs adorn the floorboards and, from what she can see of the living room, there is an array of knitted blankets slung over the backs of the armchairs and sofas. Stefani knew Cynthia's mother, Peggy – everyone in town did – and she imagines this is exactly how she had the house before she died. She doubts the decor has changed even in the slightest. It suits Peggy to a tee.

Stefani moves through the hallway and follows Bradley into the living area, where her eyes land on Cynthia, huddled up on the sofa clutching a mug, and two other people who she recognises as Alex and Jase Forrester. Before she says anything, she takes a moment to observe the occupants of the room closely, as she always does when entering a potential crime scene. She knows these people already, has seen them at parents' evenings and school fetes, at the annual carnival and queuing up at the butcher's. That's what you get when you live in a small village with only one school. Everyone knows everyone. This makes it harder to remain impartial, so she must be careful to approach the situation with a completely objective eye.

'Before I begin, I must make it clear that I'm not on duty. I can't make any formal investigation, not yet.'

She waits for a response, but there is none, just the soft sniffling of Cynthia.

'Well then,' Stefani continues. 'Why don't you tell me what happened?'

The four of them glance between each other, as if unsure of who should speak. Cynthia looks up from her cup for the first time since Stefani arrived, and stares blankly at her. Her eyes are red raw around the rims and bloodshot; her skin is washed out. Certainly a far cry from the put-together, sophisticated woman Stefani is used to seeing around town. Clearly, no matter what the police say, she is extremely worried about her daughter. Finally, Cynthia clears her throat.

'I was having drinks with Alex out at the firepit in the front garden. Just after she went home, I left to pick up Bradley from a club in the city. Hannah said she was going out with friends, but then she never came home. I've phoned around everyone she spends time with. No one seems to know where she went . . .' She falters, her voice cracking, and Stefani feels a wave of sympathy. She can't imagine what it must be like to return home to find your daughter gone without a word, to not be able to get hold of her. The whole situation makes her want to run straight to her own daughter.

Cynthia shakes her head. 'It's not like Hannah. She never stays out all night. She's always home before I go to bed, and if she's staying at a friend's house, she always calls to let me know.'

Stefani swallows hard, forcing herself to remain professional. 'What time did you leave to pick Bradley up?'

Cynthia's eyes glaze over, and she looks to Bradley for an answer.

'Mum texted me to say she was on her way about 10.45 p.m.,' he says, clearly agitated. 'I'm not sure what time we got back. I guess just after midnight.'

Stefani pulls a small notebook from her pocket and begins to jot down the times. She moves her gaze to the other two in the room.

'Where were you both around this time?'

Jase runs his hand through his hair. 'I was at a meeting, which finished about seven thirty, but I had coffee with one of my colleagues after and then got called back into work later on in the evening. Didn't get back until three yesterday morning.'

Stefani nods. She expected that to be his answer. She knows he's a consultant at the hospital and often works long hours.

'And you?' she prompts Alex, who is staring glumly at her feet.

Alex starts, as if she's forgotten she's even visible. After a while, she says, 'As Cynthia said, I was outside with her and then I went home.'

'You live on site, is that correct?'

She nods.

'Did you see or hear anything after you arrived home?'

'No.' Alex returns her gaze to the floor. 'Our house is right on the other end of the field. Too far away for me to have seen or heard anything, especially at that time of night.'

Stefani cocks her head to the side and peers out of the window, across the vast green land stretching out before them. Alex is right; the converted barn is a fair distance from the farmhouse.

'What did you do when you got home to find your daughter missing, Cynthia?' She's trying her best to keep her tone friendly, supportive. The last thing she wants is for Cynthia to feel threatened by her questions.

'I called her mobile a few times, but it just went straight to voicemail.' Her hands are starting to shake. The liquid in her cup is sploshing over the sides. 'Then I went round to Alex's to see if Hannah might be there. I thought she may have gone to see Daniel.'

At this, the atmosphere in the room shifts. Jase and Alex exchange a glance that the average person would probably miss, but Stefani catches it. She'd forgotten about their son.

'Where is Daniel?' she asks.

After a moment of thinking neither one of them is going to answer, Jase clears his throat. 'He's gone camping.'

'Camping?'

'He goes a fair bit.' He shifts from foot to foot. 'But he didn't tell us where exactly he was going and now we can't get hold of him.'

Stefani lowers her eyebrows, studies the Forresters. Alex is flushed, a deep redness creeping from her cheeks right up to the top of her ears.

'When did he leave to go camping?'

Jase opens his mouth to respond, but Alex gets in there first. 'Before I went to have drinks with Cynthia last night. He got home from his shift at the pub, left to go camping, and then I came here for the evening.'

'You didn't think to ask where he was going?'

Alex tucks a loose strand of hair behind her ear. 'Taking himself off to camp in remote places is his way of clearing his head. It's not unusual. I'd much rather he do that than resort to the coping methods other teenagers tend to use.'

Stefani nods slowly, not taking her eyes off Alex. If she's to be believed, Daniel left to go on his mystery camping trip long before Hannah went missing. But she's acting shifty, and Jase doesn't exactly look comfortable either. It could simply be a case of them worrying about Hannah, that they're not sure what they can do to help, but Stefani senses that something is off here.

'Can I take a quick look around the house?' she says.

CHAPTER FIVE

ALEX

Two Days After the Murder

I step into the relative safety of my home and breathe a sigh of relief as I close the door behind me, pressing my fingers to my temple. I've had a permanent headache since Wednesday. After I disposed of Hannah's body, I returned to the farmhouse and scrubbed the floor until my breathing grew wheezy and my eyes were stinging from all the bleach, then placed the rubber gloves, Hannah's mobile and every item of clothing I was wearing, right down to my shoes, into the black bag. When I got home, the clothes went in the washing machine on a hot spin, the gloves and phone went through the grinder with the livestock feed, and I spent a good half an hour picking up the mess in Daniel's room before scrubbing myself practically raw in the shower to get rid of the smell of disinfectant.

I had to pretend I was asleep when Cynthia knocked. I couldn't face her. She was obviously looking for Hannah, and I'd have broken down the second she mentioned her name. I needed at least one night before I had to start lying to my best friend. Jase came home just after 3 a.m. and didn't even question why I was up. It's not an uncommon occurrence for me to be sat up at ungodly hours of the morning with my cross-stitch. Luckily, he was far too tired to try to engage in any proper conversation with me; he went straight to bed and I didn't have to pretend I was OK. But now I do, and I'm already exhausted.

I move to the window and watch Jase close up the garage. He hasn't said a word to me since Stefani left, and that makes me uneasy. She didn't find anything in the farmhouse, thank God. I had a moment of sheer panic when I thought I might have missed something. Maybe there was something, some shred of evidence that I hadn't spotted in the house, which proves that Hannah is dead and that my son is to blame. But every time those anxieties nag at me I reason with myself that I was thorough; I checked each room twice before I left, ensured there was no trace of myself or of Daniel beyond what you'd expect to find from us living on the farm. They won't find anything.

I glance down at my phone, praying there might be a missed call or a text from Daniel, but the empty screen stares back at me. As Jase returns from the garage, I head to the kitchen and start boiling the kettle, trying to control my breathing. More than once this morning I've found myself hyperventilating; desperate gasps coupled with sweat that drenches my forehead and drips off my nose. I need to pull myself together, stop looking so damned guilty, even though I know the memories of what I did will haunt me until the day I die.

My muscles tense as Jase enters the house. I keep my eyes fixed on the steam rising from the kettle, but I can sense him behind me.

'Tea?' I say, trying to keep the nerves out of my voice.

There is a pause where I think maybe he didn't hear me, and then, 'You were telling the truth, weren't you, Alex?'

My blood runs cold and my breath catches in my throat. I purse my lips, take a second to compose myself before turning to face him.

'What?'

He narrows his eyes. 'When you said Daniel left long before Hannah went missing. That was the truth, wasn't it?'

I take in his pale, tired face, and I can already tell where his head has gone. It's gone exactly where my mind went when I found Hannah's body. He knows what Daniel is like. Part of me wants to be angry with him for thinking so little of our son, for jumping to conclusions without giving him a chance to explain himself, but I know I'm just as bad, if not worse.

'Of course it was the truth.'

We stare at each other, his gaze burning into me so that I want to look away, but I force myself to remain rigid. Endless seconds tick by, and then, as if the universe can tell I'm about to break, the doorbell rings.

Both of us start, take a second to register that there's someone at the door. Jase gives me a look that says, *We'll talk about this later* and goes to answer it, while I turn back to the tea. Small droplets splash over the side of the cups as I shakily fill them.

'Mark.' Jase's voice echoes through the open-plan living area. My head snaps up at the mention of Cynthia's husband's name. 'I thought you weren't back until next week?'

'That was the plan, but . . . well . . . with everything going on . . .'

My shoulders curl forward. I need a break from pretending, just for an hour. This is all too much. I give myself a little shake and paste on my friendly yet sorrowful smile, before joining Jase at the door.

'Mark, how are you doing?' I say. 'I've just boiled the kettle. Want a cuppa?'

He shakes his head and takes an almost nervous step back, as if the prospect of entering our home is a terrifying one. 'No, thank you. I just wanted to talk to you both quickly. Check a few things, if that's OK?'

Jase and I exchange a quick glance.

'Of course,' Jase says. 'Anything we can do to help.'

There is an awkward silence while Mark shuffles from foot to foot, seemingly searching for the right words. I've never seen him so unsure of himself. Mark Butler is a director at one of those big tech firms in the city, I forget which one, but his demeanour has always suited that sort of career. Strong and self-assured. Like Jase, he's tall and muscular, dark-haired, and he's a real presence in the room, which only adds to his usual air of confidence. He and Cynthia have only been married for two years, and Cynthia chose not to take his name so as to still have the same surname as her kids.

'Obviously, I've spent the last hour since I got home going over all the details with Cynthia. Trying to figure out if we've missed anything,' he begins, 'and she remembered that you called her Wednesday, Alex.'

My stomach roils and bile collects in the back of my throat. I'd completely forgotten about the phone call. That was before I'd even found Hannah. I try to look nonchalant while I frantically try to recollect what was said.

Mark clears his throat. 'She said you asked her if she knew where Daniel was. We checked the call log; it looks like you called her at about 11.45. The only reason it stuck out to us was . . . well, because you said to the police officer earlier that Daniel left before you went for drinks with Cynthia.'

He stares at me expectantly, and I can sense Jase waiting for my response too. My heart is thudding in my ears so fast, I can't hear myself think. I need time to slow down, to just stop so that I can gather my thoughts.

Finally, after what feels like an eternity, I twist my facial expression into one of confusion. 'I didn't ask her if she'd seen Daniel. She was on the motorway, I think she was struggling to hear me. I was asking if she'd seen Daniel's debit card anywhere. He realised before he left to go camping that he'd lost it and the last place he had it was at yours.'

Once I've stopped talking, I hold my breath to stop myself from descending into a puddle on the floor.

Mark narrows his eyes. 'You called her about that at 11.45 at night?'

'Well, yes. The last thing I want is for it to be stolen. If it doesn't turn up today, I'll have to ring the bank and cancel it.'

I hold perfectly still while I wait to see if Mark will believe me. *What if there's a way to get a recording of an old phone call?* I think, light-headed with nerves. Given Mark's line of work, for all I know, that's something he can do. I feel like the floor I'm standing on is wonky and uneven, tilting underneath me. I didn't kill Hannah. I'm innocent of murder. But I am guilty nonetheless, and I fear that guilt is painted plain as day on my face.

'I see,' Mark says finally, and my shoulders relax a little. 'Just a case of crossed wires, I suppose. Have you heard from Daniel at all?'

I shake my head and glance down at my phone in my pocket. 'I've tried calling him, but it goes straight to voicemail. The signal usually isn't great when he goes camping.'

At least that's the truth. I've been desperately trying to get hold of him since Wednesday. What I'd give to just hear his voice right now.

'OK. If you hear from him obviously let us know. For all we know Hannah could be with him.'

I nod and swallow the lump in my throat. 'Of course we will.'

He gives a brief nod to both of us, then retreats towards his car. As Jase closes the door, I let out as subtle a sigh of relief as I can manage. Once the door has clicked shut, Jase turns towards me, his face stony. Then he reaches into his pocket and pulls out his phone.

'What are you doing?' I ask.

'Calling Daniel.'

'He won't answer,' I say, suddenly panicked. 'I've tried.'

'No harm in trying again.'

I wait with bated breath, my palms growing hot and clammy. Part of me desperately wants him to answer, but the other part of me knows that if he does, Jase will jump straight down his throat. He won't give him a chance to explain. I need to be the one to speak to him. I'm the only one who knows how to talk to him.

Jase shakes his head. 'Voicemail.' He replaces his phone in his pocket and gives me another of his looks. 'If you hear from him, you must promise to tell me straight away. OK?'

'I promise.'

Before my body has a chance to descend into shakes, I turn away from him, pick up my cup of tea and settle myself in the armchair.

'Tea's on the side,' I say, while I pick up my cross-stitch.

The sun is setting. Its glow is emitting from the horizon, blazing and hot, taking with it the second full day without Hannah. It's too bright, too cheery, so I glance down and focus on sliding my needle through the next hole. I'm on the red leaves section. It looks like a splash of blood.

@WMerciaPolice: We are growing increasingly concerned for missing Hannah Carmichael, 18, from #Herefordshire. She was last seen on Wednesday 19 April at her home in Ledbury, Herefordshire. Please call 999 with any info, ref 68MIS11592

@nadinestevens38: Where were her parents when she went missing, that's what I want to know! #Herefordshire #HannahCarmichael #WhenWillWomenBeSafe

@rightthewrongs862: Take it you don't have kids @nadinestevens38. She's 18. Try keeping an 18 year old wrapped up in cotton wool! #nooneaskedforyouropinion

@BBCbreaking: Hannah Carmichael was last seen in her home on Wednesday 19 April. The family has yet to comment. More news as we have it.

@groundhog1989: She's dead. Guarantee it #RIPhannah

CHAPTER SIX

STEFANI

Three Days After the Murder

'No, absolutely fucking not.' Stefani's chief, DCI Walton, tends to shift from his usual phony posh accent to his natural south-west London accent, littered with curse words, when he gets angry. Since he discovered that Stefani conducted her own private questioning of the Carmichaels, he's shouted just about every curse word under the sun, loud enough for them to be heard through his office's closed door, much to the squad's amusement.

'Sir, I'm the right person for the job. I know these people.' Stefani talks in a warm, calm tone, as if she were talking to an insolent child. She has learnt over the years that this is the approach you need to take with the chief; assertive yet composed. Eventually, he'll say that whatever she was trying to convince him to do was his idea, and she lets him believe that.

Chief Walton shakes his head, rubbing his temples with the tips of his fingers. 'That's exactly why I shouldn't assign you to this case. You're too close to it. There's no way you can be impartial. Besides . . .' He moves to the other side of his desk and sits in his chair; a not-so-subtle cue that he's just about done with this conversation. 'Why should I let you take it when you deliberately disobeyed orders and went behind my back?'

And there it is. That's what this is really about. It's nothing to do with his lack of confidence in her ability to conduct this investigation. He's bitter that she didn't do as he wanted. Stefani would have thought he'd be used to her way by now. They've worked together for over ten years, and she's lost count of the number of times she's taken his orders more as suggestions.

'Sir, you know I'll always be impartial,' she says, keeping her tone even. He does know. He's just putting on a show because he's annoyed at her. 'I'm the best person to do this. All I care about is seeing that girl come home safely.'

She watches for any alteration in his expression. He sticks out his lips slightly as he mulls it over, and fiddles with the pen on his desk, clicking the top in and out. Finally, he leans forward and meets her eye.

'Don't ever go behind my back again.'

She nods and smiles before exiting the office, and they both know full well that eventually she'll do it again, and he'll let her off then too.

The first twenty-four hours since Stefani officially took this case have been infuriatingly slow. They had to speak to each of the family members again and take their official statements, speak to Hannah's friends to see if any of them had heard from her, and search her social media profiles for any clue as to where she might be. Nothing has come up. Hannah hasn't used any of her social media accounts since the day before she went missing, which Stefani knows is a bad sign when you're talking about a teenage girl. As yesterday came to an end with no sign of her and no leads, Walton agreed that it was time to step the search up a gear, and now here they are.

Stefani sits with Cynthia, Mark and Bradley in the waiting room, acutely aware of the growing group of journalists gathering in the adjacent media room. Cynthia is gripping tightly on to Mark's hand, her chest rising and falling at an alarming rate. Beside her, Bradley is deathly pale, twisting his hands together, his face a picture of turmoil. They say twins can feel each other's emotions. Stefani wonders if that's true; if he's got some kind of sixth sense, a gut feeling of whether Hannah is alive or dead. She can only imagine how churned up he must be for his sister to be missing for this long.

Stefani takes a polystyrene cup from the water dispenser and fills it before passing it to Cynthia.

'Here, take a few slow sips. It'll help to regulate your breathing, calm you down.'

Cynthia takes the cup wordlessly, eyes fixed ahead. She had initially recoiled at Stefani's suggestion that they should make an appeal to the press. She eventually agreed when Stefani pointed out that now that it's been over seventy-two hours since Hannah was last seen, these are now their prime, and quite possibly final, hours for finding her alive. They need someone to have seen something. From what the initial investigation has garnered, they're not much further ahead than they were yesterday.

Mark picks up the piece of paper off the coffee table which contains the prepared statement Stefani helped to craft. His eyes flick side to side as he reads it for the sixth time.

Stefani glances at her watch. 'A couple of minutes and then we'll head out. Are you all ready?'

Cynthia stares at her as if she's just asked if she's ready for her execution. 'I don't know if I can do this.'

Bradley edges closer to his mother and she turns her head, almost seeming to look right through him, but when he reaches out to place his arm around her shoulder, she flinches, recoiling back towards Mark. The twins share a striking resemblance. When Cynthia looks at her son, is she consumed with thoughts of Hannah? If this turns out badly, will she ever be able to look at him again? Seeing the hurt in his face, Stefani tries to offer him a reassuring smile. He hasn't said much since she first arrived at the farm yesterday, but the love for his mother is evident in his body language.

Stefani can't help but feel a sense of trepidation herself. This is the first time her squad has been faced with a missing teenager since she joined the force eleven years ago. They're lucky enough to live in an area where most missing persons reports end in their safe return within twenty-four hours. She's never seen it get to press level before.

'You'll be fine,' she says, nodding at Mark to signal that he needs to take the lead here and make sure that Cynthia gets into that room. 'Just keep to the statement and don't try to answer any questions. Once you've finished, come straight back here. I'll be with you the whole time.'

Cynthia forces a nod and stands to leave, clinging on to Mark's arm as if she is a frail old lady, with Bradley trailing behind. Stefani positions herself in front of them and leads the way to the media room, where a dozen or so reporters are gathered. Cameras flash as soon as they're in shot, and for a terrible moment, Stefani thinks Cynthia might turn and run straight back out of the room. She doesn't though. She steps forward and takes a seat at the table, gripping on to the statement so hard the paper is crumpling in her hands. There had been some discussion about whether Mark should be the one to read the statement, since Cynthia is in such a state, but Stefani gently suggested that it needed to be Cynthia. As much as Mark is undoubtedly worried about his stepdaughter, he has only been in her life for a couple of years.

A recent picture of Hannah is enlarged on the screen behind the table. It's the same photo that's printed on the flyers that the community search party is currently handing out, the same one that's on their fireplace mantel back at the farmhouse. It's Hannah's last school photo, and she looks painfully young despite the picture only being a year old. Her blonde hair sweeps down over her forehead, giving way to rosy cheeks and a mouth spread out into an earnest smile.

Stefani looks away from the photo, a silent reminder to herself to stay strong. Emotions can't play a part in this. She needs to remain focused on finding Hannah, no matter what. If she has anything to do with it, she'll see that Hannah's face is plastered on every newspaper and TV screen. The advantage they have in this instance is that the missing girl comes from a fairly well-to-do, middle-class family. It's a sad fact Stefani has learnt over the years that these girls tend to get more media coverage.

Stefani lifts her hand to signal she's going to speak, and the room quietens down.

'Good afternoon. We are currently appealing for any information about the whereabouts of eighteen-year-old Hannah Carmichael, who went missing from her home on the evening of the nineteenth of April.' She pauses unexpectedly; a vision of her daughter Cassie flashes into her mind, and she has to fight a wave of nausea, the impulse to wobble. Her boss will be watching this. She must remain professional.

Taking a sip of water, she clears her throat before continuing. 'She was last captured on CCTV getting off the bus at Lyne Down Road at 9.45 p.m. She is thought to have walked towards her home in Ledbury – a journey which should have taken about ten minutes. It is totally out of character for Hannah to go missing. Her mobile phone hasn't been used, she hasn't been in touch with family or friends, and she hasn't used social media. Have you seen Hannah, or spoken to her? We would like to hear from anyone with CCTV or dashcam footage from any time after 9.45 p.m. on the nineteenth of April in the Ledbury and surrounding areas. I will now pass you over to Hannah's mother, Cynthia Carmichael.'

She gives a friendly smile to Cynthia and holds her breath while she waits for her to speak. Cynthia blinks rapidly, as if she can't quite see the words on the paper in front of her. She takes a few slow breaths, clears her throat, crosses and uncrosses her legs under the table.

Finally, she speaks.

'Our daughter Hannah is a loving, caring and bubbly eighteen-year-old. She would prefer to curl up in her room with a book, or spend time with close friends, than to go to pubs or clubs. If she ever does go out, she is always home by her midnight curfew. She cares deeply about her family and her friends and was looking forward to spending some time at home before starting at university next year.'

A small crack emerges from Cynthia's voice and she pauses, closing her eyes and running her fingertips along her temple before continuing.

'We cannot believe she hasn't been in touch with anyone, not even on social media. She wouldn't want to cause this worry. She'd find all the fuss embarrassing. There has to be a reason for her highly unusual disappearance. Hannah, if you can hear me or see me as I read this, please come home. Get in touch. Just let us know you're safe. We love you so much.'

A few tears roll down her cheeks as she approaches the end of the statement. She places the sheet down on the table to signal she's finished, and forces her eyes up to the sea of faces staring back at her, the camera lenses.

Stefani tilts her head to the side, investigates the expressions of all three of them. They all look equally anguished, displaying the expected level of worry and concern. But there's something else. Stefani can't quite place her finger on it, but something is off. Something doesn't feel right.

CHAPTER SEVEN

ALEX

Four Days After the Murder

I'm trying not to look at the photo of Hannah on the flyers as I hand them out to passers-by. I still can't believe that Hannah is dead. It doesn't compute. I won't let it. Because if I allow it to sink in, I'd have to come to terms with what I did.

Jase and I have positioned ourselves outside the little row of shops that serve the entire village. Nothing special. A butcher's, a greengrocer's, an impossibly small convenience store with a post office attached, and a pharmacy. There's nowhere else to go without driving to the adjacent town though, so this small street is often bustling, though being a Sunday, it's unfortunately not as busy as usual. Not that it's going to make the blindest bit of difference whether it's busy or not. Hannah is gone, and no amount of flyers is going to change that.

I peek at Jase through the loose strands of my hair, but he's not looking at me. He's barely acknowledged my existence since this all started. I feel like I should say something, point out to him that this behaviour is just making us look like we've got something to hide, but every time I go to open my mouth around him, I clam up, as if a chain has wrapped itself around my throat.

I pass the last of my flyers to Jenna Driscoll, one of the sixth-form mums. She shakes her head and tuts as she looks at Hannah's beaming face.

'God, I heard. Isn't it just awful?'

'Yes,' I say, praying she won't want to engage in conversation. 'It's horrendous.'

'Do give Cynthia my best wishes, won't you? I just keep thinking what if it was my Lauren. I don't know what I'd do.'

'I will. Thank you. She's talking to the press at the moment, but I'll let her know you're thinking of her when she gets back.'

I try to take a step to the side to indicate that we're getting ready to leave, but Jenna doesn't pick up on the hint. Or maybe she does and just chooses to ignore it.

'Maybe I should cook up a lasagne and bring it round. What do you reckon? I bet she's not eating properly, poor love.'

'I don't think the police really want other people near the house at the moment.'

'Oh, of course. I suppose it's considered a crime scene, is it? Or is that not unless she's found . . . hurt?'

I swallow hard, scrunch my hands into fists to stop myself from snapping at her to mind her own business. My nails dig into my palms so hard, it stings.

'I'm really not sure what the process is,' I say, purposefully looking at my watch in an over-the-top fashion. The press conference should be done by now, so Cynthia and the others are probably on their way back. I wonder if the search of the farm is still going on. I had desperately wanted to stay behind and watch them, just to get an idea if they were on to me, but I knew if I did, it would be suspicious. I have to be seen as helping out, no matter how pointless and heartbreaking it is.

A thoughtful expression crosses Jenna's face, and she tilts her head to the side. 'Hannah was dating your Daniel, wasn't she?'

The muscles in my cheek twitch. I can feel Jase looking over at us, can sense him waiting to see my response. It's a cool day, there's been a steady pleasant breeze all morning, but I'm starting to sweat. Heat is rushing from my core up to my head, and I am acutely aware that my chest and face are reddening.

'Yes,' I say, my voice catching in my throat. I feel like I should say more, but I can't find the words. Jenna is surveying me, her eyes flitting across my face.

'How's he coping with it all? I haven't seen him around.'

There's that chain around my throat again, tightening so that I feel like I can't breathe. I rub my hand along the back of my neck as I search for something to say.

'He's away on a trip at the moment,' Jase cuts in, coming to stand beside me. 'We decided to wait to tell him until he gets back. Hopefully, she'll be back by then.'

I want to fall into Jase's arms. My legs are like jelly. Instead, I reach down and grip on to his hand, squeeze it to offer him a silent thanks for stepping in. He flinches but doesn't try to move away.

'Oh.' Jenna's eyes are wide. I can practically see the cogs in her head turning as she decides whether we're telling the truth or not. 'Well, I should probably get going. Do let me know if there's anything I can do.'

And with that she saunters off, with the flyer gripped tightly in her hand.

I let out a breath, the chain around my neck loosening. 'Thank you,' I whisper to Jase. He looks down at me and pulls his hand out of my grasp.

'We should get back.'

The walk back to the farm is thick with tension, a heavy presence sitting in the air around us. Jase hasn't explicitly asked me about that night again, not since he asked if I had told the truth to Stefani, but I can feel it every time I'm with him. He doesn't trust me. He knows I'm covering up for Daniel. I desperately wish I could talk to him about it all. I need someone to confide in, to share this horrendous burden, this guilt that I'm lugging around with me. But I can't talk to Jase. He wouldn't understand.

The road leading to the farm has no pavement, just a grass verge, so I walk in single file behind him. I scoot over to the grass as a car approaches, heading towards us. The lack of speed cameras, road bumps and traffic means cars often thunder down this road, but this particular car is moving at an unusually gradual pace. It's as if the driver has slowed right down to look at something. And then I realise what they're snooping at.

When we left to hand out flyers, there had only been a couple of police cars at the farm, just a few officers of Stefani's team who were there to conduct the search while she accompanied the family to the press conference. Now, however, there are at least five cars pulled up in the main driveway, and across the main entrance gate, a blue and white tape is flapping in the wind.

Police Line – Do Not Cross.

'What the...' Jase's voice seems far off, as if there's a wall between us. 'Do you think they've found something?'

I can't answer. My mouth has completely dried up. I feel like I've been chewing on sand. All I can do is stare, the hairs on the back of my neck standing to attention, as we move trance-like towards the tape.

Stefani is standing with another officer between two of the cars. I can't see Cynthia anywhere, but if Stefani's back, I assume she's here somewhere. Stefani's eyes flick up and immediately meet mine. She murmurs something to the other officer, then comes to meet us at the gate.

'What's happened?' Jase says, once again saving me from having to attempt speaking.

Stefani's face is sombre, her lips pulled into a flat line. 'We're going to need to speak to you both formally at the station.'

'Stefani, please...' I manage to force out. 'We've known each other for years. Please tell us what's happened.'

She presses her lips together so hard, they disappear altogether. She glances from side to side, checking there's no one else in earshot.

'We found human remains,' she says finally. 'In the pigsty.'

CHAPTER EIGHT

STEFANI

Four Days After the Murder

Stefani presses her fingers to her forehead, the glare of the fluorescent strip lights of her office suddenly too bright. She barely slept a wink last night, worried sick about Hannah, about the hours slipping away with no trace of her. And now this. It's not yet been confirmed that the teeth and bone fragments found in the pigsty are indeed those of Hannah Carmichael. They're still with forensics. But it's only a matter of time.

A shudder travels down her spine and she gulps down the remainder of her coffee to mask the sickly taste gathering in her mouth. The thought of the pigs devouring Hannah, the sheer hideousness of it, is almost too much to bear. Her poor family won't even have a body to bury.

She can't believe they've wasted two whole days trying to track down Daniel Forrester. The parents are sticking to their story that he's gone camping and they have no idea where, which Stefani doesn't buy for one second. They're covering for him. She just needs to figure out how involved in this whole sorry situation they actually are. She's known them for years, would never have pegged them as murderers, but if there's anything she's learnt since becoming a police officer, it's that you can never truly know anyone. Her to-do list now involves searching Daniel's usual camping spots, getting his photo up on social media, TV if possible, and scrutinising Alex and Jase until one of them slips up. Which they will do. She's sure of it.

She also needs to figure out where Hannah went that evening.

According to Cynthia, Hannah went out with friends, and the CCTV footage they recovered from the bus confirmed that she did indeed travel a few towns over, though they lost her after the bus stop. When she returned at 9.45 p.m. she was alive and well, so ordinarily Stefani wouldn't be quite so concerned with figuring out where she went, but none of her friends have admitted to seeing her. In fact, nobody has come forward to say they spent time with Hannah the night she disappeared. That in itself sends questions firing in Stefani's head.

'Stef!' Her colleague's shout snaps her out of her thoughts. She blinks and looks at DS Davies, standing in front of her desk with his brows knitted together.

'What?'

'I said, how's Cassie? Are you OK? You look miles away.'

Stefani gives her head a shake, attempting to snap herself out of her brain fog. 'Sorry, sorry. I'm just thinking about finding this kid.' She takes a large swig of coffee and leans back in her chair. 'Cassie's good, thanks. A typical eighteen-year-old. She's staying with me next weekend.'

At this, Stefani allows herself to feel the faintest flutter of excitement. She's meant to see her daughter every other weekend, but a combination of work and Cassie teetering on the edge of adulthood means it doesn't always happen. She makes a mental note to send a text to Cassie's dad later and check what time he'll be dropping her off.

DS Davies nods. 'Good, good. Are you ready? Alex Forrester is in Room Three. Jase Forrester is in Room Four.'

Stefani nods, takes a final sip of coffee before dumping the stained cup in the sink and making a start down the hall. They will be interviewing Alex first, then Jase.

'How was the mother when you escorted her out?' she asks. They did the formal interview with the family earlier, though they didn't gather any information from it that they didn't already know. Stefani has to admit she would have been useless if it hadn't been for DS Davies leading on the questions. Telling Cynthia what they found in the pig barn was without a doubt the worst moment of her life so far, one that she'll never fully recover from. She can still picture the way the poor woman dropped to her knees and howled, the way Mark and Bradley wrapped their arms around her shoulders and they clung to each other. If any of them are lying, they're bloody good actors. Now, the thought of facing Cynthia again makes Stefani feel sick to her stomach.

'A complete wreck, as you'd imagine.'

'And the brother?'

'Didn't get much out of him. He reckons he should have known she was dead since she's his twin.' He pauses. 'Was his twin.'

Stefani sighs, then says, 'What about Alex Forrester? How does she seem?'

'It's hard to tell,' DS Davies says as they turn the corner. 'Upset, that's for sure. But doesn't everyone seem like that when we bring them in?'

Stefani nods, pressing her lips together. The alibis of both the Carmichaels and the Forresters all seem to check out, to a point. They've recovered CCTV of Cynthia picking Bradley up from the club, of Mark at his hotel, of Jase at his meeting and then at the hospital later on that night, and of Daniel at work at the pub. They've also spoken to Jase's colleague, who has confirmed that Jase was with him between the meeting finishing and him getting called back into work. Alex is the only one they don't have anything concrete on, although Cynthia has confirmed she was with her for some of the night. But there are gaps in every single person's story; snatches of time where their movements can no longer be verified.

Being in the middle of the countryside, there is a point where CCTV coverage becomes non-existent, and no one has come forward with any dashcam footage. Any one of them could have been on the farm at the time of Hannah's death. On top of that, they haven't found a single trace of blood in the house or any of the farm vehicles. Assuming she wasn't attacked outside somewhere, the killer has done a thorough job of covering their tracks.

'Let's see what she's got to say for herself, shall we?' Stefani says.

She steels herself before entering the interview room. Alex is sitting hunched over the table, picking at the polystyrene cup of water in front of her. Little flakes of white fall to the table like snow, creating a small mountain at the base of the cup. She doesn't seem to have even noticed they've entered the room.

'Thank you for coming in,' Stefani says, and Alex's head jerks up with a start. She doesn't say anything in response, just keeps her eyes fixed on them as they take their respective seats opposite her and press the record button.

Stefani clears her throat. 'Interview commenced at' — she checks the time — '14.05 on Sunday the twenty-third of April. Those present are Detective Sergeant Warner and Detective Sergeant Davies. You are currently not under caution. Please can you state your name for the tape?'

Alex gulps. Stefani can see it physically travel down her throat.

'Alexandra Forrester.'

'Mrs Forrester, can you please take us through the events of Wednesday the nineteenth of April?'

Alex sighs, and Stefani can't quite tell if she's simply tired of reiterating her story again, or if she's taking a moment to recall what she's said previously.

'My son Daniel came home from his shift at the pub and picked up his camping gear.'

'And what time was this?'

'I can't really remember. It was before I went to have drinks with Cynthia, so I guess about nine forty-five.'

Stefani makes a mental note to check with the pub what time Daniel finished his shift. She nods encouragingly at Alex, hoping she's masking her suspicion well enough. 'What happened after he left?'

'I went to have drinks with Cynthia outside the farmhouse. As far as I knew, Hannah was in her room while we sat outside. I came home at about ten forty-five.'

'That's a very short time to be having drinks. Why did you leave so early?'

There is a pause. Alex returns her fingers to the cup and starts picking at the edge again.

'We had a slight disagreement. It was silly really. We've been friends for like . . . thirty years, and you know how old friends get.'

She's brushing it off. There's something more here.

'What was the disagreement about?'

'Does it matter?'

Stefani's eyebrows flick up and Alex's cheeks redden. She appears to shrink back in her chair a little.

'Sorry,' Alex mumbles, not meeting Stefani's eye. 'I just mean, I don't see how this information will help figure out what happened to Hannah.'

Stefani exchanges a quick glance with DS Davies, and she can tell from his expression he's thinking the same thing as her.

'It might not,' she says, 'but the clearer a picture we can get of that night, the better.'

Alex chews on her lip for a moment, then says, 'It was about our children.'

'For the benefit of the tape,' DS Davies cuts in, 'the children mentioned are Daniel Forrester and Hannah Carmichael, the deceased.'

Alex blinks before continuing. 'Yes. As you know, they've been seeing each other for some time.'

She pauses, a thoughtful look crossing her eyes, and Stefani leans forward. 'Go on,' she prompts. She doesn't want to allow Alex too much time to craft an answer.

'Cynthia has been very focused on getting Hannah to choose a university recently. She was worried Daniel was . . . distracting her.'

'Distracting her how?'

'By being in a relationship with her. They're teenagers. At that age a relationship seems like the most important thing in the world. I know you think my son had something to do with this but . . .' She trails off, a slight quiver interrupting her words. She swallows hard again, before meeting Stefani's eyes for the first time since she entered. 'He loved that girl. He would never have hurt her.'

Her voice rises at this, the wobble in her throat becoming more pronounced. For a moment, Stefani feels a pang of sympathy for her, but quickly realigns herself, reminding herself that this is not Alex the mum she'd chat to at the school gates, but a suspect.

She looks down at the notes in front of her and flicks to the second page.

'According to Cynthia, you stormed off. Seems a rather dramatic reaction to a disagreement about Daniel distracting Hannah.'

She tilts her head to one side, keeping a keen eye out for any kind of reaction. She's leading Alex in a certain direction and how she responds will tell a lot.

'I . . . I don't really remember. Perhaps the alcohol made me overreact.'

'How much alcohol did you consume?'

'I . . .' She's getting nervous, attempting to predict where the conversation is headed. Tiny beads of sweat are dotting her brow. 'I really don't remember.'

'Was it enough to skew your perception of that night?'

'What? No!'

'But it was enough to cause you to overreact?'

'It was . . . perhaps two or three glasses. As you know, I wasn't with her for long.'

Stefani pauses, allowing a silence to settle over the room. She's rattled Alex by asking about the alcohol, but the next question is the one that will really get under her skin. After a moment, Stefani leans back in her chair.

'You and your son were involved in a serious altercation a few years ago, weren't you?'

The colour completely drains from Alex's face in seconds. Her eyes are wide saucers in her head, her jaw gaping open as if she's gone to speak and someone has come along and snatched the words right out of her mouth. Stefani doesn't say anything else, just waits.

'I'm sorry?' When the reply finally comes it's a whisper, barely audible.

'We've recovered a few news articles. It was quite serious, wasn't it?'

'I don't see what that has to do with anything.' Alex is still pale, and Stefani recognises the look on her face. The look of a lioness protecting her cub.

She softens her tone, changes tack just a little. 'Was your disagreement to do with it? Is that why Cynthia had an issue with their relationship?'

Alex shrinks in on herself, her fingers digging into the table in front of her. The tips of her fingers are starting to turn bright white. She doesn't even seem to realise she's doing it. Stefani eyes the scars that snake their way around Alex's forearm, before she tugs her sleeve down. After a few seconds, Alex's chest starts heaving and her eyes travel the room wildly.

'We know this is difficult, Mrs Forrester.' Stefani nudges the cup of water closer to Alex with her fingertips, but she doesn't notice. Her whole body is starting to tremble. 'Alex?' Stefani exchanges a quick glance with DS Davies, whose brow is furrowed with concern. She gives him a nod and he turns to the recorder.

'Interview paused at 14.10.'

CHAPTER NINE

ALEX

Four Days After the Murder

I don't know what happened. One moment I was answering Stefani's questions, the next it was as if the room was shrinking, the bland windowless walls of the interview room crushing me. Suffocating me under the gravity of what I've done. According to Stefani, I had a panic attack. I've never had a panic attack before. I've always been fairly level-headed, able to keep my cool in stressful situations. Even when I found Hannah, I managed to force myself to think straight. But in that room, when Stefani mentioned the altercation, I had no control over my body.

I'm now in the truck, my temple pressed against the window as the street lights flash past. It's cool, soothing for my headache. It took another couple of hours after my episode before we were allowed to leave – Jase still had to have his interview and the station medic had to check me over – and we grabbed a McDonald's on the way home because neither of us had eaten all day.

I just want to get home. I want to change into my pyjamas and hide under the bedcovers. Pretend that this hell I'm living is some kind of bizarre nightmare. I imagine walking into Daniel's room and seeing him there, playing his guitar or listening to his music. I've always been such an outdoor lover. I usually hate being cooped up in my house. Now I never want to leave.

'Yeah, I'll update you as soon as we hear anything,' Jase murmurs down the phone to his mum. I'm not sure what time it is in Australia, but it must be early. She called as soon as she saw the news and Jase has been trying to reassure her the whole journey home. Ordinarily, I'd tell him off for not using the hands-free while he's driving, but I'm too exhausted to care. I just want him to get her off the phone. Thank God they live so far away. I don't want any family members involved in this mess. Not his parents, and certainly not mine. No matter how well intentioned they may be, any phone calls or visits would just be laced with it. Judgement. That I could let my child turn out like this. Of course, it's my fault Daniel is how he is in the first place.

'Daniel will be fine, Mum. It'll all work itself out,' Jase says, and hearing Daniel's name again makes me tear up. As I close my eyes against my headache, they spill over onto my cheeks. 'Look, I've got to go, I'm nearly home. We'll call you later.'

Eventually, he manages to convince her to hang up and lets out a long exhale. Neither of us says anything else for the remainder of the journey. It's like we've forgotten how to be a couple. Forgotten how to even be in the same space together.

'What's Mark doing there?'

I open my eyes to see we're travelling down the dirt path. The sight of home is welcoming in the distance, albeit slightly blurry from the tears, but as my vision clears, I see him too. Mark is sitting on our front step, his elbows on his knees and his head bowed low. As we approach, he looks up. His face is stony, deep lines etched into his forehead. His stubble is getting long too. He seems to have aged at least ten years over the last four days. I don't imagine I look much better.

We pull up to the garage and Jase is the first to open his door.

'Hey, Mark,' he says, his voice laced with sympathy. 'How's everyone doing?'

For a moment, I don't think he's going to respond. He hauls himself up from the step, a grunt escaping him as he does so, and shuffles towards Jase.

'Not great, as you can imagine.'

I feel like I should get out of the car and offer him my sympathy too, but my body has stopped responding. There's a nagging thread of anxiety pulling at me. All I can do is sit and watch.

'I'm sure. I'm so sorry, mate. If there's anything we can do . . .'

Mark isn't meeting Jase's eye. His gaze is cast down, hands bunched into fists by his sides. Something's wrong.

'Look, Jase. I'm really sorry to have to do this. Everything is just really shit at the moment and . . . both Cynthia and myself think that it would probably be better if you found an alternative living situation for now.'

My stomach turns. Finally, my body snaps into gear and I throw open my door, stumbling to my feet.

'What?'

Mark gives me a double take, as if he'd forgotten I was even here. 'Just until this all gets sorted out.'

'Mark, you can't. Please.'

'Alex . . .' Jase places a hand on my shoulder, but I shake it off.

'No, you can't make us leave. Please. This is my home. It's been my home since I was sixteen.'

My voice is growing shrill, carrying over the quiet of the surrounding fields. A dull heaviness is settling into my core. This farm is everything I've ever known. I've poured my heart and my soul into it for as long as I can remember. It's where Jase and I had our first kiss. It's where I gave birth to Daniel, hunched over in a blow-up birthing pool in my living room. It's where he took his first steps.

'I'm sorry,' Mark says, the lines deepening. 'We just can't have you here right now. Not while . . .' He trails off.

'Not while what?' I stare at him, waiting for his response, but I already know what he was going to say. 'Not while you think Daniel killed her?'

'I didn't say that.'

'That's what you mean though!' The tears are welling up again, threatening to burst free, so I turn my back to Mark and suck in a shaky breath. My eyes scan the landscape. The barns with the animals that I tend to every morning, who keep me company when Jase is working his stupidly long hours. The crops I've lovingly nurtured from seeds. My life being ripped out from under my feet. And finally my eyes land on the farmhouse. 'I need to talk to Cynthia.'

Before Jase or Mark can stop me, I'm clambering into the driver's seat of our truck and lurching it forward, nearly stalling. I can hear

Jase calling me, but I ignore him. Dust kicks up behind the truck as I power back down the path and skid to a halt by the house.

'Cynthia?' I call as I climb out. I stagger to the door and bang my fist against the wood. 'Cynthia, it's me! We need to talk!'

An engine rumbles behind me. Jase and Mark have followed me in Mark's truck, but I don't turn around. I continue hammering the door, attempting in vain to peer through the netted curtains hanging up in the windows.

'I know you're in there, Cynthia! You can't just kick us out without talking to me. I've been your best friend since we were kids! The least you can do is face me!'

'Hey!' Hands grab my shoulders and yank me back. Mark's face is no longer stony. It's filled with rage. 'What the hell do you think you're doing?'

'I just need to talk to her. Cynthia!' I try calling again, but Mark shakes me, my head snapping back and forth. His fingers dig into the soft tissue beneath my collarbone.

'Shut up! What's the matter with you? That woman in there is grieving!'

'Mark, get off her!' Jase is here now, pushing himself between us. Mark releases my shoulders, the spots where he was holding me suddenly throbbing.

'You need to get off our property. Now,' Mark says.

'OK, OK.' Jase puts his hands up. 'We're going to go. Can we just grab some of our stuff?'

Mark swallows, then nods. 'Make it quick.'

The air of the approaching night is muggy. A thin layer of sweat clings to the back of my neck. After our week of heat there's going to be a thunderstorm. I can feel the rain swelling in the sky above me. I hope Daniel will be OK in his little tent. I worry about it every time he goes camping and there's poor weather. My initial instinct is to wonder if I should get up early tomorrow to check the fields for any flooding, but then I remember it's not my responsibility now. It'll be Erin or Steve, the two youngsters I hired last year. Neither of them will be able to manage the farm without me. All my hard work and graft is going to disappear down the drain and I'm powerless to stop it.

We lug our suitcases – filled with the bare essentials we managed to scrape together in the ten minutes Mark gave us to pack – into the lobby of the first bed and breakfast we'd googled in the car. A place halfway between our town and the next.

'Oh, I wasn't expecting anyone this late.' The knit-wearing owner shuffles out from his office.

'Yes, we're sorry to turn up at this time of night.' Jase lowers his suitcase and the floorboards beneath it creak. 'We need a room if you've got any. Probably for a few nights. Maybe more.'

I glance at Jase, wondering how much truth is in that statement. Mark said if there's anything else we need from our house, we are to call and he'll arrange to have it sent to us. That's all very well, but just how long will this go on? Our entire lives – our furniture, our evening clothes, our cookware – it's all there in that barn. We can't live out of suitcases for long.

The man studies us, and I see his expression falter, his mouth pressing together so hard his lips disappear. He recognises us, I'm sure of it.

'This is . . . awkward,' he says, and that familiar sense of dread I felt when we first pulled up to see Mark sitting outside our house returns. 'You understand, word travels rather fast in a small village such as this and . . . I'm very sorry, but I can't give you two a room. No one would want to stay here.'

'Please. We've got nowhere else to go.'

'I'm sorry, I really am.' The man shakes his head and gestures towards the door.

'No, you're not,' I snap.

Jase touches my arm, a silent message to calm down. I know I need to. I know this isn't the time or place to make a scene, but everything that's happened is piling up inside me like a bull trapped in a pen.

The man winces, the guilt in his expression evident. 'I hope this all gets sorted for you soon.'

He moves past us, opens the door and holds it wide. For a moment, Jase and I stand still, dumbfounded, but there's nothing either of us can say or do. We pick up our suitcases and trudge outside into the cold, back to our truck.

As we travel out of the small town, I keep my head bowed, terrified I might accidentally catch the eye of someone we know. As that man said, word travels fast around here. They must all know, must all suspect my son. And it'll only be a matter of time before they put two and two together and assume I'm helping to cover his tracks, just as the police do. They're certain I know where Daniel is. If only that were true.

The Premier Inn we finally find a room at is right on the far end of the next town. The room is nice, clean and orderly, as hotel rooms always are, but the air feels stuffy and I find myself equally desperate for a shower but too drained to face it. As we unpack, Jase grumbles about how long it will take to get to work in the morning, and I have to bite my tongue to stop myself from snapping at him. At least he'll be going to work in the morning. What am I to do besides sit on this bed that isn't my own and think about my son, who is out there somewhere probably terrified that the police will track him down at any moment? And what of his mental state? Has he come to terms with what he's done? Has he seen the news and figured out that I must have been the one to clean up the crime scene? Is he worried that I'm going to get in trouble? I wouldn't know because I can't talk to him. If only he would pick up the damned phone.

I jump as a hand rests on my shoulder, and turn to see Jase looking down at me. His eyes are actually meeting mine for the first time since this all happened. Neither of us says a word, but we don't have to. We're both thinking the same thing, wondering how we're going to get out of this, terrified of what tomorrow will bring. And then we're holding each other, his strong arms wrapped around me, my face burrowed into his shoulder, and I never want to let go.

CHAPTER TEN

HANNAH

The Day of the Murder – 7.20 p.m.

'Won't be long,' I say, keeping my head bowed low as I move swiftly towards the front door. I'm hoping if I move quickly enough, Mum won't have time to stop me. She's like a hawk though, swooping in at lightning speed, her presence behind me instantly making me feel on edge.

'Where are you going?' she asks.

I don't turn to face her, but I can picture her perfectly. She'll be stood with her arms crossed, her face stony, lips pursed as if she's been sucking on a lemon. Bradley and I have a way of doing that to her apparently.

'Just out with friends. I won't be late back.' I try to sound as nonchalant as possible as I edge towards the door, making it clear that I'm not asking for her permission.

'You've been going out a lot recently. Shouldn't you be working on your personal statement?'

A flash of annoyance hits me and my stomach tightens. This is why I need to get out of here. I feel like I'm drowning and she's the one holding my head under the water.

'It's basically done,' I say, trying with all my might to keep my tone even. Mum and I have been arguing a lot lately and I hate it. I don't want to argue with her. It's Bradley who's always causing issues, not me. I'm the good girl. I'm the one she's proud of. Though, of course, she doesn't know what I've been up to lately. 'I just need to do a quick grammar check and then it'll be good to go.'

I'm about to open the door when she appears right beside me. 'You can't be so casual with this, Hannah. It's too important. A quick grammar check just isn't good enough.'

'For God's sake, Mum! I've still got weeks to perfect it. Will you just back off?'

Before she can respond, I yank open the door and storm out, slamming it behind me. I fix my eyes on the entrance gate and don't dare look back at the house. My stomach is doing flips. I've never snapped at her like that. I shouldn't have. But there's nothing I can do about it now.

I walk quickly, hugging my jacket around me. It's my favourite jacket. Designer. Way fancier than anything I could ever afford. It was a present from him after he saw me looking longingly at it through the window of the House of Fraser in town last month. Luckily, Mum is so behind the times she'd never know where it came from, so I don't have to dodge any questions about how I managed to pay for it. It's certainly worth its price tag at the moment – I'm bloody freezing.

The bus takes me as far as the next town over, but I have to walk the final bit. It's a pain that it's so far away, but we chose our special place for a reason. We have to make sure there's no way we'll bump into anyone we know.

I check the time again and send him a quick text.

Nearly there xxx

After hitting 'send', my finger hovers over Mum's number. I should probably apologise for storming out like that, but part of me is too proud to, and the other part of me is too scared of what she'll say. I know how it would play out. She's a master of mind games. She'll find a way to make me feel so guilty that I never go out again until I'm receiving my degree.

I shake my head and slip my phone back into my pocket. It's not worth it. She's meant to be having drinks with Alex tonight. Hopefully by the time I get back she'll be tipsy enough that she'll have forgotten what I said, or at least care less.

As I walk, a sharp gust of wind pelts me and my hair whips around my face. I curse, attempting in vain to smooth it down again, and fumble about in my bag for a hairbrush. I can never seem to turn up at our special place these days without looking like I've been dragged through a hedge backwards. Between the walk from the bus stop and the film of farm dirt that seems to constantly cling to my skin no matter how often I shower, I never look nice by the time I get there. I can't wait to get out of this shitty place. Soon, we're going to escape together, just the two of us. He's promised.

I'm finally here. I walk up the steps and move into the shelter of the lobby, giving the bored-looking receptionist a cheerful smile. She doesn't really acknowledge me. It's not much warmer in here than it is outside, but my mind isn't on the cold anymore. It's on seeing him.

I'm just about to pass the reception desk when hands land on my shoulders, gripping on to me and spinning me around. I let out a yelp, lifting my fists in the air, ready to fight off my attacker, when my eyes land on his face.

'You scared the crap out of me!' I exclaim, blushing at my overreaction. I can see the receptionist watching us out of the corner of my eye, so am quick to make it obvious that I know this man and that he's not a threat.

He has an amused look on his face, his eyes twinkling and the corners creasing.

'Oh come on,' he says, and the warmth in his voice allows the thudding of my heart to calm a little. 'You know I'd never hurt you.'

CHAPTER ELEVEN

ALEX

Six Days After the Murder

Not one word. We didn't hear a single update yesterday. Nothing this morning either. Not directly anyway. The only information I've managed to obtain is what's been plastered on the internet. Cruel words about Daniel, about us. Tweets from people who think they've got this case all figured out. Plus, a text from Jenna Driscoll:

> How are you holding up, Alex? The girls are coming round later for a cuppa. Do join us if you need a bit of friendly natter!

I scoffed at it and deleted it straight away. I've never been invited round for tea before. The only reason she wants me to come over is so she can try to dig out the gossip.

I haven't been sleeping. The bed at the Premier Inn is plenty comfortable, but my mind won't shut off. It swirls and jumbles, a torturous mix of visions of both Hannah and Daniel. It doesn't help that the thunderstorm that settled over England after we left the farm has made it near impossible to go out for any kind of fresh air. Even now, the wind is battering against the windows. Jase left for work at four this morning and I've been lying here ever since, staring up at the ceiling, listening to the rainfall. My limbs ache despite the unusual lack of physical labour the past couple of days.

I stretch, rub the crusty residue from the corners of my eyes and roll out of bed. I take a shower, turn the showerhead onto the most powerful setting so that the droplets beat down loudly on my head, hoping it might help to drown out my thoughts. I go about a few mindless morning tasks; make myself a coffee at the little self-serve station, brush my teeth, tie my hair into a ponytail. And then, just like yesterday, I find myself with nothing to do, and so I sit down at my laptop and open up Google.

Hannah Carmichael Murder.

My fingers tremble as I type the letters, even though I've typed them more times than I can count since we arrived here. Every time I do this search, I'm terrified that a photo of Daniel in handcuffs is going to come up with a headline saying they've found and arrested him. But no, the same articles stare back at me. Timelines of the murder case, all identical despite being from different newspapers, as if they've all filled each other in on the details. Updates as they come in.

I click into the first one, a BBC report, and my heart sinks. There, at the top, is the smiling photo of Hannah, the one that was used on the flyers we handed out. And next to Hannah is a photo of Daniel, one they took off social media. In it, he has his arms wrapped around her. Protective. The words underneath the photos read: *'Human remains have been found by police investigating the disappearance of Hannah Carmichael. On the right, Hannah's boyfriend Daniel Forrester.'*

Every time I come to this page I hope Daniel's photo might have been replaced by someone else's. That they've found evidence there was another person involved, that it wasn't my boy after all. But I know in my heart of hearts I'm clutching at air. Hannah was murdered in her home on the farm, and there was only one person angry enough to kill her that night.

I scroll a little further and my throat constricts. There's a photo of me. It's slightly out of focus and dark, most likely taken in the early evening, but it's definitely me walking from our truck to the Premier Inn entrance. My hair is bundled into a messy knot on the top of my head. My face is washed out, devoid of life. Underneath this photo are the words: *'Pictured: Alex Forrester, mother of the chief suspect.'*

Anger curdles in my stomach. They've taken that picture outside in the car park. The papers have actually resorted to hounding me here, to the place we're staying because no one in our home town wants to know us, and have been watching me without my knowing. They could be out there right now, waiting for me to leave.

I stand up and move at a snail's pace towards the window, keeping myself well hidden behind the wall, and peer out. There's nobody out there. The vehicles in the car park are all empty. Yet still my skin is covered with goosebumps.

Satisfied that there's definitely no one watching me – not now, at least – I return to the bed and my laptop. I scroll down the article a little further, but no new information arises. A related article draws my eye over to the side of the screen: **HANNAH CARMICHAEL VIGIL TO BE HELD TONIGHT.**

Pursing my lips, I click into the article and scan the details. As I read, every fibre of my being tells me to shut the laptop. I know without a hint of uncertainty that my showing up at a vigil for Hannah would be a terrible, terrible idea. But even so, as the hours of the day slip away unproductively, I find myself pulling a black dress out of my suitcase, running the hairbrush through my peppered strands and heading to the bus stop.

There aren't that many people at the church when I arrive. I'm early by about half an hour, but things seem to be getting started regardless. You can practically feel the shock waves radiating through the community, the disturbance in the air. The vicar is by the door handing out candles, the glow of each one like a halo bobbing around the church grounds. More candles are grouped around a floral display next to the graveyard, and despite the dim light of the incoming evening, I can see Hannah's face staring back at me from within an ornate frame.

I don't go to collect a candle from the vicar. Instead, I keep to the opposite side of the street, in the shadow of the bus stop, and simply watch. Hands clasped, head bowed. I haven't come here to speak to anyone or to throw my hands up in prayer. I'm not sure I believe in all that anyway. The only reason I am here is to pay my respects to Hannah as quietly and surreptitiously as possible. I owe her that much after what I did.

'Alex! Do you know where your son is?'

Before I can fully comprehend what's going on, a microphone is being thrust into my face. The dark eye of a lens blinks at me and another camera flashes, reflecting off the wet ground. It's blinding, turning the street around me into a bright fuzzy haze. I can't believe I hadn't noticed them before. There are three or four blue vans all lined up along the edge of the road with news-station logos emblazoned on the sides, all presumably filled with press hoping to capture an award-winning snapshot of Cynthia and Mark's grief. But I've given them something even better. Maybe they were hoping I'd turn up.

'Do you know where he is?' the reporter asks again, pushing the microphone even closer, nearly batting me in the mouth with it. She's exactly how I picture reporters: sleek, straightened hair, thin red lips, a tailored suit-jacket and skirt. I stare at her, wondering if she has kids. She can't. If she did, she surely wouldn't be able to harass a mother in this way. Surely she'd show me a hint of humanity.

'No . . . I . . . No comment.' I don't mean to stutter, don't want to seem unsure of myself, but this has completely knocked me off-kilter. I take a few steps back, distancing myself from the cameras. I'm suddenly acutely aware of the church congregation staring at me, whispering and murmuring, the attention well and truly pulled away from Hannah's memorial. Mortified, I duck my head low and turn on my heel, trying to scan the return bus times. The numbers blur before my eyes.

'Are you hiding him, Alex? Are you covering for your son?'

'No comment!'

'Do you think he's capable of murder?'

The reporter's words slice through the air. My body tenses as heat flushes through me, causing every muscle to quiver. And then, before I know what I'm doing, I'm whipping around. The sting seems to come seconds before the impact of my knuckles on the reporter's cheek. Gasps sound from the crowd as the reporter stumbles backwards, crashing into her colleague holding the camera.

For a moment, I am frozen solid, the heat of anger still pulsing through my veins. Then, after what feels like an eternity, my eyes travel to the crowd and fix on Cynthia's blotchy, tear-stained face. It's the first time I've seen her since Hannah was found apart from the photos online. I can't quite place the look she's giving me, but it's one I've never seen before in all our years of friendship. It's like . . . like we're enemies. And that's when I notice it. The hatred on each person's face. Women I've chatted to at the school gates, have gone on coffee dates with, whose children I've babysat. They all hate me.

I return my gaze to the reporter, who is tending gingerly to her swollen cheek.

'I'm sorry,' I whisper, before walking, running, sprinting in the opposite direction.

CHAPTER TWELVE

STEFANI

Seven Days After the Murder

Stefani's tense reflection stares back at her as she waits outside her ex's glass-paned front door. She didn't text him to tell him she was coming, which she realises is rather inconsiderate, but she's hoping Luke won't mind too much. She just had to see Cassie. All this business with Hannah Carmichael is making her re-evaluate her priorities.

Luke's distorted outline appears through the glass after a couple of minutes. 'Hey, Stef,' he says as he opens the door, confusion etched across his face. 'What are you doing here? You're not having Cassie until Saturday.'

'I know, I'm sorry for turning up unannounced. I'm on my way into work and I just wanted to see her. I thought perhaps I could drop her into school.' Stefani secretly wishes Cassie was still young enough to be taken to and from school. Now that she has a nearly adult daughter readying herself to leave education, she misses the school run, stress and all.

Luke raises an eyebrow. 'She doesn't even let me drop her in these days. Apparently, I cramp her style. But come in, maybe she'll be in an agreeable mood.'

Relieved, Stefani steps into the warmth of the house and follows Luke through to the kitchen. It looks completely different from when she lived here. Luke and Amanda have just added an extension onto the back of the house, making the kitchen twice the size and completely remodelling it with sleek built-in units. It matches Amanda perfectly, who is sitting at the breakfast bar in the angel-like glow of the skylights, her engagement ring glinting in the sun. Seeing her, Stefani is seized by a sense of inadequacy.

Amanda glances up from her phone as she enters.

'Stefani, lovely to see you!' She moves over to her and plants a kiss on each of her cheeks. Stefani forces a smile. She doesn't dislike Amanda. Of the three women Luke's dated since their separation, Amanda seems to be the nicest, and she hopes for Cassie's sake that she'll be the one to stick around. But Stefani is acutely aware every time she sees her that this woman spends more time with her daughter than she does.

'I'm really sorry to just drop by,' she says again, starting to regret the rash decision.

Amanda waves her hand dismissively. 'No bother at all. Cassie's in the shower. She shouldn't be long. Would you like a coffee while you wait?'

Stefani nods, more out of a want to have something to do with her hands than anything. Amanda floats around the breakfast bar and presses a few buttons on their fancy coffee machine, while Luke disappears into his office. Stefani secretly wishes he'd stay in the kitchen while she waits so that she isn't alone with Amanda. At least with Luke she doesn't feel the need to fill awkward silences.

Amanda places a double-walled glass mug filled with frothy barista-style coffee in front of Stefani, and she sips it gratefully. It's certainly a step up from the instant stuff she has at home.

'Oh, by the way,' Amanda says, as she perches herself on the opposite bar stool, 'Cassie's doctor's appointment went fine. No problems.'

Stefani frowns. 'Doctor's appointment?'

'To get her birth-control pills.' There is a brief silence, and Amanda's cheeks start turning pink. 'She said she'd told you?'

'Oh, yes! Sorry. I'm miles away.' Stefani looks down at her coffee, focusing on the beige and white pattern in the foam so that Amanda can't see her eyes glossing. 'Good. Thank you again for taking her.'

'No problem at all,' Amanda says, the relief evident in her voice. 'I'm just glad she's being careful. You know what teenage girls are like these days. Though she says the main reason she wants to go on the pill is to clear her skin up . . .' Amanda pauses, clearly anxious that she has revealed something else Stefani doesn't know. Cassie's struggled with her skin for a couple of years, so this at least isn't a surprise, but still, Stefani feels outside of her daughter's life again.

Somehow, she manages to get through the pleasantries with Amanda that follow without betraying the humiliation building inside her. It should have been her who Cassie confided in, who took her to the doctors and talked her through all her options. This was a mother–daughter experience, but another woman got there first. And now the time has passed.

'Mum?' Cassie finally appears at the kitchen door after ten or so excruciating minutes.

'Hi, sweetheart.' Stefani smiles warmly, gulping back the lump in her throat. 'Fancy a lift to school?'

Cassie presses her head against the car window as they drive, clearly not thrilled about being dropped in. But at least she didn't flat out turn her mother down.

'Are you taking on the Hannah Carmichael case?' she says as they come to a halt at a red light.

'I am. Did you know her?'

'No, not really.' Cassie turns away from her to look at her reflection.

Stefani nods, quietly glad. This case is almost certainly a murder case, and she doesn't want Cassie having to deal with that. It's bad enough that it's happened to someone at her school. She shakes her head, swatting thoughts of Hannah away. The whole reason she wanted to drop Cassie in was so that she could spend some time with her and forget about the case for just five minutes.

'So,' she says, turning options of what to say over in her mind. 'How are things with Ethan?'

Ethan is Cassie's boyfriend of three months, though she's never called him as much. He's not exactly the boy Stefani would like to see Cassie with – he wears his trousers ridiculously low and doesn't seem to be a huge fan of washing his greasy mop of hair – but as long as he treats her well, Stefani hasn't got an issue with him.

'Fine.' Cassie shrugs.

Stefani shuffles in her seat, trying to figure out the best way to subtly mention the birth control without dropping Amanda in it. 'You've been together for a while now. Are things starting to get serious?'

'I don't know.'

If only there were an instruction manual for how to talk to teenage girls. It's like trying to squeeze blood from a stone.

'You know you don't have to do anything you're not ready for, don't you?' Stefani says, noting Cassie's seeming disinterest in Ethan.

Cassie doesn't answer this, except to roll her eyes so hard they nearly disappear into the back of her skull.

'You can drop me here. Saves you having to fight through the traffic.'

Before Stefani can say anything, Cassie is already unbuckling her seat belt.

'OK, I'll speak to you later?'

'Yeah, talk to you later.'

She hauls herself out of the car and gives Stefani a quick wave before shutting the door and walking off in the direction of the school.

Stefani slumps back in her seat, wishing she'd told Cassie she loves her. For some reason, whenever they're together, she can never quite get across what she wants to say. It's as if, a lot of the time, they're a couple of strangers rather than mother and daughter.

'Give me some good news, Warner.' DCI Walton's shadow stretches across the desk in front of Stefani, and she can already tell without even looking up that he's got his arms crossed – his favourite intimidating posture. He's getting more and more impatient by the day. His boss is on his case, even more so since the tabloids have started phoning the precinct. Not to mention the false leads, the idiots making stories up for their five minutes of fame, the psychics assuring them they know where Daniel is.

Stefani winces before lifting her gaze to meet his, hoping her face is coming across more confident than she actually feels. 'I got a message from Davies just ten minutes ago. There's an update on Daniel Forrester's phone.'

They've been attempting to track Daniel's phone for the past couple of days, but tech said it must be switched off. She had hoped they'd be able to pick up at least his last known location, but so far she's not heard anything. DS Davies' message this morning is the first flicker of hope she's felt since this investigation started.

Walton raises an eyebrow at her. 'I expect an update report on my desk by 2 p.m.'

Stefani releases a breath through her teeth as he walks away. She begged for this case, assured him she was the right person to tackle it, but the lack of progress is making her doubt her abilities. DS Davies keeps reminding her to not be so hard on herself, that this is a particularly tricky case, which is true. Though the human remains they found in the pig barn were enough to confirm it was Hannah, any trace of evidence they'd usually look for on a dead body was gone. No skin under fingernails, no stray strands of hair on clothing, no signs of sexual assault. Everything mutilated. Her social media hasn't provided anything useful either. Just your average teenage girl's collection of selfies. In all the photos Daniel appears in, he seems to adore her, though Stefani knows that doesn't mean anything.

She leans back in her chair and glances over the profile on Daniel's parents once more. Luckily for Alex, the reporter she walloped isn't pressing charges, but she's most definitely made things worse for herself. The story has now evolved from 'loving mother protecting killer son' to 'killer son gets his anger issues from his mother'. But, if Stefani is honest with herself, she doesn't blame Alex for lashing out like that. She hates journalists too.

When DS Davies finally emerges through the precinct doors, Stefani practically falls out of her chair. He takes a wary step back as she lunges for him.

'Please tell me something good,' she says, her nails digging into the palms of her hands.

DS Davies hesitates. 'We found Daniel Forrester's phone.'

His words are despondent, lacking the enthusiasm she'd expect from him right now.

'And?' Stefani prompts.

He shakes his head. 'You're not going to like it.'

'I can't cope with this anymore.' Cynthia presses her fingers to her temples, and Stefani's eyes are inadvertently drawn to her thinning hairline. 'I just need this to be over. I just need you to find him so that this can be over.'

Stefani nudges the box of tissues on the coffee table closer to her, wishing she could break professionalism for just a moment to offer her a hug. She can't imagine how conflicted Cynthia must feel in all of this. Obviously, she wants Hannah's killer caught, but she's known Daniel since he was a baby. He's her best friend's son. It must be heartbreaking to contemplate that he's the one who took her daughter from her.

'The phone was out of battery, hence our technical team's struggle to track it.' Stefani straightens herself, running through her rehearsed speech in her head. 'I assure you we're doing everything we can to find him. We've been following his movements on CCTV, and have obtained some dashcam footage from people who were out on the roads that night, and we've managed to place his last known location as somewhere in Brecon Beacons. I've got a team there currently scouring the area. Unfortunately, he seems to camp at a different spot each time he goes, so we haven't got a whole lot to go on.'

'OK, that's good.' Mark squeezes Cynthia's shoulder and she seems to relax into his hand. 'They're closing in, Cynth. They'll get him.'

Stefani, relieved at Mark's ability to pacify his wife, takes a breath before she moves on to her next point. 'In the meantime, we'd like to start looking into Hannah's phone records.'

Cynthia's forehead creases. 'I thought you couldn't find her phone either?'

Stefani winces at the way Cynthia says 'either'. Another reminder of her failures on this case so far.

'We can't,' she says carefully. 'But we will be able to access records without the physical phone.'

It's Mark's turn to frown. 'You want to look at her last contacts?' he says.

'Exactly. We need to know if she spoke to anyone else in the lead-up to her death. It will help us to eliminate any other suspects.'

With this, the hostility in the room seems to swell around her, and Stefani shares a nervous glance with DS Davies.

'Other suspects? You can't be serious!' Cynthia's eyes widen and she starts blinking rapidly. 'We already know who did it!'

The force in Cynthia's voice is one Stefani hasn't heard in any of her interviews with her. Previous to this, she's come across as frail and vulnerable. Now, her nostrils are flaring and the vein in her forehead practically pulses. It's taken Stefani aback somewhat. When she came to tell Cynthia that Daniel's phone had been found in his bedroom, and that her team had missed it during their first search of the converted barn, she had expected more tears from Cynthia. She's not quite sure how to respond to the anger she's getting now, as much as she understands it.

Mark places his hand on Cynthia's arm again, but this time it doesn't seem to possess the same appeasing qualities. 'Cynthia, darling. Calm down.'

'No! I won't calm down!' She pulls her arm away from Mark and glares at Stefani. 'Look, Daniel's always been a good kid, but ever since... well, he's also been volatile. It might have been an accident, who knows.' She shakes her head, looking down at her lap. 'I don't understand why you're wasting time looking into other suspects when it's so obvious who did it. Why else would he disappear off the face of the earth?'

'Mrs Carmichael, we understand what a difficult situation this is,' DS Davies interjects, clearly eager to defuse the situation. 'We assure you that our top priority is finding Daniel Forrester.'

Cynthia lets out a laugh and turns away from them.

Stefani swallows hard before continuing. 'Unfortunately, at the moment, even if we find Daniel Forrester, we don't yet have enough evidence to convict him. Hannah's records may well help us to find the evidence we need. They could also help us figure out who she was with that evening before she died.'

There is a pause as Stefani's words hang in the air. After a long, long moment, Cynthia turns back to face them.

'Or maybe you're looking for other suspects because you don't want to convict him?'

Stefani blinks, taken aback. 'I'm sorry?'

'You've been a part of this community for years. You've chatted to Alex at the school gates. Maybe you're going lightly on her son because of personal loyalty?'

'Mrs Carmichael, I can assure you I have no personal loyalty to anyone involved in this case. My one and only priority is finding justice for Hannah. But I cannot do that without full cooperation.'

Stefani is trying hard to keep the bitterness out of her voice, to remain neutral, but Cynthia's words have touched a nerve. That was her chief's exact worry when she first asked for this case. Does he think this of her too? Is he concerned her lack of progress is because of some kind of misplaced loyalty towards the Forresters?

Cynthia is still staring at her, but she doesn't say anything else. Instead, Mark steps forward.

'We really appreciate all your hard work, DS Warner. Please, keep us updated.'

CHAPTER THIRTEEN

ALEX

Seven Days After the Murder

I've just settled down to my usual dinner of a chicken and mayo sandwich from Tesco – the only thing I can stomach at the moment – when Mark's name flashes up on my phone. A piece of crust lodges itself in my throat and I cough and splutter while trying to swipe to answer the call.

'Hel—hello?'

Mark's voice, when it comes, is raspy, as if he's been shouting. 'Hi, Alex. It's me, Mark.'

'Mark,' I repeat, as if he's spoken to me in a foreign language. Dread is pooling in my stomach. I've nearly called them so many times. It's been gnawing at me, the conflict I feel between protecting Daniel, and myself, of course, and the pain I feel for Cynthia and Mark. But each time I've picked up the phone, I've chickened out.

I clear my throat as I realise he's waiting for me to speak. 'Mark. Yes. How is everything?' It's my first instinct to ask the question, but I immediately regret it. I can already guess how everything is.

'Um, not great,' he says. 'Can we have a chat?'

The ball of anxiety expands inside me. 'Sure, I'm listening.'

'I mean in person.' Mark pauses. 'Where are you staying?'

I fall silent and my throat constricts. The noises from the neighbouring rooms suddenly seem amplified, their movements and muted chatter pounding through my head. The last time I saw Mark, when he yelled at me for trying to talk to Cynthia, I witnessed a side to him I'd never seen before. An edge that frightened me. The last thing I want is to be alone with him.

'I'm not sure that's the best idea,' I say eventually. 'The police wouldn't like us meeting up privately.'

I'm sure that's probably true – after the incident at the memorial, Stefani expressly forbade me from going anywhere near the family until this is all resolved – but it's not the real reason I don't want him to come here, and Mark knows it. The thought of facing him again makes me feel queasy.

'Please, Alex,' he says. 'It won't be for long.'

There's a desperate tone to his voice and I soften a little, swallowing down my doubts.

'All right. But if the police catch on that you've been—'

'Ten minutes,' he says. 'That's all I need.'

I spend the next half-hour while I wait for Mark's arrival pacing the hotel room. A few times I pull out my phone and consider texting Jase to let him know what's going on, and a few times I consider calling Stefani, but each time, I change my mind. No matter who I call they'll tell me not to meet with him, and as much as I really don't want to, I can't help but be curious as to what he's coming to say. Mark made it very clear he didn't want me anywhere near him or Cynthia, but perhaps he's questioning Daniel's guilt now?

The sound of a car pulling up outside the Premier Inn draws my eye outside. I pull the mesh curtain to one side, peeking around its edge. It's chucking it down outside. Thick streams of water drizzle down the window, obscuring the figure getting out of the car, but I know it's him. Suddenly, I'm overcome with the urge to rip the curtain closed again and to hide down the side of the bed, curl up in the foetal position and pretend I'm not here. Instead, I stay frozen to the spot until I hear the gentle *tap, tap, tapping* at the door.

Mark is drenched when I open the door to him. Little droplets of rain drip off his hair and clothes, and a small puddle is already forming at the base of his feet. I move to one side, opening the door wider to allow him to pass and then closing it behind him. For a moment, we just stare at each other, and I'm unsure whether I'm supposed to be the first to speak or not. Should I offer him a cup of tea from the self-service station?

Fists curled, I peel myself away from the wall and press the speed dial on my phone for Daniel. I've done this every day, but never with this level of desperation. Deep down, I know I'm going to hear his voicemail again and, sure enough, his recorded message trills back at me. My grip tightens on the phone.

Mark is right about one thing. This has to stop. I will not allow my son to go down like this. I won't let Mark, or the police, or anyone else, wreck this family any more than they already have. There's still hope. The police are looking into other suspects. That means they don't have a shred of evidence against Daniel apart from his disappearance. So, as far as they're concerned, someone else could well have killed Hannah.

I navigate to Stefani's number, allowing all the anger, all the fear, all the desperation I've felt since this all started to bubble and rise to the surface. It rings just three times before her voice sounds on the other end of the line.

'DS Warner.'

'Hi,' I say, taking a steadying breath. 'I think there's something you should know . . . about Mark Butler.'

@mama799: How have the police not found the boyfriend yet? How do they expect young girls to feel safe these days?? #JusticeForHannah

@zobobo: Useless. Bet we'd have better luck finding that son of a bitch #JusticeForHannah

@news_junkiee: I don't reckon it was the boyfriend. Too obvious. My bets are on the parents!

@zobobo: The dad isn't even her dad. Her real dad died years ago. Maybe the mum killed them both off LMAO!

@mama799: Hardly a laughing matter @zobobo . . . #JusticeForHannah

CHAPTER FOURTEEN

STEFANI

Eight Days After the Murder

'What exactly did Alex Forrester say?' DCI Walton hands Stefani a cup of coffee before taking a swig of his own. She accepts it gratefully, allowing the warmth to filter through to her hands and make her fingers tingle. The weather has definitely turned. The rain hasn't let up for the past couple of days, and the village's plumbing is struggling. Stefani had hoped the poor weather might draw Daniel Forrester out of his hiding place, but it doesn't seem to have done so far.

'Apparently, Mark called her out of the blue. Asked to chat in person. When he got there, he started ranting and raving, threatening to hurt her if she didn't tell him where Daniel was, threatening to kill the boy if he found him.' She sighs and shakes her head. She can't quite picture it, Mark going into a rage like that. From what she knows of him, he seems a mild-mannered bloke. But then he is under a lot of strain. 'Alex reckons he's got anger issues and a drinking problem. Of course, that could just be her trying to shift the suspicion away from her son.'

'Any witnesses?'

'DS Davies pulled up the CCTV from the Premier Inn. He was there all right, at the exact time she said.'

He nods, deep in thought. 'When are you bringing him in for questioning?'

'Later today. I've got an appointment at the school just after lunch. I'm speaking to some of her friends, teachers. Maybe they can shed some light.'

'Be sure to mention Mark, won't you? See if anyone's ever said anything about him. Man's obviously got a temper.'

'I was planning to,' Stefani says. 'Although, we haven't found any kind of motive for him to kill Hannah. Unless it was accidental, in a fit of rage kind of thing.'

'You never know. How long has he been in her life again?'

Stefani consults her notes. 'Only two years. His marriage to Cynthia was a bit of a whirlwind by the looks of it.'

'It's not unheard of,' DCI Walton says, 'a new stepfather trying to show his dominance in the household. Maybe she kept talking back to him. Wouldn't let him boss her around.'

'Maybe.' Stefani swirls her coffee in her mug, watching the frothy top separate. She agrees that they need to seriously consider Mark as a suspect. After all, he says he didn't return from his business trip until after Hannah went missing, but there's no proof of that. There's no traffic cameras on these kinds of country roads, and there were snippets of time where he left the hotel for one reason or another. For all they know, he could have driven back home, killed her and then returned to his hotel room to give himself an alibi.

Something just doesn't sit right in her head. There's more to this case. It's becoming more complicated, and more tricky to solve, as each day passes.

The stale smell of old sweat hits Stefani as soon as she opens Hannah's locker door. Her PE kit is still in there, sitting unwashed in her bag. With a white-gloved hand, Stefani rifles through the contents. It's all the things you'd expect to find in a teenage girl's locker. A pencil case, a small toiletries bag with a few bits of make-up inside, a collection of textbooks and workbooks. She pulls out a few of them, flicks open the first couple of pages and scans Hannah's swirly writing. Her heart hurts to look at it. There's something strangely haunting about seeing the writing of someone who is no longer alive, especially when that someone was so tragically young. Stefani gives herself a little shake, places the books back into the locker and sighs.

She had hoped, as awful as it sounds, there might have been a diary tucked away in there. A diary would reveal Hannah's innermost thoughts in the lead-up to her death, things that she possibly didn't share with anyone else. If Mark had a history of being violent with her, it might be in a diary. She'd also thought that maybe Hannah's phone would be in there, even though logic would suggest Hannah would have her mobile glued to her, like every other teenager, but no such luck. Hopefully, the phone records will be back later today.

'DS Warner? DS Davies?' Stefani turns to see the headmistress, Alison Taylor, striding towards them. They smile at each other warmly, though the undercurrent of tension is thick.

'We're all done with Hannah's locker,' Stefani says. 'Thank you.'

Alison nods. 'I hope it was... helpful?' A not so subtle way of asking if they've found anything. Stefani chooses to ignore the question.

'Are we able to speak to Hannah's form tutor yet?'

'Yes,' Alison says, trying to conceal her disappointment in Stefani's change of subject. 'That's what I came here to tell you. Registration is just coming to an end and Mr Woodward has a free period.'

Mr Woodward is a red-haired, slight man with freckles dusting his nose. He sits across from Stefani and DS Davies, crossing and uncrossing his legs as if he's not quite sure how to behave in front of two police officers. The classroom they're sat in is presumably that of Hannah's tutor group, the room in which she would have sat twice a day for registration. Stefani allows her eyes to wander, glancing at the chairs tucked behind the desks, and wonders which one was Hannah's.

'Thank you for talking to us,' she says, keeping her tone warm so as to help Mr Woodward feel less on edge. 'We're hoping you can help us get a clearer picture of who Hannah was at school. How did she behave in class? Who did she spend time with? Things like that.'

The teacher nods, his foot tapping on the floor. 'Of course. She was a very bright girl. One of the best grade reports out of her whole form. And very well liked, as far as I could tell. One of the more popular girls in the class. Lots of friends.'

'Any boys?' DS Davies asks, and Mr Woodward frowns.

'Well, yes. The Forrester boy.'

Stefani nods. 'We know about Daniel, but we're interested to see if there was anyone else she was close to who we should be speaking with.'

At this, Mr Woodward appears to blush a little.

'I try not to pay too much attention to my students' love lives, but, as you know, she was a very attractive young girl. I think most of the boys had a thing for her.'

'But no one specific? No one she was openly involved with?'

'No.' Mr Woodward shuffles awkwardly in his seat. 'She didn't seem interested to be honest. She seemed more interested in her schoolwork. Honestly, she was the perfect student.' His voice cracks at these last few words, and Stefani feels a wave of sympathy for the man. It must be terrible, seeing a young girl every day for years, watching them grow and reach their adult years, only to have their life ripped away in such a violent fashion.

'And her friends?' Stefani says, her pen poised above her notebook ready to write down names. 'Who did she tend to spend the most time with?'

At this, Mr Woodward goes bright red and stares down at his feet. Stefani frowns. Why is he so nervous talking to them? She doesn't say anything, just waits for his response, which takes a good ten seconds to come.

'There is someone we think she was closest to. In one of the other tutor groups. Apparently she spent most of her break times with her.'

Stefani leans forward, watching Mr Woodward intently.

'And who was that?' DS Davies prompts.

'It's . . . awkward.'

Stefani shakes her head. 'Sorry, what's awkward?' she says, but as the words leave her mouth, she's already worked it out; why he hasn't been able to meet her eye since they came into the classroom.

'Well, as I said she was friendly with most of her fellow students,' Mr Woodward says. 'But the person she was particularly good friends with was your daughter. Cassie.'

CHAPTER FIFTEEN

ALEX

Eight Days After the Murder

The tension is thick as I swirl my teaspoon around my cup, the soft *clink* of the metal against china the only sound in the room. I hate this room. My life now is just staring at the four walls of the Premier Inn, endless cups of tea growing cold in my hand. That's all it's been since we arrived and I'm not used to it. Ordinarily, I'd be out in the open, breathing in the country air, moving my body. But since the vigil, the press have started to gather outside the entrance, and now I'm a prisoner. Even my cross-stitch doesn't do anything to calm me anymore. It has sat untouched on the desk, reminding me of the joy I'd felt when I started it, back when things were still normal.

Jase is getting ready for work. I watch him as I sip my tea, take in his strong jaw and slightly wonky nose. I was so head over heels for him when we first met. All he had to do was give me one of his looks and I'd go weak at the knees. He never seems to give me that look anymore. In fact, since that godforsaken day four years ago when our lives got turned upside down, I could probably count on one hand the number of date nights we've had. On the rare occasion we do have sex, it feels more like fulfilling an obligation to each other than anything deep and meaningful. I suppose what happened with Daniel affected us in more ways than we care to admit. And Jase's workload has been pretty intense since he was made a consultant.

'I hope you have a good day at work,' I say as he emerges from the bathroom and pulls his coat over his shoulders. I present my cheek to him and he places a small kiss on it. A small, insignificant, efficient kiss. As he pulls away my eyebrows knit together.

'What's the matter?' he says.

'Are you still angry with me?'

He sighs, runs his hand through his just gelled hair. 'You should have told me. The second he said he was coming round, you should have called me.'

'I know. I'm sorry.'

There's a pause, the silence stretching thin between us. Finally, he wraps one arm around me and gives me a squeeze. It's only a half-hug, but I melt into it nonetheless.

'Anything else happens you have to promise me you'll tell me,' he says. 'Any update, no matter how insignificant it may seem, you tell me. We need to be a team. That's the only way we're going to get through this.'

I nod, tears stinging my eyes. He does still love me. I know he does. Our relationship is just another casualty of this awful situation. Another reason to go full self-defence mode. I will save my family.

Jase drops his arm from my shoulder and heads towards the door. Part of me wants to beg him to stay, to suggest we spend the day cuddled up in bed watching trashy TV like we used to when we first got together, but the words won't come. Instead, I watch him go, and I'm alone again.

I move to the bed with my cup of tea and settle myself with my back up against the headboard and my knees pulled up. My usual morning routine at the moment consists of scrolling through social media and upsetting myself with all the terrible things people are saying about me and my family. But today I choose not to. My finger drifts to my gallery, and as it opens, my screen fills with my efforts at artistic sunset shots, awkward selfies that I'm probably too old to attempt and family pictures. It's these that I want to see. I scroll as far back as I can, watching the date in the corner descend. Two years ago, four years ago, five.

These photos only go back to when I discovered the joys of cloud storage, six years ago. All my other photos, the ones of Daniel when he was really little, are in albums back at the farm. I might ask if I can have them. Mark did say if there was anything we needed I should call and they'll forward it to us, though I doubt he'll be quite so accommodating now I'm accusing him of having a drinking problem.

The images before me blur as my eyes glass over with tears. Despite them only being from six years ago, Daniel looks so painfully young. The difference between a thirteen-year-old boy and a nineteen-year-old is huge. In these photos he's still so slim, with knobbly knees and a layer of baby fat puffing out his cheeks. Now, he's tall and is starting to get muscular, no longer my little boy but a man.

Just as I'm scrolling into the five-year-old photos, a call comes through. The answer or reject box pops up over a photo of us at Disneyland, and it takes me a moment to register that someone is calling me. It's a number I don't recognise. My finger jabs at the decline button. I've had a few of these calls over the last couple of days; three journalists hungry for an inside scoop, and two threats from anonymous cowards. I don't need to hear from either right now. I resume scrolling, but only for ten or so seconds before my phone starts ringing again. Same number as before.

I roll my eyes and this time hit the accept button.

'Whoever this is, leave me alone!' I growl.

'Mum?'

My chest tightens and tingles start dancing across my skin like a million tiny ants.

'Daniel?'

'Hey, are you OK?'

I don't know what to do. I don't know what to say. I've been waiting to hear his voice for so long I'm speechless. Perhaps I've finally cracked and I'm imagining things. I want to scream and laugh and cry all at once. I want to ask if he's OK, but I also want to shout at him for abandoning us like this. Every fibre of my being is at odds with one another.

I drop my head forward and pinch the bridge of my nose, willing my brain to cooperate. Daniel is on the phone. This is the moment I've waited for, prayed for.

'I'm so happy to hear your voice,' I eventually stammer through the tears now streaming down my cheeks. Shouting isn't the angle here. If I start on him, he might hang up and I can't afford for him to do that. He needs to know how loved and missed he is.

'Mum, what's the matter?'

I shake my head, my mouth opening and closing like a goldfish. 'What do you mean what's the matter? What do you think?'

There's a pause, and for one horrifying moment I think the call has disconnected, but then a deep, throaty sigh sounds from the other end of the line.

'Yeah, I know. I know I shouldn't have just disappeared like that. I was going to call you once I'd cleared my head, I promise, but I must have left my phone at home. I've just managed to find a pay phone.'

My jaw gapes open. I'm not sure what to say. He sounds so calm, so composed.

'I'm really sorry if I worried you,' he continues. 'I just needed some space. I'm all good now. I'll be coming home soon. Can you tell Hannah I'll be back at the weekend and that I miss her?'

The walls around me seem to cave in, the bed I'm perched on opening up into a black hole, swallowing me up. I can't breathe. I can't think.

'Hannah?' is all I can manage.

'Mum, seriously, what's going on? You sound weird. I know you must be mad at me for running off like that, but I'm nineteen, for God's sake.'

My mind unwittingly shifts back to that night on the farm, the night I've tried so hard to suppress from my memories. How I knelt beside Hannah's lifeless body and was so sure my boy was the one who had killed her.

'You don't know?' I eventually breathe down the line.

'Know what? Will you just tell me?'

He's getting frustrated now, the annoyance in his voice carrying over the line, but I don't know how to tell him. My brain isn't processing this information. I'd say he was lying, pretending to not know about Hannah to cover up his involvement, but I know him. I can hear it in his tone. He has no idea.

'Daniel,' I start, forcing my brain and my mouth to cooperate. 'I'm so, so sorry but . . . Hannah's dead.'

The silence on the other end of the line is excruciating. I know he's still there, can hear him breathing, but he doesn't say a word. I try to picture his face, imagine what he must be doing right now. I should be there with him. This shouldn't be something he has to hear over the phone. But he has to know before he comes back. He has to understand the gravity of the situation, that he is the prime suspect.

'Daniel?' I say after a moment.

There is a hitch in his breathing, and then, 'What are you talking about?'

The tears are unstoppable now, dripping off my chin and creating soggy patches on my clothes and the bed sheets.

'I've been trying so hard to get hold of you,' I say. 'She was found the night you left . . . Someone attacked her . . . killed her. The police are all over it and they . . . they don't know who did it.' I can't quite bring myself to say they think he did it.

To begin with, there is nothing but more stone-cold silence, but after a moment or two, another sound crackles through. Sobbing. My heart shatters. I want to reach through the phone and grip on to my boy, pull him into me and never let him go. My arms ache from the desperation. It's the most unnatural thing in the world to hear your child cry and not be able to comfort them.

I swallow hard and dig my nails into my palm, forcing myself to focus. 'Daniel, listen to me. You disappearing like that on the same night, it doesn't look good . . .'

'What? They think I killed her?' His voice is shrill, panicked.

'Apparently they're also looking into other suspects,' I add quickly, 'but our main priority now has to be clearing your name. You need to come back and tell them absolutely everything. Every tiny shred of information you can think of that might help them to solve this. I promise you, I swear I will not let anything happen to you.'

'I didn't kill her, Mum,' he says. 'I'd never have hurt her.'

He doesn't sound like a man anymore, but a small boy. My small boy.

'I know, sweetheart. But you're going to have to come home. That's the only way we're going to be able to work this out.'

'Mum, I'm scared.'

I close my eyes, shaking my head. 'I know. Breathe. Remember your exercises. We'll get through this together. Just come home. Please.'

There's another pause, and it takes all my might not to shout at him to do as he's told.

'OK. I'll pack my stuff up right now.'

The sense of relief that floods me makes me feel light-headed. He's coming home. My boy is coming home.

'I love you, Daniel. I'll see you soon.'

'I love you too, Mum.'

And then the line goes dead. I collapse back against the headboard and bury my face in my hands. A shriek escapes my lips, half a cry and half a laugh, and before I know it, I'm giggling like a child at the ceiling, utterly hysterical. He's coming home. Daniel didn't kill Hannah. He's innocent!

The realisation hits me like a ton of bricks, and I sit bolt upright. The sharp movement makes my stomach turn.

Daniel didn't kill Hannah.

So whose crime scene did I help to clean up?

CHAPTER SIXTEEN

HANNAH

The Day of the Murder – 8.15 p.m.

We're walking down the hallway when my phone buzzes in my pocket. I pull it out, expecting to see an angry text from Mum wondering when I'm going to be home. But it isn't Mum. It's Daniel.

> Hey, gorgeous. I think I might get off early tonight. Want to come round while my mum's with your mum? I miss you.

I swallow, my stomach turning. He's so sweet. He's always treated me like I'm a queen; romantic gestures of flowers and jewellery, bending over backwards to meet my busy schedule, a genuine interest in my life. *And look how you've repaid him*, a voice grates in my head. *He's only ever treated you with utter adoration, and look what you're doing.*

I know what I'm doing isn't fair to him. I know I should break it off with Daniel, and I do keep meaning to. Every single time I'm with him I go to say something, but the words just won't come. He loves me so wholly and with such passion, I can't bear to break his heart.

To be honest, I was never particularly invested in our relationship. We've known each other forever, since we were babies. As kids, we were in and out of each other's houses all the time, and I've always loved him, but in a kind of brotherly way. I'm not really sure when it became more than that. We just kind of drifted into it, I guess because we were so comfortable with each other and that's just what you do when you're fourteen and the hormones start kicking in. We had been flirting for a few months when he had his accident, and then when he woke up and he was so poorly I guess I felt like I had to be with him. I couldn't exactly dump him. Not when he told me that it was me being by his side that was helping him to get better. I felt trapped. I suppose that's how I've justified what I'm doing. But the guilt weighs heavier and heavier on me every time I see him. That's why I keep blowing him off. I'm so sick of being full of self-loathing, and until I can grow a spine and actually pluck up the courage to end things with him, I'd rather avoid him. But he knows something's up. I can tell. And things are even more complicated now. I'm not sure how much longer I can get away with sneaking around like this.

We're approaching our room now.

'You OK?' he says, snapping me out of my thoughts. I thrust my phone back into my pocket, my ears burning.

'Yep.'

He raises an eyebrow, but doesn't push the matter. He knows better than that. This is our time. When we're together, any thoughts about how wrong this all is get pushed to one side. I can deal with the guilt another time.

'What's with the tie?' I ask. He's dressed in chinos and a blue shirt, and the burgundy-coloured tie isn't his usual style.

'I came from an external meeting after work.'

I nod, wishing I had as good an alibi as him for where I keep disappearing off to. Whenever Daniel asks me where I've been I have to make up some crap about studying with my phone switched off.

I'll break it off with Daniel tonight, I decide. *I just have to get it over and done with.*

CHAPTER SEVENTEEN

STEFANI

Eight Days After the Murder

'Stefani, I don't know what you want me to say.' DCI Walton slides his fingers back and forth over his forehead, his body hunched over his desk. 'I knew I shouldn't have put you on this case. You're too ingrained in the community.'

Stefani groans and begins to pace the office. 'Oh, I wish everybody would stop bloody saying that! I can do my job perfectly well. I'm not an amateur. I know how to remain impartial!'

'Be that as it may' — Walton leans back in his chair and crosses his arms — 'you know full well I can't let you sit in on an interview with your daughter. That's not me making the call. That would be the same no matter who you worked for.'

Stefani shakes her head, hands pressed to her hips. She knows he's right, but she can't stand the thought of Cassie being questioned without her being there. She's about to try to argue with him, suggest he at least let her see her before the interview, when DS Davies knocks at the door.

'Sorry to interrupt,' he says. He's holding a folder, and Stefani has to stop herself from snatching it straight from his hands. This case is doing her head in. 'Hannah Carmichael's phone records are in.'

Walton gives Stefani a look that says 'we'll talk about this later' and ushers Davies in. He shuffles forward, clearly sensing the atmosphere in the room, and spreads the contents of the folder across the desk. The three of them scan the sheets, mainly focusing on the top two which show the couple of days before Hannah's death. One of the numbers

Stefani quickly recognises as Daniel Forrester's. The sequence of end numbers is burned into her brain from when they were searching for his phone. But there's another number that appears almost as much as Daniel's, one that she hasn't seen before. The calls are all very short, mere seconds each, but the number is there again and again. There's even a couple of unanswered calls from the day Hannah was killed. Stefani flicks back a few weeks and there the number is again, still the same regular yet short calls.

'Is that the mother's number?' Walton asks, and Stefani checks their record.

'Nope. It's not Mark Butler or Bradley Carmichael's number either.'

'Davies, run it through the database.'

'Yes, sir.' Davies scoops up the sheets as quickly as he placed them down and hurries out of the room, ever eager to please.

'And, Warner?'

Stefani tilts her head towards her boss.

'Go and speak to Mark Butler as you'd planned. Focus on that. I'll give you an update on Cassie when you're done.'

Stefani crosses and uncrosses her legs under the table, trying to do as she's told and focus on her current interview rather than the one she knows is happening a few rooms away. Mark is looking at her expectantly. Understandably, he was slightly taken aback by their request to speak to only him, as opposed to both him and Cynthia like they have done previously.

Mark is forty-three and looks good for his age. He'll definitely be one of those silver-fox types when he allows himself to go grey, but Stefani has a sneaky suspicion he dyes his hair and isn't planning to age gracefully any time soon. According to the village, he's a stand-up guy. Comes home from the office each day and pops into the pub for a pint, where he's always the one cracking jokes and livening the place up, though Stefani can't get anyone to admit to him drinking excessively. Apparently, he was one of the best things to happen to Cynthia. Pulled her out of her depression after her mum died and has been an unwavering source of support.

Stefani certainly got that impression when she first spoke to the two of them after Hannah's disappearance. Mark's arm never left Cynthia's shoulder. He never dropped his protective stance. Could his visit to Alex have been another example of that protectiveness, or something more than that?

Stefani stares at her notes, forcing herself to focus.

'Mr Butler,' she says finally, 'where were you yesterday evening between seven thirty and eight?'

Mark flinches, the crease between his eyebrows deepening. 'I went to see Alex.'

'Why would you do that?'

'I . . .' He trails off and sighs, looks down at the table, clearly realising what a stupid thing it was to do. 'I don't really know. I was just hoping if I appealed to her better nature, explained what a mess Cynthia is in, she might tell me where Daniel is.'

Stefani sighs. It's pointless telling him he shouldn't have done that. He already knows exactly how stupid he's been.

'And how did that conversation go?' she says instead.

'The same as it always goes. She claims she doesn't know where he is.'

'And what was your response to that?'

He shrugs. 'Nothing. I went home, having wasted my time.'

There is a pause. Stefani allows it to sit between them, percolating. There is a slight sweat breaking out on Mark's upper lip, and an alarm bell rings in Stefani's head, but she quietens it. She mustn't jump to conclusions.

After a suitable amount of time has passed, she leans back in her chair. 'According to Mrs Forrester, you started threatening to hurt both her and Daniel.'

Mark stiffens, his lips pressing together. 'I didn't threaten her. I was just frustrated. Obviously, I'd never hurt either of them.'

'Alex Forrester said she thought you were drunk. That she could smell alcohol on your breath. Had you been drinking before visiting her?'

'No . . . yes . . . I mean . . .' He's going very red now. He rubs his face in his hands. 'I had a few, yes.'

'Is that a regular occurrence? Drinking and then having these little . . . outbursts?'

'No!'

Time to change tack. 'Mr Butler, what was your relationship with Hannah like?'

The redness changes to grey as the colour washes out of his face. 'It was fine. We never had any issues.' His eyes dart between Stefani's and Davies' again. 'You can't think I had anything to do with this, surely.'

Neither of them answer this.

'Did you ever have any disagreements? Power struggles? It's not uncommon when a step-parent comes on the scene,' Stefani continues. 'Especially in the early days. You've only been in Hannah's life for two years, is that correct?'

'This is ridiculous!' He recoils from her so sharply, his chair tilts back on its hind legs. He shakes his head in disbelief. 'No, we never had any disagreements. You're asking me if I killed her and the answer is emphatically no. Ask Cynthia! I'd never hurt Hannah and I'd never hurt Alex or Daniel. I'm not a violent man!'

The room falls silent, and Stefani taps her foot lightly on the floor. She's seen many people sit in this room and protest their innocence. Oftentimes she can tell they're lying, but sometimes it's not so clear. This is one of those times. She just can't quite make her mind up.

Mark rubs his hands over his face. 'I'm not answering any other questions without a lawyer present.'

CHAPTER EIGHTEEN

ALEX

Eight Days After the Murder

I've been sitting on the end of the bed staring at the clock ticking away for the past hour. I can't concentrate on anything other than Jase coming home. I'm going to call Stefani, of course I am. But I need to talk to Jase first. I need to tell him I've heard from our son.

He was due home from work seventeen minutes ago, and with each tick of the clock, I feel more and more sick. I keep running things over in my head, trying to solve the case as if that's not what the police have been desperately trying to do for the past week. I think back to the last time I saw Hannah alive. It was the Tuesday before she died. I'd gone to knock at the farmhouse to hand back the keys to the gun shed and nearly crashed straight into her. She'd stormed out of the house angry, tears staining her cheeks. When I asked her if she was OK she just said that Cynthia had been on at her again about making her university choice, but what if it was something more? Is there a clue hidden there? If I hadn't got rid of all the evidence, maybe they'd have the killer by now. I've allowed a murderer to walk free in our village.

I clasp my hand over my mouth as the nausea travels from my stomach to my throat, but before I can actually throw up, footsteps sound in the hallway and the beep of Jase's keycard unlocking the door pierces through my thoughts. He steps inside and gives me a double take.

'Jesus, what's the matter?'

'Close the door,' I say.

He does so warily, not taking his eyes off me. I take a deep breath. I've rehearsed what I'm going to say to him as I've sat here waiting for him, but now he's actually here, my mind is blank. I cough, give myself a shake, blink a few times.

'Daniel called.'

'What?' He practically falls forward to come and join me on the bed.

'I know. I couldn't believe it either.'

'Well, what did he say? What did he say about Hannah?'

I offer him a small smile. 'He didn't do it, Jase. He didn't even know she was dead.' The words still sound alien in my mouth. Everything I've done since I found Hannah has been about hiding what Daniel had done, and now my purpose has completely shifted, turned on its head. Now I need to prove his innocence.

Jase looks down at his lap and exhales slowly, his cheeks puffing out. 'Do you believe him?'

'Yes,' I say, my voice strong and assured.

'What now? Have you told the police?'

'Not yet.' I shake my head, not wanting to focus on that right now. Our boy is innocent and he is coming home. That's all I want to talk about. The details can wait for half an hour more at least. 'Isn't it amazing, Jase? He's coming home!'

Tears gloss my eyes once more and I look up, expecting to see Jase welling up right along with me. But he isn't. His face is set in stone, sombre and thoughtful.

'He said he was coming home?'

'Yes. I think he was hesitant at first when he realised the police suspected him, but I begged him. I made him see reason.'

Jase narrows his eyes, his expression pinched. 'I told you to call me if anything like this happens,' he says.

I frown at him, completely confused. Why isn't he as relieved as I am that Daniel's been in touch?

'I know, I just . . . I couldn't think straight. It was all too emotional.'

Jase shakes his head, then trudges into the bathroom. I watch his reflection in the mirror as he splashes his face with cold water and starts removing his shirt. Bewildered, I slide off the bed and edge towards the bathroom door. He ignores me.

'I don't understand,' I say. 'Why are you angry?'

'I'm not angry, I just . . .' He trails off, leaning on the edge of the sink and hanging his head. 'I'm not sure Daniel coming back right now is the best thing.'

I gawk at him, my jaw dropping. 'What are you talking about?'

'I mean, if he comes back now, he'll be arrested and tried as an adult. You know what the police are like. They're desperate to put someone behind bars for this. The media is pressuring them to arrest someone and it doesn't matter who it is. Even if that person is innocent, they won't care.'

My head is swimming. I can't comprehend what Jase is saying. What does he want Daniel to do? Stay away forever? Hide out in the woods like some criminal on the run?

'If he comes home he'll have a chance at proving his innocence and the police can then focus on finding the real killer. All the time he stays out there, they'll think it's him. All those police officers searching for him and it's a total waste of time.'

'He says he's innocent.' Jase turns to the shower and flicks on the hot water, then faces me again. 'But we don't know that for sure. Can you actually look me in the eyes and say that you've believed he was innocent right from the get-go?'

He waits for my response, the vein in his temple pulsing, but I don't say anything. Just avert my gaze. Because though I do believe Daniel now, I can't pretend that's the way it's always been. Not after what I did.

Jase leans in to check the water temperature, his eyes still on me; a look on his face that's telling me to leave him alone to shower. But I can't. This isn't how this conversation was supposed to go.

'Even if I didn't believe him,' I say eventually, 'I'd still want him to come home. He's our son. Our flesh and blood. Whatever he has or has not done.'

Jase shakes his head. 'We've had nothing but issues with him since he was fifteen. I kept on trying to tell you we should seek help beyond that idiot psychiatrist, talk to someone else about him, but you wouldn't listen. Now look what's happened!'

Suddenly, it's as if my body is a separate entity, disconnected from my brain. My hand flies through the air before I even realise it's moving and connects with Jase's cheek so hard, his head snaps to one side. Red-hot fire pulses through my bloodstream.

'Get out!' I shriek, pointing frantically at the door.

Jase stares at me, aghast. 'What?'

'I said get out! Get out! Get out! Get *out*!'

My voice is rising in pitch, higher and higher until I'm screaming. Jase, his face pale apart from the smarting red mark on his cheek, pulls on his shirt, angrily turns the shower off and pushes past me. He rips open the door and nearly crashes straight into someone in the hall.

'Jesus . . .' He staggers back, takes a moment to register who he almost collided with, then grunts and continues to storm out.

'Have I . . . come at an awkward time?' the woman in the hallway says, and I try to hide my grimace. Maybe I'd be better off sticking with Jase.

I retreat back into our room, still trembling with rage, leaving the door open by way of half-hearted invitation to come in.

'What are you doing here?' I mutter.

'Well, isn't that a nice way to greet your mother.'

My eyes roll as I make a beeline for the self-service station and flick the kettle on. If I don't make tea within the first two minutes of her arrival, I'll be criticised for my poor hosting skills.

'I went to the farm first,' she says, shuffling into the room and sliding her coat off her shoulders. 'The gentleman there told me where you were staying.' Her eyes roam the unmade bed and the simple furnishings, her mouth pulled into a frown. She's trying to find somewhere acceptable to set down her coat, but seeing as I specifically asked housekeeping to stop making their daily visits so that I didn't have to worry about making myself look presentable each day, she'll struggle to find a worthy spot.

The first time she came to visit me, she threw a fit because her heels had sunk into the mud on the walk between the car and the front door. She then proceeded to point out how much dust there was behind my radiators and mentioned how she 'wasn't expecting it to smell quite so strongly of . . . animal'. I'm not entirely sure what she expected. She'd never be seen dead in a Premier Inn under normal circumstances.

Still clutching her coat, she perches on the very corner of the bed, placing as little of her behind as possible on the mattress. I hand her the cup of tea and remain standing, arms crossed.

'So,' I say, 'were you just passing through or . . .'

She raises an eyebrow, the way she always did when I gave her lip as a teenager. 'He's my grandson, Alexandra. I have a right to be concerned.'

'No, you don't.' I turn back to the kettle and start making myself a tea, not because I particularly want one, but because I know if I continue to look at her, I'll end up tearing up. 'You lost that right when you decided to not show up at the hospital. You didn't care then, so why do you care now?'

'Oh come on, that was four years ago. You're not still sour about that, are you?'

Despite myself, I spin around and gape at her. Insults fill my mouth, but I swallow them down. There's no point in rising to it. I straighten myself. 'Always lovely to see you, Mum. Have a safe journey home, won't you?'

Considering we haven't seen each other in nearly a decade, I have surprisingly little to say to her. When we first fell out, I never expected it to last this long. She had turned her nose up at Jase, said she got a bad feeling from him. In actual fact, she didn't like that he had no problem calling her out for making me feel like an utter failure every time she visited. The day I told her to not bother coming round anymore if she had such a problem with Jase, I thought the silent treatment would only last for a few weeks, months at most. But no, the years went on with both of us being too proud to apologise. Then the accident happened, and I thought it might be enough for her to get in touch, but apparently not. I imagine the only reason she's come out of the woodwork now is because the press are involved. She's after her five minutes of fame.

'Don't be like that, please,' she says, snapping me out of my sour memories. 'I know things have been difficult between us these last few years, but I really do care.'

I return to making myself a cup of tea.

She lets out a long sigh. 'Jase didn't seem in the best of moods when I arrived.'

The teaspoon clatters on the counter. 'Really? You're going to start on him already? You've not even been here five minutes!'

'No, I just meant this must be so hard on the both of you. You have to remember he'll be struggling too.'

I'm not sure how to respond. Having her stick up for Jase is uncharted territory. I search for something to say, attempt to force my way past the lump in my throat, but I can't, and before I know it the lump turns into a sob. I angle my head down so that she can't see me welling up.

'Oh, darling, I should have come sooner.'

'Yes, yes, you should have,' I say, swiping angrily at my face.

Out of the corner of my eye, I see her stand up and take a wary step towards me. Her hand rests on my shoulder and my initial instinct is to jerk it away, but something stops me. I'm so angry all of the time. Angry at whoever killed Hannah. Angry at Cynthia for kicking us out. Angry at the police for hounding Daniel, and now I'm angry at Jase too. I'm so tired of being angry.

I soften against her touch and peek up at her through wet, sticky eyelashes.

'Want to tell me what happened?' she says, offering me a meek smile. 'You don't have to. We can talk about something completely different if you want.'

I'm not going to talk to my mother about the argument with Jase. I'm not stupid enough to give her more reasons to hate him. But just thinking about what he said has me quivering with rage once more. It's like I don't know Jase at all. What kind of father is he?

CHAPTER NINETEEN

STEFANI

Eight Days After the Murder

Stefani sits in Luke's living room opposite her daughter, hands clutched around a steaming cup of tea. It's too hot and it's burning her hands, but she doesn't care. As soon as she was out of her interview with Mark, she was on the phone to Luke and asking to see Cassie, even though she knows full well how much trouble she'd be in if Walton were to find out. Luke had just got home with Cassie and was not pleased to hear what Stef had to say.

'Jesus Christ, Stef. You could have at least given us a heads-up that they wanted to talk to her!' he'd said.

'I couldn't! Walton made me stay away from it. Conflict of interest and all that.'

'Well, maybe it's best you don't see her then.'

Stefani's blood had run cold at that comment. It's always the thing that lurks in the pit of her stomach, that nags at her brain late at night. What if Luke tried to stop her from seeing Cassie? Of course, deep down she knows she'd have a fair case if they took it to court. She's always kept up her child-support payments, even when things were really tight, and aside from her work snatching away her weekends occasionally she's – she hopes – a good mum. It would never get to court anyway. Luke has always been amazing, bending over backwards to accommodate Stefani's ever-changing schedule. They've got a really solid co-parenting relationship. But the worry still sits there, waiting to sneak up on her every now and again.

'Please, Luke. I won't be long. I'll just pop in for a quick cup of tea, check she's OK. I won't talk about the case or anything. I'm not allowed.'

And that's how she has ended up sitting here on Luke's sofa. She offers a small smile to her daughter, whose hazel eyes are red-rimmed. She's been crying.

'How are you holding up?' Stefani asks, choosing her words carefully so as not to say anything that'll get her into trouble at work.

Cassie shrugs.

'The school said they've got a counsellor on site. She can help you deal with any grief or sadness. I thought you said you didn't really know Hannah?'

Cassie flinches at Hannah's name, and Stefani is overcome with the urge to throw her arms around her daughter and squeeze her tight. She wouldn't like that though. She's such a typical teenager at the moment, too cool for her lame mum, as evidenced by the fact that she clearly never talks to her about anything substantial. Every time Stefani sees her, she asks what's new, how's school, who does she hang out with, and every time, she gets the same responses. 'Nothing much.' 'It's fine.' 'Lots of people.' Stefani realises, with a pang of guilt, that she really doesn't know her daughter at all anymore.

'I don't know who killed her,' Cassie blurts out suddenly, the words short and sharp.

Luke leans over the sofa and squeezes Cassie's shoulder. 'Cass, we spoke about this. You can't talk about the investigation with your mum. She's on strict orders from her boss.'

'But that's why you're here, isn't it?' she says, her eyes locking with her mother's. 'To find out what I know?'

Stefani blinks, taken aback, and shakes her head. 'No, it isn't. I came to see you. To see if you're OK.'

'Yeah right.' The dismissiveness in Cassie's tone cuts Stefani like a knife, slicing straight into her heart. Has she really been that distant?

'Cassie, I'm your mother before I'm a police officer.'

'Except for the times you blow me off for work.'

Each jab is a poison dart flying through the air, burrowing into her skin.

Luke straightens himself. 'OK, that's enough, young lady. You don't talk to your mother like that.'

Stefani tries to force a weak smile of thanks. It's a shame they seem to make a better team separated than they did when they were together. But even though Cassie seems to have taken his warning, and is now slumping back into the sofa with her arms crossed, the damage has been done. The hurt is already there.

Stefani tries to divert the subject away from Hannah and instead talks about their upcoming weekend. She asks what Cassie wants to do, if she wants to go anywhere in particular, and though she's met with the usual 'I don't care', the tension thankfully starts to dissipate. By the time she's finished her tea and Luke has shown her Cassie's most recent school report, things seem to be mostly back to normal.

She places her cup in the sink before heading to the door.

'Cass, your mum's just leaving,' Luke calls to the living room, before turning to Stefani and lowering his voice. 'Don't forget her football match tomorrow – 5 p.m.'

As she looks in at the living room, for a moment Stefani fears Cassie's not going to come over to say goodbye, but she pulls herself up off the sofa and shuffles towards her. Stefani kisses the top of her forehead and tilts her chin up so that they're looking at one another.

'I'll see you at football, OK? And you're with me this weekend. We'll do something special.'

Cassie nods, and Stefani notices a slight sheen to her eyes.

'Darling, I am so sorry if work's been getting in the way recently. I promise you, you are the most important thing in the entire world to me.'

Cassie nods again, her lips twitching at the edges. Not quite a smile, more a sign of acceptance. Stefani turns to leave, thanking Luke again for letting her pop round, when suddenly Cassie grabs her wrist.

'I told the police, but I think I should tell you too. Hannah was seeing someone.'

Stefani tilts her head to one side. 'Yes, Daniel Forrester.'

'No, not him. Someone else. She was seeing someone on the side.'

'Cassie, you can't be talking about this right now.' Luke pulls her back a little. He's right, she shouldn't be divulging any information to Stefani. But now that she is, Stefani can't bring herself to stop it.

'Do you know who?'

Cassie shakes her head. 'She wouldn't tell me who. Just that . . . just that it was an older man.'

CHAPTER TWENTY

ALEX

Eight Days After the Murder

I've had to get the bus into the village again. Jase took the truck when I told him to leave and I haven't heard from him since. I'm not sure if he'll be coming back again later – I imagine if he was planning to, then my mother turning up might have changed his mind – but to be honest, I don't think I care. The fury I felt earlier has died down a little, but the flames are still there, flickering away in my gut. Mum offered to come with me. Apparently, she's staying at the B and B we couldn't get a room at and plans to stick around until this is all over, but I made it clear that none of this has changed anything. She can stay nearby, pretending she cares, all she wants. I don't need her hovering.

The second I step off the bus, I'm instantly on edge. The sense of being watched falls over me, as if there are eyes everywhere. I glance up to the windows as I walk, but there's no one staring out that I can see. Pulling my coat tighter around me, I hurry my pace, heading away from the parade of shops and down the lane. Towards the farm.

The entrance to the farm is barely visible underneath the bunches of flowers for Hannah. A wave of familiarity hits me as I step off the road and onto the main dirt path. It's as if the farm is greeting me after my time away. I take a moment to allow my hands to slide over the rough wood of the front gate, to breathe in the smell of the combed earth. I love this place.

'Alex?' A man's voice behind me makes me jump and spin around, but it's not Mark. It's Steve, the young lad I hired to help tend to the animals. He's a good worker, disciplined and loves what he does, but doesn't always do things in the most logical order. I often felt like a surrogate mother to him, guiding and steering him to allow him to flourish. I wonder how he's getting on without me.

'Hey.' I smile as warmly as possible, even though my heart is still racing.

But Steve doesn't smile back. He looks nervous.

'You're not meant to be here,' he says quietly.

'I know. I'm sorry. I just need to grab a few things from my house.'

I take a step closer to him, a sudden gust of wind sending a shiver down my spine. He lifts a hand to rub the back of his neck, his Adam's apple bobbing up and down as he hesitates.

'I don't know. Maybe I should go ask Cynthia.'

'Please, Steve. I promise, I'll be in and out. They won't even know I've been here.'

Even if he refuses, I can just come back later and sneak past, but my worry is if he tells Cynthia I was here, then she'll tell Stefani. I smile pleadingly at him, hoping he'll remember how good I've always been to him.

Finally, he moves to the gate. 'Just make it quick. And if they see you, I didn't know you were here.'

'Thank you, Steve.'

I fight my urge to give him a hug and start hurrying down the dirt path before he has the chance to change his mind. I don't risk looking towards the farmhouse, just keep my eyes fixed on my destination; our beautiful barn house, sitting there on the other end of the field, abandoned. Waiting for us to come home.

My heart flutters as I insert my key into the door, panicking for a moment that they might have changed the locks, but they haven't. The door swings open and I scurry inside before anyone can see me. Yet more tears prick at my eyes as I turn to face our large, open-plan living space; the kitchen that Jase and I have our 'cooking dates' in, the armchair positioned a perfect distance from the fireplace, the high ceilings that always made the space feel so open and welcoming. It seems all I ever do these days is cry.

Everything is exactly as we left it, except for the thin layer of dust coating the furniture, and my fingers twitch with the desire to grab the duster out of the cupboard and run it over everything. The kitchen tap has been dripping. A shallow puddle has formed in the bottom of the sink. I fight past the urge to tidy, and head straight to Daniel's room.

I'm not entirely sure what I'm looking for. Just something, *anything* that might help our case. It feels alien stepping into his room while he's not here and rummaging through his things, like I'm invading his privacy. I've never been the type of mum to pry through his personal belongings or keep tabs on his phone. Jase always said I should be. He thinks I'm too soft on Daniel. Maybe I am.

I work methodically, starting to the right of the door and searching in a clockwise fashion, top to bottom. The expected discoveries are made: a pile of dirty clothes that have been kicked under the bed, his missing coursework from last year that we had to redo tucked behind the wardrobe, a few unwashed cups that are starting to form a blanket of mould. But nothing that will prove helpful. Tired and frustrated, I flop down on his bed and sob. My head presses against his pillow and I can smell him. I pull it closer to me, tug the duvet up over my head, imagining he's here with me.

Something crinkles under me and I feel about the mattress. I pull my hand back and inspect the piece of paper I've retrieved. It's a receipt of some kind, though I can't see what for under the duvet. I prop myself back up and shake my head. What's a receipt doing in his bed? I get up and take it over to the window and squint at it. It's a hotel receipt, the cheap one out on the edge of town, a total dive, not somewhere Jase and I would ever go, or my son. I can't for the life of me figure out why Daniel has it.

I'm just about to screw it up and throw it in the wastepaper basket when I see it. The date of the stay, printed in black boxy letters in the upper corner. Just the one night's stay. The night that Hannah died.

It's getting late by the time I get to the hotel. Nearly dinner time. That's the joy of public transport; everything takes about five times as long. Jase may be wondering where I am, though he hasn't called me. Maybe he hasn't even returned to the Premier Inn to notice me gone.

I step off the bus and look up and down the old building before me. It's sandwiched between a Nisa and a betting shop, both of which look as if they've been built fairly recently, which only adds to the broken-down appearance of the hotel. A neon sign hangs in the smeared window, saying 'Vacancies', and a row of old, cracked steps, slippery from the recent rain, lead up to the metal front door. I can't help but grimace a little as I approach. Why would Daniel have been in a place like this?

The woman behind the reception desk doesn't even glance my way as I enter. She's too busy flicking through a magazine, chin propped up with her forearm.

'Um, excuse me?'

'How many?' she says, still not looking up from her magazine.

'I'm sorry?'

She lets out a long sigh, as if my very presence is a nuisance. I bite my tongue to stop myself suggesting she get some additional customer service training.

'Nights. How many nights?'

'Oh, no. I don't need a room here.' I realise a little too late how appalled at the prospect I sound, and when the woman finally looks up at me, it's not with a particularly cheerful expression.

'What do you want then?'

I fumble around in my bag and pull out the receipt and my phone.

'I wondered if you remembered this boy staying here? On this night?'

I bring up my most recent photo of Daniel on my phone. She peers at it for a few seconds before shaking her head.

'Don't recognise him.' She goes to return to her magazine.

'Please,' I say, pointing to the date on the receipt. 'It's really important. Were you working on that night?'

Her eyes narrow. 'What is this, lady? Are you the police?'

Her voice is sharp and snappy, and I know I haven't got much time before she's going to tell me to get lost. I hate this feeling, this helplessness. Knowing that this rude receptionist could be my last chance to save my son.

'No, of course not. Just a worried mother.'

The woman narrows her eyes again. Her long red nails click against the reception desk as she considers me. Finally, she lets out another sigh and grabs the receipt out of my hand.

'What's your boy's name?'

'Daniel. Daniel Forrester,' I say. Relief laps in tiny waves over the frustration, causing my voice to tremble and ruining my attempts at appearing calm and level-headed.

She taps away at her keyboard for a few seconds, then shakes her head. 'No one called Daniel Forrester checked in that night.'

My heart sinks, and I'm about to thank her for her time when another thought occurs to me. I scroll through a few more photos on my phone until I land on one of Daniel with his arms around Hannah.

'What about her? Did you see her?'

She rolls her eyes but leans forward to look at the photo. I expect instant recognition and for her to shout, 'Ain't that that girl from the news?' but she doesn't. Clearly *Cosmo* is more her cup of tea than a newspaper.

She doesn't dismiss it in the same way she did with Daniel's photo though. This time her brow furrows and she tilts her head to one side, taking in Hannah's beaming young face. I hold my breath as I wait.

'Here, I do recognise her!' she says finally. 'She was here that night. Not with him, mind you.'

Tingles start to race over my skin, and every hair on the back of my neck stands to attention.

'Are you sure? Can you look again?'

'Lady, I'm not blind. It wasn't your boy. She was with another guy, older. The only reason I remember them is because I thought it was a bit weird. Quite a noticeable age difference, if you know what I mean. More like father and daughter.'

My palms are starting to sweat. Not only was Hannah with someone else, someone the police have no idea about, but she was with him the night she died. This is it. This is my way to save Daniel.

'Can you check your records? Tell me the name of the older man?'

'We're not really supposed to . . .' She trails off as she sees my eyes starting to water, my hands tightening around my phone until my skin begins to turn white. Desperation seeps off me.

I bite down hard on my lip as she returns to her computer.

'Mr John Smith,' she says eventually, and my shoulders drop.

'That's obviously a fake name. Do you people not need some form of identification when you check in here?'

'*We people?*' The woman adopts her sullen, annoyed scowl again and I'm quick to backtrack.

'I'm sorry. I don't mean to be rude.' I shake my head, the feeling of walking into yet another brick wall causing my head to pound. Why is the world so against us? So determined to see my son go to prison for something he didn't do? Am I being punished for what I did?

'Look,' the woman says, crossing her arms. 'I can't help you on the name front. Bloke paid in cash. All I can tell you is he was tall, dark hair . . . I reckon he was in his late thirties, maybe early forties. He looked smart. Not the sort you normally see here. Does that help at all?'

Acid curdles in my stomach, and it's all I can do to not vomit all over this woman's magazine. The man she is describing sounds exactly like Mark.

CHAPTER TWENTY-ONE

HANNAH

The Day of the Murder – 8.45 p.m.

I lie with my head on his chest, breathing him in. This is my favourite place to be. His strong arms wrapped around me make me feel so safe, like no one in the world can touch me. I definitely needed to be with a real man. Daniel is lovely, but he can't compete with this. I'm too mature for my age to be with a nineteen-year-old.

My eyes are starting to droop, the gentle thud of his heartbeat lulling me to sleep, but just as I'm considering giving in to it, he shimmies out from underneath me and flicks on the light. I squint, my heart growing heavy as I watch him pull on his shirt and start buttoning it up.

'Do you really have to go?' I ask, wishing I didn't sound so desperate. 'You can't stay for ten more minutes?'

He shakes his head, not meeting my eye. 'You know I can't.'

My gaze drops to his left hand, to the wedding ring he refuses to take off. More guilt. More asking myself how I could do this to the people I love. The ring glints against the light, taunting me. It's as if that small metal band symbolises all my doubts. All my fears that his promises are empty. A way to keep me happy while he has no real intention of us running off together. But I'm always quick to push those thoughts right to the back of my mind, to lock them in a small cobweb-covered box and forget that they exist. My trust in him is louder than the doubts. It drowns them out. Of course he means it when he says we'll be together. We just need to find the right moment.

I pull myself up and reach for my bra.

'Have you thought any more about when you're going to tell her you're leaving?'

I keep my eyes fixed on the grimy wall ahead of me while I wait for his answer. This place really is rank. The wallpaper is peeling at the edges, and a family of spiders appear to have made the crevices in it their home. The garish carpet is worn and threadbare, and the toilet is so stained with I dread to think what, I refuse to use it, opting instead to hold my pee until I'm home. We only come here because we know we won't bump into anyone. Another thing he's promised is that once we're together properly he'll treat me to a weekend at a fancy spa resort. But, in all honesty, I don't mind this shitty little excuse for a hotel. It's still our special place. It's where all my best memories with him have been made.

He hasn't answered my question, so I shuffle round on the bed and steal a glance at him, attempting to judge his reaction. He's fully dressed now, just zipping up his fly.

'Did you hear me?' I ask.

He lets out a sigh. 'We've discussed this. I don't know why you have to keep pushing the matter. Let's not ruin our evening together.'

'But—'

'Hannah, I can't tell her yet. It's just not the right time. I still need to figure out a plan for us before I can leave. You don't want to just leave home with nowhere to live, do you?'

I shake my head, picturing us wandering the streets with our suitcases and wondering if we've made a mistake. He's right, as always.

'You are looking for places though, right? Maybe I should start looking too.'

I pull out my phone and start typing Zoopla into the search bar, but he leans over the bed and places his hand on my wrist. The hairs on my arms stand up at his touch.

'It's fine. I'll find us somewhere amazing. Just you wait.'

I smile meekly, then nod. 'OK.'

I watch as he straps his watch around his wrist and picks up his jacket, still not rushing to put my own clothes on. The conversation isn't finished. There's still so much I need to tell him, and it's sitting heavy in my core, weighing me down.

'Before you go . . .' I say eventually, eyes fixed on that damned wedding ring. 'I need to talk to you.'

@itsmeg175: What the hell are the police even doing? Can't pull their finger out! #JusticeForHannah

@carocarobear: @WMerciaPolice why don't you just admit you're absolutely f***ing clueless??

@vegan_lover: The parents look proper shifty. Have they even been questioned? Bet they're throwing all sorts of money at this to make it go away! #JusticeForHannah

@simonLpaul: Nah it's 100% the boyfriend. Why else would he disappear like that? #JusticeForHannah

@carocarobear: @WMerciaPolice not going to explain yourselves??

CHAPTER TWENTY-TWO

STEFANI

Nine Days After the Murder

'Apparently there was an older boyfriend she was seeing on the side. No doubt the person she was travelling on the bus to meet.'

DCI Walton has chosen to accompany Stefani to see Cynthia at the farm. He says it's to update her on the case since Cassie's interview, but Stefani has a sneaking suspicion it's more so he can check up on her. She feels like a trainee police officer again, right out of school, unprepared and unequipped to handle big cases. They've finally made some progress, but not quick enough for the senior commissioner's taste.

Stefani keeps her eyes fixed on the road, pleased that driving gives her the excuse to avoid eye contact. He can't know she's already very aware of Hannah's older boyfriend, and has thought of nothing else since Cassie told her. Whoever it is potentially had a motive to kill Hannah. It's especially suspicious, seeing as this mystery boyfriend hasn't come forward.

'Did you hear me, Warner?'

Stefani blinks and nods, putting the right amount of shock into her expression. 'I was just taking that in, sir,' she says. 'Any thoughts on who it could be?'

'No, I was hoping Cynthia might.'

'Surely she would have said something if she knew about an older boyfriend.'

'You'd have thought so, but maybe it's something she's suspected but had no proof of.' He glances sideways at Stefani. 'Maybe by mentioning her suspicions she might feel she's betraying Hannah, even now.'

They haven't actually spoken to Cynthia in a couple of days, and she looks a little better than the last time Stefani saw her. She's out of her dressing gown at least and her hair has been tidied up, but the dark shadows still line the bottom of her eyes and dried blood stains her nail beds from where she's chewed them so much. She is painfully thin.

'Mrs Carmichael,' Stefani says, 'it has recently come to light that your daughter may have been romantically involved with someone other than Daniel Forrester.'

Cynthia's eyes widen and she shakes her head. 'No. Hannah would never have cheated on Daniel. That's ridiculous. Where are you getting that information from?'

'I'm afraid we're not at liberty to say. But do you know of anyone, anyone at all, that Hannah saw regularly other than Daniel and her friends? Particularly . . .' Stefani hesitates, unsure of how best to phrase it and what kind of reaction it might garner. 'Particularly any older men?'

Cynthia jerks back and her lips curl. 'What are you insinuating, DS Warner? My daughter was a good girl. She was headed to university, she was going to make a good life for herself.' She straightens her posture, her muscles visibly tense. 'She wasn't seeing anyone other than Daniel. She didn't keep secrets from me. She told me everything. I think I knew my own daughter better than you people!'

A thick, heavy silence hangs in the air. It's clear Cynthia had no idea about Hannah's private life, but trying to tell a grieving mother that is pointless and wouldn't get them anywhere anyway.

DCI Walton clears his throat. 'Let's move on for now. Mrs Carmichael, as you know we spoke to your husband yesterday.'

Cynthia responds with a snort of derision. 'Bullied him more like, from what he told me.'

'We wanted to get your view on his actions the night he visited Alex Forrester,' Walton says, choosing to ignore Cynthia's snipe. 'Has he ever shown signs of having an anger issue before? Or a drinking problem?'

'No!' Her voice is so sharp and sudden, it echoes through the old farmhouse. 'Trust me, detectives, you do not need to be looking into my husband. He is one of the kindest, most supportive people I have ever met. I don't know how I would have got through all this if it hadn't been for him.'

She looks down at her lap and starts picking at a loose flap of skin around her already battered thumbnail, before she looks up again and at Stefani.

'You of all people know what it's like to live in this town. Ever since Mark came home in the police car people have been talking, saying awful things about him. It's not what this family needs right now.'

Stefani swallows and gives DCI Walton a sideways glance. His face is stony, expressionless, but she can tell he's picked up on Cynthia's obvious familiarity with her. Yet another strike against her professionalism.

'We understand how difficult this must be for you, Mrs Carmichael,' Stefani says, rigidly sticking to formality now. 'But it's important for us to look at all angles, just in case.'

Cynthia doesn't respond to that, just shakes her head, as if Stefani and DCI Walton are a couple of imbeciles sitting in front of her.

Stefani shifts in her seat. 'Is Bradley home?'

'He's upstairs, why?'

'I wondered if we could have a chat with him.'

'He's been traumatised. I don't—' Cynthia stands, that lioness look back on her face again. Stefani feels for her. One of her children is dead. It's no surprise she's grown suddenly protective of her son.

'I promise you, we will be gentle,' Stefani reassures her. 'Just a few questions, that's all.'

Cynthia shuts her eyes and sighs. Opening them again, she gives Stefani a curt nod.

'OK, but he's very fragile right now. I don't want him upset. At all.'

'Understood.' Stefani smiles as Cynthia goes to the hall to call Bradley down from his room.

Hannah's twin, Bradley, is the family member Stefani has heard the least from during this investigation. Though they'd spoken to him briefly when Hannah was first found, it hadn't garnered any useful information. Not surprising, given his shock at what had just happened to Hannah. Stefani couldn't imagine how it must feel to have your twin die, let alone be murdered. Other than that, Bradley seemed like a classic teenage boy, his face permanently pulled into a sullen expression, quiet, moody. He'd told them he wasn't even home that evening. He was at a club, which they know is true from Cynthia's account. Now, though, given the recent information they've discovered about Hannah's apparent older boyfriend, Bradley just might be able to throw some light on the man's identity. Hannah's mother may not have known about her secret love life, but her brother might have.

'Thank you for agreeing to chat to us again, Bradley,' Stefani says in her friendliest voice as he joins them in the living room.

He nods silently, with his head bowed, his left foot jiggling.

'We wondered if you knew anything about Hannah being involved with someone romantically. Someone other than Daniel Forrester.'

His cheeks flush bright red in an instant, as if he's come face to face with a furnace. He still doesn't say anything.

'Bradley,' Cynthia says, her voice harsh and snappy, 'tell them. Tell them Hannah would never cheat on Daniel.'

Stefani bites back the flash of annoyance and keeps her eyes fixed on the boy in front of her. 'You can tell us, Bradley,' she coaxes, 'even if Hannah asked you to keep it a secret for her. It's more important we know now. You understand that, don't you?'

His head bobs up and down the tiniest bit, but Stefani can't tell if he's nodding or if it's from jiggling his foot so violently. She presses her lips together and waits, prays.

'She was . . . She was seeing someone else,' he murmurs finally, and Cynthia lets out a shocked squeak. Both Stefani and DCI Walton sit up a little straighter.

'Do you know who that other person was?'

Still nothing.

'Bradley, this is really important,' Stefani pushes. 'If you want justice for your sister, you need to tell us what you know.'

Her whole body is aching from the tension in her muscles. This is the most frustrating part of police work, that feeling of being within grasping distance of the answers but not quite being able to reach them.

'I don't know who it was.'

Stefani's shoulders slump, and she feels Walton beside her do the same. She was so sure Bradley was about to give them the name of their next suspect. His foot is still jiggling wildly, and it's hard to tell whether it's simply a nervous habit or if it's because he's hiding something. She swallows, tries to figure out whether to push him or not. Before she is able to, he looks up, his eyes glassy, and she thinks he might be about to cry.

'But I do know something else. She made me promise not to say anything.'

'Go on.' She feels for him, she really does. To make a promise to your sister like that and then be put into such an impossible situation. But secrets won't help Hannah now.

He gulps, suddenly looking very small as Stefani, Walton and Cynthia all stare at him, waiting for him to speak.

'She was pregnant,' he says.

The silence that falls over the room is deafening, like everything has been muted. The atmosphere is so shell-shocked, Stefani jumps out of her skin when their radios crackle.

'Excuse me for a moment.' Walton stands up and edges out to the hallway, leaving Stefani to sit face to face with Cynthia and Bradley. She's not sure what she should do or say. Should she continue her questioning or wait for Walton to return?

She doesn't get a chance to make a decision, because before she knows it, Cynthia is launching into her son.

'What the hell are you talking about? You're making that up!'

'No, I'm not.'

'You are! You're a spiteful little boy! Always making up things about her and now you're dragging her name through the mud!'

'She wasn't the good girl you thought she was, you know—'

This is met with a swift slap across the face.

'Hey!' Stefani stands, her motherly instinct kicking in before her police officer one.

They both turn to look at her, stunned, as if they'd forgotten she was there. For a moment, they all stare at each other. Stefani straightens herself.

'I think we'll need to continue this conversation at the station.'

As she says this, Walton appears at the door, his face flushed. He beckons her over and she shoots a warning glance at Cynthia before joining him in the hall.

'We're going to have to return to this later,' Walton says. 'We've got Daniel Forrester.'

CHAPTER TWENTY-THREE

ALEX

Nine Days After the Murder

I bolt through the door of the police station so fast it nearly swings back and hits me square in the face. Narrowly avoiding it, I hurry to the front desk, gripping on to its edge until my fingers start to burn.

'My son. You've got my son,' I pant, my brain not quite computing the words I need to say to my mouth. 'Can I see my son? Daniel Forrester.'

The man behind the desk raises an eyebrow at me. He knew full well who I was the second I burst through the doors, I'm sure of it.

'Take a seat, Mrs Forrester.' He gestures to the row of plastic chairs screwed to the wall, and my breath hitches. Jase is sitting there, staring back at me.

'Hey,' he says.

I swallow and shuffle towards the chairs, the adrenaline still rushing through me so that my entire body trembles.

'How did you get here so fast?' I pull the seat flap down and position myself awkwardly next to my husband.

'I drove.'

Stupid question. I forgot he had the truck. I'm still stuck with bloody buses.

I take a deep breath, trying to calm myself. I feel as though I might faint. The thought of Daniel being in this building, beyond just a few walls and doors, is more than I can bear. It's all I can do not to push past the officers and fight my way into whatever room they're holding him in, just so I can wrap my arms around him and never let go.

'How have you been?' Jase says, and I shake my head. I'm not sure I can engage in conversation. Between the fact that I haven't seen Jase since I screamed at him to get out of the hotel and the fact that I know Daniel is here being questioned, I can't think straight. I'm locked in some bizarre nightmare with no way to wake up.

'Fine,' I say, which he knows is a lie, but it's all I can muster the strength to say. I look up at the clock, grey metal to match the dingy atmosphere of the waiting room, and watch the seconds tick by. It's 4.30 p.m. Ordinarily, at home I'd be preparing dinner right about now. Daniel would be straightening up the living room and setting the table. Jase, if he wasn't at work, would be washing up as I cooked so there was less to do after eating. We were a pretty perfect team.

Despite myself, or maybe to distract myself, my mind wanders back to meeting Jase for the first time, an event he constantly teases me about. I'd somehow not ordered enough feed for the goats and was stressing about getting to the farm store before it shut. This was back when I was in my mid-twenties, still attempting to prove myself as capable of running the farm to Peggy. I tapped, and I do mean tapped, Jase with my truck as I rounded the corner. Even though he said he barely felt a thing and was fine, I insisted on taking him to the hospital to get checked out. It was only once we got there he started laughing and said, 'Thanks for the lift.' That's when I discovered he was a junior doctor at the hospital and had basically used my desperation to make sure he was OK as a way to get into work quicker and make a good impression. I would have been annoyed, but his grin was so cheeky, and when he said he should take my number just in case he started showing signs of injury later, I couldn't help but laugh along with him.

'Have you heard from him?' Jase says now, and I flinch out of my memory.

'Who?'

'Daniel. Since he called you, I mean. Have you heard anything since?'

'Oh. No.' I look down at my lap and start fiddling with the hem of my shirt. I hate feeling awkward around Jase. He's always been the person I could be totally myself around. 'Where did you end up sleeping last night?'

'In the truck.'

For a moment, I'm hit with a pang of guilt, but I'm quick to shake it away. Good. I'm glad he spent the night in the truck. I hope he got a stiff back out of it too, after what he said.

'What about your mum? Was that the blissful reunion I imagine it to be?'

I give him a sideways glance. I'm not sure he's earned the right to be joking around just yet. He seems to pick up on my annoyance because he shrinks back against his chair.

'I am sorry, you know,' he says, as if reading my thoughts.

I stiffen at this. A rope coils itself around my stomach. My eyes prick as I look up at him, my heart pounding.

'I'm sorry for saying he shouldn't come home.'

I nod. 'You should be.'

He winces, but I don't feel bad about it. No matter what, Daniel is our flesh and blood. There were days, back when Daniel was a toddler, when I would secretly watch Jase as he hunched over the kiddy bed and stroked our little boy's hair, kissed his forehead, his deep voice warming me as he told him how much he loved him. How can you go from that to saying what he said?

'You know I didn't really mean it,' he says, the guilt evidenced in the lines on his forehead. 'Everything is just . . . It's all so shit. I don't know how to deal with any of this!'

He hunches over and for a moment I think he's going to cry. My anger softens a little. I can't stand it when Jase cries. I've only ever seen him cry twice: once at his mother's funeral, and the other time four years ago when we were sat together at Daniel's hospital bed, praying he'd pull through.

Taking a deep breath, I reach forward and squeeze his hand.

'I know. I don't know how to deal with it either.'

His fingers tighten on mine, and it's only now I realise how much I've been clamouring for his touch.

But I can feel that Jase is shaking, and I don't think I have ever seen him in such a state. I'm used to him being the calm, collected one.

The one who calms me down. Things have been a bit weird between us lately, even before Hannah was killed. We've disconnected, argued, but he's always been so together.

'Jase...' I hold his hand tighter. 'I know this is hard on you, too. I'm sorry...'

He looks up at me, an unreadable expression there. I can only describe it as distraught.

'I'm sorry...' he repeats, and tears course down his face.

'It's OK,' I say. 'We have to stick together, Jase, for Daniel's sake. We can't let this break us.'

He nods, wipes his face with his sleeve, then says, 'Let me come back, babe.'

I don't say anything, find that my fingers are drifting over the sleeve covering my scarred skin. All I have to do is close my eyes and I'm right back there, back leant against the cold brick wall of the pub.

It's a Saturday, Daniel's fifteenth birthday. The five of us have come here for a celebratory meal; myself and Daniel situated on one side of the table and Cynthia, Bradley and Hannah on the other. Jase wasn't able to get the evening off, though us adults may as well not be here anyway with the way Daniel is giving Hannah the lovey-dovey eyes that teenagers do when they have a crush. Cynthia and I have a bet to see how long it will take for the two of them to start dating. They've grown up together, so it's taking that leap from being childhood friends to something more than that. Bradley is clearly also aware of the romantic tension between them; he keeps rolling his eyes and burying himself so far into his phone, it's a wonder he can read what's on the screen.

I've stepped outside for some 'fresh air', which is my code word for a cigarette. I hardly smoke anymore, only when I'm out like this and the smell is drifting in from the gardens and clinging on to the coats of passers-by. I don't want Daniel to see me smoking, so I always make sure to slip away as discreetly as possible.

'All right, Mrs Forrester?'

It takes a moment for me to register who's speaking to me. My eyes land on a group of four boys crowded underneath the space heater surrounded by a haze of cigarette smoke, and I recognise them instantly. They go to Daniel and Hannah's school. A few times they've catcalled after me as I've walked past, referring to me as a 'milf' and making crude remarks. They are definitely not old enough to be smoking or drinking the lagers cupped in their hands, but I'm not their mother.

I pull my phone out and start pretending to text, hoping they'll get bored and focus their attention elsewhere. They don't. Out of my peripheral vision, I can see them approaching, two of them moving to stand on my left side and the other two on my right.

'Don't feel like talking?' the tallest boy says.

One of the others sniggers. 'That's all right. We prefer 'em quiet anyway. You don't got to talk for what we want to do!'

At this, there is a chorus of laughter, and all four of them lean around me to high-five each other, as if they've just come out with the wittiest one-liner in history.

I roll my eyes and push past them, taking a step towards the cigarette bin. I stub mine out and flick it inside. As I do so, a hand grabs my right butt cheek and squeezes.

'Hey! What the fuck do you think you're doing?' Daniel's voice cuts through the muffled thumping of music coming from inside the pub. I spin around to see him standing in the doorway, eyes fiery, fists clenched. I've never seen him like that before. He's a gentle soul, certainly not the type to get into fights. I purse my lips together, willing him to stand down and go back inside. He's tall for his age, but much thinner than these lads, still yet to grow into his height. There's not a scrap of muscle on him.

'You what?' One of the boys turns on him, the jokiness suddenly stripped from his voice.

'Daniel, it's fine,' I say. 'I'm coming back inside now anyway.'

'Yeah, that's right. Go on back inside, Danny boy. Tell your old man if he don't look after your mum here, we will!'

I'm at Daniel's side now, hand on his arm, pushing him back inside the pub, but this last snipe has him spinning back to face the boys.

'My mum's not the one spreading her legs for all of Herefordshire,' he retorts.

There's an eruption of movement as the biggest boy launches towards us, his beer sploshing over the rim of his glass. 'Say that again! Go on, I fucking dare you!'

'Daniel, leave it alone!' I press my hand against his chest. 'Just ignore them.'

He stares at them for a moment, hostility hanging in the air between them, but eventually he relents. We make our way back inside and to our table, the boys' taunts slowly getting drowned out by Tina Turner's 'Simply the Best'.

We try to keep the remainder of the evening as pleasant as possible, not wanting a bunch of silly boys to ruin Daniel's birthday. Cynthia, Bradley and Hannah head back to the farm just after ten, leaving Daniel and I to enjoy some real conversation for once. It's a rarity now he's old enough that spending time with his mum is decidedly uncool, so I cherish every second of it. By the time we've settled our tab and stepped out into the chill of the night air, we've as good as forgotten about the run-in with Daniel's classmates. But as we're heading down the country lanes towards the farm, where the street lights become fewer and farther between, we become aware of four dark figures tailing us.

The biggest boy throws the first punch from behind. Daniel's grunt rips through the night as his head snaps to one side and he topples to the ground. A strangled cry escapes my mouth as I lunge forward, craning my body over Daniel to protect him from his attackers, but I'm promptly yanked away. I stumble backwards, and as I fall, my forearms grind against the sharp ground, the gravel slicing into my skin. Two of the boys hold me back, twisting my bloodied arms behind me into an excruciating armlock. I thrash and writhe under the rough hands gripping onto me, my screams echoing through the surrounding fields, but it's no use. All I can do is watch as my boy is stamped on and kicked and beaten, trampled until his beautiful face is unrecognisable.

My temporary ceasefire with Jase dissolves as I feel my anger returning at the vivid memory of that night.

'You're so hard on him,' I say abruptly, and Jase lifts his head, exhausted, to look at me. 'And you're hard on me. Can't you see how

I would worry about him after what happened. How scared I was, and still am, that he's never going to be the same as he was before, that what happened has ruined his life.'

It's true. Every time there's a mention of Daniel's issues – his aggression, his outbursts, his overreactions – I feel that familiar sense of dread flooding my insides, swallowing me whole. The words his consultant said to me ring in my ears. '*Daniel suffered substantial trauma to the frontal lobe.*' He was assigned a cognitive behavioural therapist before leaving the hospital who only told me what I already knew. Over the next few years, we battled the stigma of Daniel's brain injury: the way parents would cross to the other side of the road so that their precious offspring wouldn't pick up any of his 'bad habits'; the way teachers would give me pitying stares as they asked yet again if we had considered a special school for him; the way so-called friends would question whether he'd ever live any kind of normal life. Every issue he's faced since that day has been my fault. If it hadn't been for him standing up for me that night, those boys would never have jumped him. Everyone judges him so harshly because of something he cannot control, something that I couldn't protect him from. And the worst part is, the moment I thought he'd killed Hannah, I did exactly the same.

'I know, I'm sorry.' Jase pinches the bridge of his nose, brow furrowed. 'It still affects me too, but I know it's been especially hard on you, and I understand why you are how you are with Daniel.'

'Do you? Really? Because if you did, you'd understand that I will do anything to protect my son. *Anything.*' I try to put as much power behind that last word as possible. Jase needs to know how serious I am. He needs to know that if push came to shove, Daniel would come before him every single time.

Jase sits silent for a moment, and then nods. 'He's our son. And I'll do anything to protect him. I'll do anything to keep this family together.'

'No more fighting each other,' I tell him. 'We're in this together. And we need to figure out who really killed Hannah so we can move on from this hell.'

Jase puts his head in his hands, and I reach out to touch him, but his body feels rigid.

'We've got each other,' I tell him softly. 'We're a family, and nothing will change that.'

CHAPTER TWENTY-FOUR

STEFANI

Nine Days After the Murder

Daniel Forrester sits in the interview room for the first time since this investigation started, and it all feels rather surreal. There was a point where Stefani wondered if they'd ever find him. A teenage boy really shouldn't be able to elude the police for as long as he did, but he knows the woodlands. He visits a different part of the county every time he goes camping, so they didn't even know where to start. The time it took to track him on dashcam footage, coupled with the fact he managed to pitch his tent in a remote patch of forest only accessible by wading through water, meant it was like finding a needle in a haystack. So Daniel's used to going off-grid, disappearing without a trace. A handy skill for someone guilty of murder.

Except Stefani isn't so sure he is guilty anymore. She had been certain. All the clues pointed to him. The timing of his camping trip, the fact they couldn't get hold of him, his relationship with Hannah that may have been on the rocks due to her heading off to uni. Not to mention her mystery lover, as they now know. But there is a seed of doubt in Stefani's mind that she can't shake, and that always makes her feel uneasy. Why would he have come out of hiding if he was guilty?

She had expected DS Davies to do the interview with her, but DCI Walton insisted. The senior commissioner is clearly breathing down his neck. Arresting Daniel Forrester is their major breakthrough, and Walton probably wants to make sure they don't mess this up. It's taken a while to actually sit down with Daniel. They had to contact his parents and arrange for a solicitor to be present, and then due to his existing brain injury there were other protocols to meet. A health practitioner had to assess him to make sure he was fit to be interviewed. They had to bring in his cognitive behavioural therapist to serve as his appropriate adult — a requirement given his condition — in addition to his solicitor. Then there was the time it took for him to actually be briefed before the interview. But now, finally, here they are.

'Pretty,' Daniel says as Stefani sits down.

'Excuse me?'

'I said you're pretty.'

Stefani exchanges an awkward glance with Walton. Dr Eriksen leans in to mutter something to Daniel, and he immediately fixes his eyes on the table. He whispers something under his breath. He's counting things he can see.

Walton clears his throat. 'Let's get started, shall we? Interview commenced at' — he looks at the clock — '4.47 p.m. Murder Investigation Team interview of Suspect A, Daniel Forrester, by Detective Chief Inspector Walton and Detective Sergeant Warner in the presence of the suspect's solicitor, and appointed appropriate adult, Dr Eriksen. You do not have to say anything, but it may harm your defence if you do not mention when questioned something you later rely on in court. Anything you do say may be used in evidence. Do you understand?'

Daniel smiles, a small laugh escaping his lips.

'Something funny?' Walton says.

Stefani shoots him a glare, and Dr Eriksen bristles. Walton can't conduct this interview the way he normally would. They have to choose their words carefully and be prepared for unusual responses.

He huffs. 'Let's start again,' he says, before reading Daniel his rights once more. 'Do you understand?'

Daniel nods, his face ghostly white.

'We need you to give a verbal response for the sake of the tape please,' Stefani says.

'Yes. I understand.' Daniel's voice is louder, husky, as if he's been shouting or crying. He sounds more like an old man than a teenage boy.

There is a brief pause while Stefani checks her notes. 'Daniel, can you please describe your relationship with the victim of this case, Hannah Carmichael?'

She tries to make eye contact with Daniel, but she can't. His gaze is fixed on the table in front of him, unblinking. He looks strikingly like Jase. They have the same dark eyes and strong jaw, though Daniel's skin is tainted by the acne and oily sheen that comes with puberty.

'She's . . . she was my girlfriend,' he says.

'And would you describe your relationship as . . . happy?'

He bristles. There is an awful, loaded silence.

Finally, Daniel gulps and takes a breath. 'I thought we were,' he says, his voice cracking.

'What do you mean by that?'

'I loved her with all my heart. I thought she loved me too, but . . .' He trails off to swipe angrily at his face, wetness transferring onto his knuckles. 'Sorry,' he grumbles. 'We had an argument.'

'When was this?'

'The night she died. That's why I went off. I needed to clear my head.'

He sniffs and rubs his nose with his sleeve. It's stuffy in the interview room, the air thick and tight. Stefani wants to pause to ramp up the air conditioning but she daren't interrupt Daniel when he's speaking so freely. She presses on.

'Can you tell us what the argument was about?'

He blanches, the memory of it clearly hard for him. Whether he killed her or not, Stefani fully believes that this boy was head over heels for Hannah.

'I found out she was cheating on me. I confronted her about it, we argued, I went home and grabbed my camping equipment and then I went off. I didn't even know she was . . . I didn't even know what had happened until yesterday. That's why I came back, because I found out.'

Stefani nods, encouraging him to go on. She wasn't expecting him to be so open, so ready to talk. His story about the argument aligns with what they know about the other man, and the camping trip aligns with Alex and Jase's story.

'Do you know who Hannah was cheating on you with?'

He squirms in his seat and braces his hands against the table. His lips press together.

'No comment.'

Stefani and Walton exchange a glance. They're both thinking the same thing. If he didn't know who the older man was, he'd have said as much. 'No comment' implies he knows but doesn't want to say.

'Daniel, this other man is another suspect in this case.' Stefani leans forward, willing Daniel to look up at her. 'Are you sure that's how you want to answer?'

Still he says nothing. The sound of his leg jiggling under the table echoes around the otherwise silent room.

'You don't know who Hannah was sleeping with?' she tries again.

Daniel's solicitor pipes up. 'I suggest you find and arrest this other man and put these questions to him rather than to my client.'

Stefani raises an eyebrow at him. 'As yet, we have been unable to identify the other man that Hannah was romantically involved with. We were hoping your client would be able to provide information that would help us locate him.'

'No comment,' Daniel says rigidly, again.

Stefani flicks through her notes, frustration eating at her. Things had been going so well. For Daniel to shut down now when they're so close is almost worse than had he stayed silent from the beginning.

'I'm going to show you something that you may find disturbing,' she says, extending him a courtesy, a kindness, that she wouldn't give to others in this situation.

Daniel shrugs, though she can see his trepidation in the set of his shoulders.

She pulls out two photographs and lays them out on the table in front of him.

'Images 6A and 6B,' she says, keeping a close eye out for any reaction to the photos. A slight frown crosses Daniel's forehead, but it's gone before she can draw any conclusions from it. 'Image 6A shows the pig barn in which Hannah Carmichael's remains were found. Image 6B shows the teeth and bone fragments we recovered from said pig barn.'

'Did you do this, Daniel?' Walton pipes up, his voice strong and accusatory, and Stefani only just manages to resist silencing him. Walton's angry, frustrated just like her, but she's pretty sure that the bad-cop routine is the wrong approach with this boy. He's too fragile, too close to teetering on the edge of telling them the truth without pressure. Walton has no such qualms. He leans forward. 'Did you kill Hannah and attempt to dispose of her body in the pig barn?'

'No . . .' Daniel whispers.

'Did you find out she was cheating on you and kill her in a rage?'

'No.'

'Did you feed her body to the pigs as if she were nothing more than an animal herself?'

'No!'

'I think we should take a break,' Dr Eriksen says, but Walton carries on.

'Did you know she was pregnant, Daniel?'

Daniel looks up at them for the first time, his eyes bulging.

'What?'

There is a long pause while Daniel digests this information. Stefani can see the concern on Dr Eriksen's face as he watches for any reaction.

'But we didn't . . .' Daniel's voice is almost a whisper. Then, before Stefani or Walton can say anything else, he clasps his hand over his mouth, hunches over to the side and vomits.

CHAPTER TWENTY-FIVE

ALEX

Nine Days After the Murder

'Alex,' Jase says.

I wake with a start at the sound of my name. My cheek is red-hot, pins and needles tingling my skin, and I realise I've fallen asleep leaning on Jase's shoulder. I rub at my eyes. They're tender, like my lids are full of sand. I take a moment to readjust myself to the sight of the police station. Realisation courses through me as I spot DS Warner standing in front of us and I sit bolt upright.

'Daniel. Where is he? Is he OK?'

'Your son is fine, Mrs Forrester,' Stefani says. 'We've had to pause our interview for now and allow him some time to rest. We'll resume tomorrow.'

'Tomorrow?' My stomach turns over at the thought of him staying here overnight.

Stefani nods. 'Since this is a murder case we have filed an application to hold Daniel for up to forty-eight hours. If we do not charge him within this time, he will be released on conditional bail.'

My throat tightens and I have to force myself to speak. 'Can we see him?'

'This isn't a prison, Mrs Forrester,' Stefani says, her face apologetic. 'We don't have the facilities here to allow for visits with detainees. The best thing you can do is go home and we'll call you if there are any developments.'

Gripping the sides of the plastic chair, something inside me snaps;

the rope that's been coiling itself around my insides giving way after being pulled tight for too long.

'No!' I shout, drawing the attention of the officer behind the desk. 'I'm not going anywhere without my son!'

'Alex, come on.' Jase's hand tugs at my shoulder. 'There's nothing we can do.' I flinch at his touch.

'He's our son, we need to see him,' I hiss at him.

But Jase looks pale and drawn and is clearly not as determined as I am.

I turn to Stefani. 'Please! Stefani, you have a child!'

Other officers are joining us now, coming to see what the commotion is all about.

'Mrs Forrester, I'm sorry.' Stefani winces. 'It isn't possible for you to see Daniel today.'

Jase is hauling me up off the chair now, his hands under my armpits. 'You're only going to make things worse,' he says. 'Come on.'

The second we emerge through the doors, we're blinded by flashing lights and shouting. Reporters fill the steps leading to the police station, spilling out onto the grass. There's been less and less media attention on us as of late – obviously other news has taken priority over us – but now Daniel is in custody, it seems the news has spread like wildfire. There are other people too, holding up makeshift signs and waving them manically in the air. A sob escapes my lips as I read what's written on one of them: LOCK THE PSYCHO UP!

'It wasn't him . . .' I whisper, too quietly for any of them to hear me over the commotion. More cameras flash, my heart rate quickens, and I say it again, louder this time. 'It wasn't him. He's innocent! My son is innocent!'

I'm screaming now. I've never been more sure than at this moment. Daniel did not kill Hannah. Mark did. Mark was terrified that Hannah would tell Cynthia about their affair and he murdered her in cold blood. These people should be demanding he be locked up, not my poor sweet boy.

I'm about to say this to them, but Jase throws his arm around my shoulders and leads me forward, heads ducked low, pushing through the crowd. The truck is waiting in the car park for us, and though I'm relieved to throw myself into the passenger seat and shut the door on the mob outside, the thought of driving away from the station, away from Daniel, is more than I can bear. It's like my body is splitting in two.

@itsmeg175: Anyone else see that news report from a few years back? Explains a lot!! #JusticeForHannah

@carocarobear: @itsmeg175 I've just seen! The boy's got no self-control. Fecking scary isn't it?

@vegan_lover: I feel sorry for him. The system has obviously let him down #JusticeForHannah

@simonLpaul: @vegan_lover Sorry for him?? The guy murdered an 18-year-old girl! Brain damage or not I don't feel the slightest bit sorry for him #JusticeForHannah

@vegan_lover: @simonLpaul So much for innocent until proven guilty I guess

@simonLpaul: @vegan_lover Oh come off it! If it wasn't obvious it was him before it sure is now!

@carocarobear: All I know is I certainly don't feel safe with people like that walking the streets!!

CHAPTER TWENTY-SIX

STEFANI

Nine Days After the Murder

Stefani leans against the exterior wall of the police station, taking in long, slow breaths. It's starting to feel stuffy and claustrophobic in there. God knows how Daniel Forrester must be feeling. She watches the reporters, wondering when their shifts might be ending. The media frenzy has died down since Alex and Jase left, but there are still a few stragglers sitting on the brick wall smoking and eating messy burgers from the nearby food truck, cameras looped around their necks. They're wasting their time of course – Daniel won't be going anywhere for them to photograph any time soon – but they don't know that.

Wearily, she pulls out her phone to check the time. It feels like it's been hours since they arrived back at the station, and she has no idea how much longer she's going to have to stay. They're pretty much done talking to Daniel for today. He's getting tired too, and they have a legal obligation to allow him to rest before continuing. But there's paperwork and planning for tomorrow's questioning session to do.

Her eyes are sore and it takes a moment to focus on the bright light of the screen. There's an unread message from Luke. She's had her phone turned to silent for the majority of the day. She taps into it, and her stomach flips.

Where are you?

Cassie's football game. Fuck.

* * *

Her shoes sink into the damp mud of the school field as she trudges towards the football pitch. The players are charging from goalpost to goalpost, chasing after the ball like a cat chases a laser beam, and the parents are sitting huddled in small groups on plastic chairs. Some are fully invested in the game. They cry and cheer and holler at the referee as if it were a championship game with thousands of pounds at stake. Others are only there out of a sense of obligation, preferring instead to chat amongst themselves rather than watch their beloved children.

Luke is in neither of these groups. He sits on the outskirts, Amanda on one side and an empty plastic chair on the other. Of course Amanda is here. As if Stefani doesn't feel bad enough already.

She bows her head and attempts to slip into the chair as discreetly as possible. Luke says nothing, but Amanda offers her an awkward smile. Stefani scans the field until her eyes land on Cassie, positioned under the goalpost, black leather gloves strapped to her hands.

'What did I miss?'

Luke sighs and leans forward, his elbows on his knees. 'A bloody amazing save. She was so proud of herself. She ran over at half-time and when she realised you weren't here . . .' He trails off, and chains of guilt wrap themselves around Stefani's chest, tightening and squeezing her. This is Cassie's fourth game. Stefani wasn't able to go to the previous three due to her shift pattern, and Cassie had been so excited when she told her she finally had this afternoon off. Of course, that was before they brought Daniel Forrester in.

There are no more shots for the rest of the game – the ball never ventures far from the centre of the pitch – so Stefani doesn't get to see Cassie in action. When the final whistle blows and the parents erupt into applause, the look Cassie fires at her is distinctly hostile.

Stefani jumps up quickly as Cassie makes her way over to them.

'I'm so sorry, darling,' she blurts out as soon as she's in earshot.

'Don't worry about it.'

Though the words are meant to sound casual and indifferent, in keeping with the 'couldn't-care-less' teenager act, there is a definite bitterness to her voice. Cassie is angry. No, worse than that. She's hurt.

'I really am sorry. Work got crazy at the last minute. I wasn't even supposed to be working this afternoon but then—'

Before she can go on she's cut off by one of the other mothers, a suspiciously perky woman, Jenna Driscoll, bounding towards her.

'Stefani!' Jenna calls. A gaggle of other women are trailing behind her, their thirst for gossip seeping off them. 'How are things?'

Stefani has to stop herself from rolling her eyes. Jenna doesn't want to know how things are. She wants to know the latest on the Hannah Carmichael case.

'Fine, thanks,' Stefani says, hoping her blunt reply will be enough to ward off further prying. It doesn't.

'Have you found him yet? Daniel Forrester?'

Stefani frowns. She sees Luke and Amanda exchange a glance.

'I really can't discuss details of the case,' she says, looking pointedly at her ex and his new partner, and then turns away from Jenna and her cronies to see that Cassie has charged off. She's marching away from them towards the changing rooms.

Stefani follows, breaking into a light jog to catch up with her. Luke is close on her heels, while Amanda hangs back.

'Cassie! Cassie, wait!'

Cassie slows only a fraction, calling over her shoulder. 'Mum, it's fine, seriously. I need to go and get showered.'

'Please, darling!' Quickening her pace, Stefani reaches her and touches her arm. This time Cassie slows to a halt. 'I really am sorry I missed the game,' Stefani says, wishing she could pick her up in her arms like she did when she was little. 'You know how hard I'm working on this case at the moment. I'm trying to get justice for Hannah.'

After a long, drawn-out silence, Cassie finally turns to face her. Tears line her lower lashes. 'Maybe I should go missing too,' she says, her voice cracking. 'Then maybe you'll care about me as much as you do about someone else's daughter.'

Stefani sucks in a sharp breath, Cassie's words winding her.

Luke winces. 'Cassie, that's enough!' he says, but it's too late. Cassie has already turned her back on the both of them and started running towards the school. As she watches her daughter disappear across the field, Stefani's heart thuds dully in her chest, echoing in her ears.

CHAPTER TWENTY-SEVEN

ALEX

Ten Days After the Murder

Jase squeezes my hand as we make our way down to the Premier Inn restaurant. Breakfast is included in the price of our stay, but we have yet to take advantage of it. I couldn't face it, knowing that all the other people tucking into sausages and eggs would most likely know who we were.

'Just remember, we've got nothing to hide,' he says as we approach. 'We have just as much right to be here as anyone else.'

Nothing to hide... if only he knew. I gulp and nod, the thought of what we're about to do completely zapping any appetite. The smell of bacon and freshly baked bread and coffee hits me all at once, and only adds to my nausea. The food station in the centre of the room houses baskets of rolls, selections of cereal and yoghurts, colourful fruit juices, while the hot food sits in metal bain-maries over on the chef's station.

'I forgot how hungry I am,' Jase says, staring at it all. 'I haven't eaten since yesterday.'

I sigh. 'Me neither, but I still can't stomach much.' The fact is, food is the last thing on my mind. All I can think about is Daniel. What is he having for breakfast this morning? Are they feeding him properly? My stomach turns.

Luckily, there aren't many people in the restaurant, just a few in suits who are either staring intently at their laptops or chatting business loudly on the phone. Jase selects a table in the middle of the room, ignoring my pleas to sit at one right over in the furthest corner, and I slide into the chair while he disappears to fetch us a full English each, despite the fact that I don't want mine. The chef's station is only on the other side of the room, but I feel like he's whole continents away from me. I don't want to be sitting here on my own. As much as I've only just decided to forgive Jase, I've enjoyed having him back with me. He has a positive outlook on things. I feel safer when he's near, like everything might actually be OK.

Jase returns with two plates piled high with food, and I grimace.

'You OK?' Jase says.

I swallow and nod. 'I'm just not feeling that hungry.'

'You should try to eat.' Jase picks up his fork and stabs one of his sausages. Bubbling oil bursts out as the prongs pierce the skin. 'You're going to make yourself ill, and that won't be any help to Daniel.'

I lower my head, wishing Jase wouldn't mention Daniel while we're out in public. The last thing we want is for attention to be drawn to us. Hoping that it will shut him up, I push a few mushroom slices onto my fork and pop them into my mouth. They're slick with grease, which sits uncomfortably on my tongue.

The text tone of my phone blares, making the eyes of a couple of the laptop users dart up at me. I shrink back into my seat and fumble to turn my mobile to silent. I'm not used to anyone texting me anymore. My so-called friends from the school have seemingly chosen to freeze me out since all this started, and the only other person who ever called or texted me was Cynthia. I wonder if any of them will apologise when they find out that Daniel is innocent after all, or if they'll just pretend like nothing ever happened. *If* they find out he's innocent.

'Who's the message from?' Jase asks, and I peer down at the screen.

I feel the blood drain from my face.

'Alex?'

'Nobody. A scam message.' I thrust the phone back into my pocket, trying to stop the mushrooms from making their way back up my throat. 'I just need the loo. I'll be back in a bit.'

The chair screeches against the tiled floor as I jump up, and I nearly crash straight into one of the staff members filling up the bread basket as I dart towards the ladies'. Once inside, I slide the lock across the cubicle door, my fingers shaking. I perch on the toilet-seat lid and grip my phone between my hands, staring at the message on the screen.

> I know what you did. Don't do anything stupid, Alex. I'm watching you, bitch.

CHAPTER TWENTY-EIGHT

HANNAH

The Day of the Murder – 8.50 p.m.

I toy with the edge of the duvet cover as I watch him pace the room, waiting for his reaction. I can't believe he hasn't said anything. When I told him the pregnancy test had come up positive, I'd expected him to freak out a bit, sure. But not go completely silent on me.

'Are you OK?' I say eventually when I can't stand it anymore.

He laughs at this, not the kind of laugh I'm used to hearing from him, but a forced, sarcastic-sounding laugh. A sense of dread pools at the bottom of my stomach. This isn't how this was supposed to go.

'I know it's a shock,' I say, 'but this could be a good thing. Think about it. You were going to leave her anyway. We were going to run off together. This could be the push we needed to actually do it.'

This is how I've reasoned it out in my head. I'd gone to Boots to get a test after feeling funny all of last week.

I'd even had to sit out of class one time, and the school nurse said it was probably due to me not eating properly. But then my period didn't show up, and I'm usually regular as clockwork. My ears burned as I handed the test over to the salesperson to pay, which is ridiculous because I'm eighteen now. Sure, it wouldn't be what I planned, but if it turned out positive, I had nothing to be ashamed of. It's not like I'm a fifteen-year-old. But the affair had made it feel nasty and sordid.

Back home, I read the instructions five times before taking the test. It really was simple – pee on the stick and wait two minutes – but I was convinced I was going to mess it up somehow. I'd bought a two-pack so that I could double-check whatever result came up, so I put the spare one on the side of the bath while I struggled to rip into the packet of the first test with my trembling hands. I momentarily considered texting him and letting him know what I was doing, but decided against it. There was no point in worrying him about something that could just be stress or something.

When those two lines first showed up, bright red and unmistakable, I was horrified. How could I be a mother? I'm eighteen years old, I've got no job. Mum would kick me out for sure, and that's before she even found out whose baby it is.

I didn't even have a chance to properly process all this, because no sooner had the lines formed than someone started banging on the bathroom door.

'Just a second,' I called out. I was in such a panic to wrap the test up in loo roll and shove it in the bin that I dropped it twice. More banging.

'Hannah, hurry up! Stop pissing around with your hair!' It was Bradley. Of course it was. He's an expert at making himself appear where he's least wanted.

I flushed and washed my hands, slid the spare test into my pocket, before breezing out of the bathroom and saying, 'Just because you like looking like a homeless person doesn't mean all of us do.'

I spent the majority of yesterday in sheer panic, locking myself away from everyone while I sobbed under my duvet. But once I'd had the evening to mull over what to do, and had taken the other test just to be sure, I realised it could be a blessing in disguise. What better way to start our new life together? Creating our own little family somewhere far away from here. Images started appearing in my mind: the three of us having a picnic in the park, him teaching our child how to ride a bike, family holidays.

I smile as I think about it, but his expression brings me crashing back down to reality with a thud.

'A good thing?' he says. 'Have you lost your mind?'

I recoil, suddenly feeling vulnerable sitting here in my underwear. He's never got angry at me before, has never looked at me the way he's looking at me right now. Like I'm a piece of chewing gum stuck to his shoe. Stupidly, I'd kind of been expecting him to say congratulations.

'It's not the end of the world . . . it could work.' My voice is barely a whisper now, and I'm not even sure he's heard me.

'You sure it's mine?' he says, and I feel as if the grungy walls of the hotel are about to come crashing down on me.

'How could you ask me that?'

'What about Daniel?'

I swallow, forcing back the tears of hurt and embarrassment that are pricking my eyes. 'He and I haven't had sex in months.'

This is true. I always say I'm too tired; I'm on my period; Mum will be home any second. Since I started cheating on him, I haven't been able to bring myself to sleep with him. It feels wrong even kissing him and pretending to still be his girlfriend.

'And I haven't slept with anyone else before you ask,' I say, anger clipping my words. 'You're the only person I've been with. The only person I've wanted to be with.'

He's staring at me with such shock, and horror, that I have to turn my head away if only so that he can't see the humiliation on my face. Shaking his head, he runs his hands through his hair and sits on the edge of the bed, back facing me. I peer over his shoulder to try to see what he's doing. He has his phone in his hand and is opening up a Google tab.

'What are you searching?' I ask.

'Abortion clinics,' he replies. 'There's no way you can have this baby, Hannah.'

CHAPTER TWENTY-NINE

STEFANI

Ten Days After the Murder

The glare of Stefani's laptop is starting to give her a headache, one that pulses right behind her eyes, but she can't bring herself to turn it off. She's not meant to be on duty for another couple of hours, but the clock is ticking on Daniel Forrester being in custody, and she needs to feel useful. Clutching her third cup of coffee in less than an hour, she scrolls down Hannah's Facebook photos. There are hundreds. All manner of selfies and pouty group shots. She's seen them all before – checking for any unusual activity on Hannah's social media was one of the first things they did before they even knew she was dead – but now she's looking at them with fresh eyes. Last time, she didn't know what to look for. She's hoping she'll come across a picture of her with an older man, but so far all she can see are fellow classmates. Hannah was a popular girl. Stefani wonders, wrongly or not, why she chose to be with Daniel when she clearly had her pick.

The fan on her ancient laptop is whirring furiously, clearly not happy with being used for such an extended period of time and at such an ungodly hour of the morning, and just as Stefani reaches the previous year's photos the screen flickers before turning blue.

Your laptop has run into a problem and needs to restart.

Wonderful. Stefani lies back against the sofa, swearing under her breath. No amount of pressing the power button seems to make a difference. She should take this as a sign from above that she needs to take a break. Clearly the universe is telling her to indulge in a Netflix box set and a sharing packet of crisps. Never one to listen to what she should do, however, she grabs her mobile and texts Luke.

The tension is thick as she walks into Luke's kitchen. She hasn't spoken to Cassie since the football game, though not through a lack of trying. Once she got home, she attempted to phone her three times, but each time the call went to voicemail. She half wishes Cassie was home now so that she could try to make amends, maybe even go in for a hug. But she purposefully waited until Cassie went out. She's at the cinema with Ethan, so Stefani has a good couple of hours before she's due back.

'Cassie's laptop's over there.' Luke gestures towards the Mac sitting open on the end of the breakfast bar. 'You know she'd kill me if she knew I'd let you use it.'

'I know,' Stefani says, picking the laptop up as he holds open the door to his office. 'I promise I'll leave everything exactly as I found it. Is there a password?'

'No. Amanda has a strict no-password rule. She says it's important we all trust each other.'

Stefani resists the urge to make a comment about Cassie being eighteen and needing privacy. At least she knows Amanda is looking out for her daughter, as much as it pains her.

'Thank you,' she says, before moving inside and settling herself in Luke's chair. He shuts the door, and she takes a moment to process that this is the first time she's been alone in this house since she moved out after the divorce. She hasn't even peed in this house since.

Her eyes roam the desk, settling on a framed photo of Cassie, Luke and Amanda swimming with dolphins in Dubai. If she didn't know better, she'd assume Amanda was Cassie's mother. She wonders, as she sits in Luke's office in his chair looking at his belongings, if Amanda is ever bothered by how friendly they still are with each other. She's not sure she'd like having her fiancé's ex-girlfriend and mother of his child nip round as often as she does. But then again, Amanda knows full well she's got nothing to worry about. She's Stefani's superior in every way.

Tearing her eyes away from the photo, she pulls open the lid of Cassie's laptop and opens up an incognito tab. She doesn't think her daughter would bother to check the browsing history, but better to be safe than sorry. The last thing she needs is for Cassie to figure out she's been looking at Hannah's Facebook profile on her beloved Mac. Or Luke for that matter. As far as he knows, Stefani's just sending a couple of emails.

It takes her a good ten minutes to navigate back to the photos she had found when her own laptop crashed, and when she finally reaches the correct place, her eye is immediately drawn to a photo of Hannah and Daniel. It's the one the media latched on to and printed in all the papers. Daniel is standing behind Hannah, his arms wrapped around her front, and she's leaning her head onto the crook of his elbow. She looks happy; her eyes are smiling along with her mouth. But it's Daniel that Stefani can't stop looking at. Something in his face makes her heart skip a beat. He looks so incredibly . . . proud. As if he's holding his entire world in his hands. He was clearly as in love with Hannah as his mother said. Stefani knows it does happen, but it just doesn't make sense to her that such absolute adoration could turn to murder.

The Facebook profile isn't garnering any groundbreaking information, so after a few more minutes of scrolling, Stefani decides it really is time to take a break. She exits out of the tab, and then proceeds to close the thirty-two other tabs that Cassie had left open. What is it about teenagers not shutting down their laptops properly? It makes Stefani itch seeing that many tabs.

The desktop is just as bad, with endless screenshots saved so that it's one huge jumble on the home screen. Stefani resists the urge to highlight them all and drag them to the recycle bin. That would be a good way to make sure Cassie never spoke to her again. She's just about to move the mouse over to the 'shutdown' button when something stops her in her tracks. Amongst the mess of screenshots there are a few folders. Clearly, at one point, Cassie started to organise her files before deciding it was a lost cause. Most of them relate to school and various papers that she's had to write, but one of them, right up in the top left-hand corner, is labelled 'Pics'.

Stefani checks behind her to make sure the office door is still firmly closed, then moves the mouse over to the folder and double-clicks. Her throat tightens. What is she doing? Probing into her daughter's business like this? She knows it's an invasion of her privacy, but she's drifted from her daughter so much these past few years. No matter how hard she tries to connect with her and find out what's going on in her life, it's like speaking to a brick wall. Perhaps her personal photos might tell her a little more about who her daughter actually is.

The folder opens up after a couple of seconds, and considering how unorganised the desktop was, it is surprisingly divided up into categories. 'Football'. 'Yearbook'. 'Parties'. 'Food porn'. 'Outfits I like'. Stefani clicks through each of them, somewhat dreading what sort of booze-infused escapades she might find, but is pleasantly surprised to see that Cassie appears to be a fairly level-headed teenager. The folders go deeper and deeper; inside the 'Parties', folder there are six others, and within those there are even more. Stefani gets so wrapped up in seeing these glimpses of her daughter's life, of who she really is when she's not with her, that she completely loses track of time. And then, in the depths of Cassie's seemingly endless files, another folder catches Stefani's eye.

'Han'.

Frowning, she double-clicks. When the folder opens it reveals row upon row of photos. She squints, leaning in to inspect the thumbnails. Not quite sure what she's looking at, she clicks to enlarge one of them.

'What the heck...' she mutters under her breath.

The photos are all of Hannah, but they're not like the photos on her Facebook profile. They're candids. Shots of her walking along the street, laughing with Daniel with her back partially turned from the camera, sitting in her car. It's as if she didn't realise these photos were being taken.

CHAPTER THIRTY

ALEX

Ten Days After the Murder

My fingers drum along the steering wheel, needing something to occupy them beyond keeping the truck straight. I reach down to the radio and turn the volume dial up so loud the angry rap song that's apparently reached number one makes my ears ring. When I get back to the Premier Inn, I'll need to do some of my cross-stitch. My anxiety is intensifying.

I tried to reply to the person who sent me the text message, but it was an unknown number and my message wouldn't send. When I got back to our room, I googled to see if there was any way I could trace who had sent it, but apparently there are actually apps that allow you to send completely anonymous messages. There's no way of telling who it's from, and no way of replying to them. It could just be a prank. I've had plenty of threats on Twitter; targeting my phone could just be taking it to the next level. But how could someone have got my number? And what did it mean when they said, '*I know what you did*'? Was someone watching me that night, without me knowing? I dismiss this idea as pretty unlikely, but still, the thought sits in my mind, dark and dangerous.

No. If it isn't a prank then the most likely explanation is that someone's worried that Daniel will be eliminated as a suspect, that I'll do whatever it takes to clear his name, maybe leaving whoever sent that message exposed as the real killer. They're desperate and trying to frighten me off. But they're wasting their time. I'm not going to give up on my son. He's innocent.

I realise, as I drive, that this is the first time I've been alone in our truck since it happened, and an odd sense of freedom comes with that realisation. I could go anywhere. Do anything. I've felt like a prisoner in that hotel room, too scared to venture outside for fear of the press or the angry protesters. What if one of the many threats I've received online is more than that? What if there actually is someone lurking outside ready to throw acid into my face? But as I drive, all of that seems to disappear further and further into the distance. The urge to continue driving, seeing where the road would take me, is strong.

But I can't leave Daniel.

We'll have to move when all this is over. I never thought I'd want to leave the farm, but there's nothing here for me anymore.

I pull into the garage and fill up the truck, before making my way into the little shop and scanning the shelves. The selection isn't great, but I don't really care. Jase suggested we try to take our minds off the fact that Daniel has been sitting alone and scared in a cold cell since yesterday, and is currently facing another night of it, by watching a movie together and gorging ourselves on salty snacks. Maybe he's secretly hoping we'll have sex too, given it's been so long since we were last intimate. It feels wrong, unethical to try to have a good night while my son suffers the way he is. But at the same time, I appreciate that Jase is only trying to bring back some normality, a reminder that we are still a married couple. 'We're no good to Daniel if we're not strong and united,' he had said. He's right, I suppose.

I can't focus on what I need to buy. The labels on the crisp packets are blurring, melting into one. I run my fingers along my brow and squeeze my eyes shut. My head hurts so much. I never again wanted to feel as helpless as I did that night Daniel was attacked, but here I am. Every attempt I make to help shift the focus from Daniel just seems to make things worse. Meanwhile, Mark is at the farmhouse, cuddled up with Cynthia with not a care in the world.

He thinks he's got away with killing Hannah.

I snatch up a couple of grab bags of Doritos and take them to the counter. A TV screen is playing the news behind the attendant's head, reporting on the latest election, but a ticker tape is running along the bottom. The words 'Hannah Carmichael' jump out at me and I squint to read it.

'Man, 19, is being held for questioning over Hannah Carmichael's murder.' My body tenses, muscles quivering. 'Man, 19'. That's all Daniel has been reduced down to. The press, the police, the Twitter trolls, they all speak of him as if he's an object for them to pull apart. There's no compassion, no consideration of the fact that he might be just another innocent victim of this case. They all seem to forget he's still only a teenager.

'Miss?'

The attendant's voice snaps me back to reality. I blink and look questioningly at him.

'That'll be £5.79.'

'Oh, of course. Sorry.' I fumble around in my purse for a ten-pound note and thrust it at him, my hands still trembling from the white-hot, burning rage that's coursing through me.

Once I'm back in the truck, I pull out my phone, scrolling down to the number for the police station. I have to do something. I can't just sit idly by while everyone tries to pin this murder on my son. I don't yet have proof that Mark was the one sleeping with Hannah, but maybe if I tell Stefani about the hotel, she'll be able to find evidence. They'll be able to pull CCTV from the lobby showing that Mark was with Hannah the night she was murdered, as opposed to on his business trip like he said.

Stefani isn't at the station, I'm told. She's due in at 11 a.m., and it's just gone 9.30. I leave a message asking her to call me back as soon as she's in. There's no point speaking to anyone else. They're all so desperate to wrap up this case I doubt they'll listen to anything that doesn't help them convict Daniel. But at least Stefani knows us. She might be more likely to listen to reason.

I run my finger along the edge of my phone and eye the packs of crisps on the seat next to me. I don't want to go back yet. I'm not ready for another day of pretence with Jase, acting like everything's all fine and dandy. Instead of starting up the engine I navigate to my texts. My finger briefly hovers over Mum's number. She's been asking me to call her since Daniel was arrested, but I keep telling her I need space.

Shaking my head, I scroll away from her and find Cynthia's number. Pressing my lips together, I tap out a message.

I really need to talk to you. Please can we meet?

* * *

She looks awful. She's attempted to cover her dark circles with concealer, but it's all gathered in the creases around her eyes, as if it's been days since she first applied it. I don't think she's showering; there is a stale whiff emanating from her as I approach.

I had expected her to say no, or to just blank me entirely. I was picking my way through a fresh, warm croissant that Jase had gone out especially to get from a bakery in town, when my phone flashed on the bed beside me with her reply. It took all my might not to snatch up the phone when I saw her name on the screen, but I didn't want Jase noticing. He keeps telling me I need to just sit back and let the police handle everything. He'd be annoyed if he knew I'd contacted Cynthia.

She told me to meet her at 12.30 at The Five and Dime on the high street. It's a good choice; away from the village, where we're less likely to be spotted by anyone we know. The Five and Dime is one of those retro American diner-style café-restaurants, and Cynthia's bedraggled appearance is a stark contrast to the vibrant pop-art posters decorating the walls and the bright red leather booth that she's currently sat in. I slide in opposite her, feeling a bizarre sense of déjà vu. Only a year ago Cynthia and I would sometimes come here, when I had an afternoon off from duties at the farm, and have 'girls' days' sipping coffees while Hannah, Bradley and Daniel were at school, enjoying the freedom of having grown kids. Sitting across from her now, the change and shift that's occurred in our relationship becomes even more apparent.

We stare at each other in silence, and I'm relieved when the waitress comes over to take our order, just for the break in awkwardness.

'Two lattes please,' I croak.

My mouth is dry, my palms clammy. I should have asked for a

glass of water while we wait for the coffees. At least then I'd have something to focus on other than the way Cynthia is glaring at me.

'Thank you for agreeing to meet me.' There is a pause as I wait for her to speak. I swallow hard, crossing and uncrossing my legs underneath the table.

'Just say what you have to say,' she replies eventually. I wince, her disregard for all our years of friendship wounding me, but let it go. I have to remember that no matter how hard I'm finding all of this, it's far worse for Cynthia.

'OK...' I take a moment to collect my thoughts. I'd prepared for this meeting. I know what I've come here to say. But now that I'm here, actually face to face with her, my brain is a jumbled mess. I force myself to focus. 'I found out something... about Hannah.'

Cynthia doesn't say anything, but her eyebrows narrow and her lip twitches. I take a deep breath, trying to pull myself together.

'Did you know she went to a hotel the night she died?'

Finally, there's a reaction, a break in her brick-wall exterior. She blanches, jerking back slightly in her seat. 'What are you talking about?'

'I found a receipt in Daniel's room from that night. When I went to the hotel the receptionist said she'd seen her.'

Cynthia is blinking rapidly as she processes this information. 'Have you told the police this?'

'Not yet. I've asked DS Warner to call me as soon as she gets into the station.'

'Why wait for her? If there's evidence that Daniel was with Hannah that night, the police need to hear it!' Her voice is hardening, getting shriller.

'It wasn't Daniel she was with. The receptionist said Hannah was with someone else. A man.'

Her face changes, greying even more as the gravity of my words sinks in.

'Who?' she says.

I shake my head, pursing my lips as I brace myself to deliver the blow.

'I think it might have been Mark.'

There is a long, long time where neither of us says anything. The air between us feels thick and heavy, as if the shock from what I've just said is a living, breathing life force. After what seems like forever, Cynthia grits her teeth.

'What the fuck are you talking about?'

I have to force my words out, fighting past the sandpaper texture that's formed in my mouth. 'That's who it sounded like when she described him. I know this is hard to hear and I am so, so sorry to have to be the one to say it, but I thought you needed to know. If it was Mark, if Mark was sleeping with Hannah, you need to get away from him. It's not safe being in the same house as him.' The words are flooding out of me now. I can't stop. 'You're my best friend, Cynthia. I could never forgive myself if he hurt you too.'

'Alex, shut up!' Cynthia stands so suddenly, she nearly crashes into the waitress approaching with our lattes. My cheeks burn as I realise every head has turned to look at us, but Cynthia seems oblivious. 'Do you even have a shred of evidence to support what you're saying? Besides a vague description from some receptionist who claims to have seen them.'

'I . . . well . . . No, I . . .'

Before I can stutter a response, Cynthia leans in towards me, her hands pressed against the table. 'Daniel did this to Hannah. Your son. And making some half-arsed attempt to pin it on my husband isn't going to change that.'

I chew down on the inside of my cheek. 'Cynthia, listen to me—'

'No, you listen!' Her words are filled with venom, spittle flying across the table as she speaks. 'Mark is a good man. Whatever you think you know, you're wrong. I know him. Leave us alone!'

And with that, she storms out of the café, leaving me to apologise profusely to the waitress, and wishing the plush leather of my seat would swallow me up whole.

Cynthia is really unravelling. She seems unhinged. Maybe I touched a nerve.

CHAPTER THIRTY-ONE

STEFANI

Ten Days After the Murder

'We're going to have to let Daniel Forrester go, aren't we?'

DCI Walton is standing hunched over his desk, his hands pressed against the wood, with Stefani and DS Davies opposite him, looking and feeling like naughty schoolchildren. Stefani already knew this was coming from the second she walked into the station. Daniel's lawyer has practically been staring at his watch since they arrested him, counting down the seconds. They've held Daniel for nearly twenty-four hours now, with not a scrap of evidence against him. One day left to find enough to convict him or they'll have no choice but to let him go.

Stefani had emailed herself the photos she found on Cassie's desktop so that she could properly pore over them later without fear of being caught, but from the quick glance she got this morning, they don't seem to show anything that would help them convict Daniel. All they do – though Stefani is terrified to even go there – is make Cassie look like some kind of stalker. Stefani's heart lurches. She has disconnected from her daughter and it's her fault. She hasn't been there for her. Whatever was Cassie doing taking those clandestine photos? Stefani knows she has to talk to her about them but she needs to find the right time.

'Fuck!' Walton slams his fist against the desk, making Stefani jump. 'How can we not have enough on this kid? He's a teenager for Christ's sake! How can he have covered his tracks so well?'

Stefani shuffles in her spot, knowing full well anything she says right now might just tip Walton over the edge.

'Maybe we're focusing too much on Daniel Forrester?' she ventures, her heart battering against her ribcage as she does so. 'If she had an older lover . . . and she was pregnant with his baby . . . well, that's a motive right there. If he was married, a baby would ruin everything for him.' As she speaks, Stefani finds herself more convinced of this. 'It would be one heck of a motive, in fact.'

Walton raises an eyebrow. 'Or maybe Daniel killed her when he found out she'd not only cheated on him but also got herself up the duff with another man's child?'

Stefani purses her lips. She knows that's a possibility, but she feels like they're doing an injustice to Hannah by not fully exploring all other options. Yes, they're desperate to pin this crime on someone, but isn't it more important they get the right person?

'If I may?' DS Davies pipes up. 'I do think DS Warner has a point. Maybe we could talk to her friends again, see if they knew anything about the pregnancy?'

Stefani gapes at him. 'If you're talking about Cassie, I assure you she knew nothing about the pregnancy. She would have told me if she did!'

They both stare at her and she feels heat flushing up her neck.

'Why?' Walton says, frowning. 'You're strictly forbidden from discussing the case with her, DS Warner.'

'Of course I haven't discussed anything with her,' Stefani says quickly. She's aware that she's sweating, the skin under her collar prickling with heat. She wishes she could remove her tie. 'I just don't think she'll give you any more information than you already know.'

Walton's gaze flicks between her and Davies. Stefani knows now is the time to tell them about the photos. That would be the responsible thing to do. But she can't until she's had a chance to talk to Cassie about it first. Maybe Walton is right. Perhaps she shouldn't be on this case after all.

Eventually, he sighs. 'Davies, you go and speak to Cassie. See what you can get out of her. Talk to Hannah's other friends too. Warner, there's been a call for you from Alex Forrester. Go and find out what she wants, will you?'

She nods, biting back the urge to argue.

'What about Daniel?'

'Unless you can find some earth-shattering piece of evidence in the next twenty-four hours, which I highly doubt given the shambles of this investigation so far, we've no choice but to let him go.' He sits in his chair, rubs his temples with his fingertips. 'But I want officers watching him from the moment he leaves this station. He is not to be out of sight for even a second.'

Stefani tries her hardest not to think about her daughter as she rings Alex Forrester, winding the cable around her finger as she waits for her to pick up. Hopefully, whatever she wants to say will be enough to distract her until Davies comes back. She wishes Cassie wasn't a part of all this. Had she known that Cassie and Hannah were friends, she might not have pushed so hard to take this case. At least then she would be allowed to be there for her daughter more than she is right now. At least she could actually be the mother that Cassie needs. But she can't give up the case now. She's in too deep, has allowed it to seep into her life too much. She thinks about Hannah constantly, every second of every day.

Alex hadn't said what she wanted to talk to Stefani about, only that she needed to speak to her as soon as possible. Honestly, Stefani's not expecting anything more than another rant about how long they've held Daniel, but when Alex answers, she can hear in her voice that it's something more than that.

'Hi, Stef . . . DS Warner . . .' Alex says nervously.

'Mrs Forrester, I understand you want to speak with me?'

There is a long pause, and Stefani has to check the phone to make sure they're still connected.

Finally, Alex says, 'I have some information about . . . about Mark Butler.'

Stefani's eyes widen. 'Mark Butler?'

'Yes . . .' Alex sounds hesitant now, as though she's getting cold feet.

'Would you like to talk to me face to face?' says Stefani. 'Can you come into the station?'

'OK . . . when?'

'Can you be here in an hour?'

'Sure.'

When the call ends, Stefani pulls out her mobile. Hands trembling, she taps out a text to Davies.

If you haven't left yet, come back. Looks like we might have some more on MB.

CHAPTER THIRTY-TWO

ALEX

Ten Days After the Murder

I keep my head bowed low as I pull up to the Premier Inn. I did consider just going straight to the station, but Stefani said she'd see me in an hour, and I don't trust myself to wait outside for that long knowing Daniel is just a few walls away. Besides, I need to grab the hotel receipt from my suitcase so that she can see I'm not just making up these accusations against Mark.

Luckily, the reporters who hounded us outside the police station don't seem to have followed us here, but I bet when Daniel is with us they will. It's only a matter of time before I'm going to have to start doing my best celebrity impression again; hand in front of the face, rim of a hat pulled down so that I can only just see, quick strides to the door while doing my best to ignore the camera flashes and bombardment of questions. I'm surprised no one started snapping photos in the café. I imagine a shot of Cynthia screeching at me the way she did would make a good tabloid feature.

Despite the car park looking relatively empty, I don't want to be outside for any longer than I have to. I park up and hurry to the lobby as fast as I can. Once inside, I take a moment to steady my breath and am met with the usual pitying stares of the receptionists.

'Any post?' I ask, and the young girl at the counter nods. She doesn't even need to ask my name or room number anymore. This is the same routine every time I venture away from my room – which is rare – or when Jase goes to work. She hands me a bunch of envelopes and I thank her before heading to our room. I wonder what that young girl at reception thinks of us. Does she think my family are a bunch of murderers, like everyone else? She masks it well, if she does.

Jase glimpses the envelopes in my hand as I enter and rolls his eyes.

'More poisonous mail?' he says wearily. 'I don't know why you bother collecting it. It's better off in the bin.' He plucks the post from my hands and flings the letters onto the writing desk. They wobble and slide across the wood surface. 'I'm not in the mood for all that crap. If we miss any important mail, we'll get a phone call or an email.'

He's right, I know he is. We agreed with the manager as long-term guests that we could put a postal redirect in place to catch any urgent letters that would otherwise be piling up at home, but I wish we hadn't bothered. All we ever receive is poisonous letters from people who don't know us, don't know Daniel. Venomous, shocking words that I don't think I could say to even my worst enemy. The courage that comes from anonymity is really something. But each day I force myself to read each one, push back the hot, angry tears that prick at my eyes as I ball them up and throw them into the recycling pile, if only to remind myself why I need to clear Daniel's name. When he does come home, I don't want him seeing what people have been saying about him. I couldn't bear that.

I sigh and pick up the top envelope, even though I know it will annoy Jase. I can feel his eyes boring into me, but I ignore him, focusing instead on ripping open the flap and taking in its contents as quickly and as painfully as I can. Hate letter number one. I screw it up and drop it in the bin before repeating the process with the next letter.

I'm five letters in when I pick up an envelope that instantly feels different. There's something inside, something small and hard. I open it and shake the contents out. A small black USB stick drops onto the desk. Frowning, I peer inside the envelope. There is a small scrap of paper that I might have missed if I hadn't looked closely. It's folded in half, but I can see the indents where someone has written on it, pressing with the pen far too hard by the looks of it.

I pull the paper out, unfold it and let out a loud whimper.

Jase is by my side in an instant. 'Alex? Alex! What's wrong?'

I can't respond. I can't do anything but stare at the writing before me, at the angry, scrawled letters. My legs buckle underneath me and it's all I can do to grip on to the back of the desk chair and lower myself, trembling, into the seat. I can't even begin to think how to answer him.

Jase grabs the paper, but my hand stays hovering in mid-air, as if I'm a film that's been paused. The panic rising inside me turns into sobs. I hunch forward, claw at my face as the tears fall and I realise just how stupid I've been. Everything I've done, all the little lies I've told since I found Hannah, it's put us all at risk. Myself, Jase . . . and Daniel. The words on the paper replay in my mind.

I told you once, now this is your final warning. Stop digging or I'm sending this to the police.

* * *

I suck in a few shaky breaths as I wait for Jase's response, wondering just how much he's going to hate me. I had to tell him. I had no choice. This isn't just threatening messages anymore. Whoever sent this has been here, in this building. Even if I didn't tell Jase, he'd have looked at whatever is on the USB, and it's clearly something to incriminate me. It was time.

I watch him pace in front of me, trying to read his expression, preparing myself for the outburst of anger I'm sure is coming. But it doesn't.

After a few minutes he returns to crouch in front of me, shaking his head.

'You should have told me straight away,' he says, prompting more tears.

'I know. I wanted to. You have no idea how much this secret has been tearing me up inside.'

He lets out a long, slow breath. 'Well, at least I understand why you've been so . . .' He trails off, but he doesn't need to continue.

'Crazy' is the word he was looking for, because I have been. I've been acting a little insane ever since I found Hannah that evening, and I've made everything so much worse for everyone.

Jase cocks his head to the side, eyeing the USB warily. I'd been so wrapped up in the letter, I'd almost forgotten about it. We both stare at it, as if we're afraid it might explode.

'Jase, I don't think I want to know what's on it,' I say, dread tugging at my insides.

He picks it up and moves to his laptop bag. His forehead is etched with the same anxiety I'm feeling about what he's going to see.

'I don't think we have a choice,' he says, gripping the USB stick so hard, I'm worried he might break it. 'Someone knows something. We've got to know what we're dealing with.'

I swallow down the argument forming on my tongue and hold my breath as he boots up the laptop. Jase's computer is fairly old and the wait for the USB to load is agonising. When it eventually does, just one file appears on the screen. It's a video.

I see him inhale a deep breath, then click to open it before I can try to stop him. A buffering wheel appears for a few seconds, and then a familiar sight flashes onto the screen. It's the farmhouse porch. The old stone steps and flower-bed borders are unmistakable, even in grainy grayscale. It looks like it's from some kind of security camera, though I can't believe I never knew there was one there. It must be well and truly hidden behind the porch light. I'm not even sure if the police know about it. If they do, they haven't mentioned it. For a moment I think the video isn't playing as the image is completely still, but after a while a movement appears in the corner of the screen. I blink rapidly as I watch the footage and my stomach lurches.

It's me. It's unmistakably me. And I'm carrying Hannah's lifeless body out of the farmhouse.

CHAPTER THIRTY-THREE

HANNAH
The Day of the Murder – 9.45 p.m.

I press my hand to my stomach as I clamber off the bus and start making my way down the country roads to the farm. It's still flat, not even a hint of a bulge there, but it feels different somehow. Like I can sense the baby – my baby – dividing and growing deep inside me. I think about the videos we've watched in our science classes of cells splitting, alien-like. A tiny fragment of him is growing inside me. And he wants me to get rid of it.

The thought makes my throat constrict. That fantasy that I had pictured to try to make myself feel better was as fragile as a balloon, and now it has burst spectacularly in my face. I'm tired and tender and hurt and fucking angry. He isn't planning on leaving her to be with me at all, is he? If he was, he wouldn't be pressuring me to do this. OK, he probably thought that part of his life was over and it's not exactly ideal timing, but we could make it work. It would certainly take a lot more thought and discussion if he was actually planning on being with me. No. He doesn't want this baby because he doesn't want her to find out. I've been trying so hard to kid myself, but I can see it now. The ugly truth of it all. I'm just a shag on the side.

The anger bubbles and boils as I approach the farm, until all I can see is red. My phone buzzes in my pocket and I glance down at it. It's him. He's been calling me since I stormed out of the hotel, but I can't talk to him. Hearing his voice would just make me break down. I jab at the decline button and pass through the old wooden gates. The glow of the firepit is still shining brightly. Mum and Alex must still be having drinks.

Another buzz, this time a text. I can see it's from him, and part of me wants to delete it without reading it, but curiosity gets the better of me. I open it and stare at the screen, biting down on the inside of my cheeks so hard it hurts.

It's for the best.

That's it. No apology. No asking if I'm OK. Yet again, all he cares about is whether or not I'm going to do something that will screw him over. My fingers type furiously. The text is littered with typos, so I have to erase it and start again. He doesn't get to do this to me.

I'm not having an abortion. I'm going to tell everyone the truth.

As I hit 'send' more tears start rolling down my cheeks. I'm so focused on staring at my phone, waiting to see if my reply has been read yet, that at first I don't even notice movement coming up behind me.
'Hannah?'
I gasp, my stomach lurching, and spin around.
Daniel.

CHAPTER THIRTY-FOUR

STEFANI

Ten Days After the Murder

'Alex Forrester reckons she has some information on Mark Butler,' Stefani says, standing across the desk from Walton and Davies. 'I think we need to prepare to get him back in for questioning.'

'Let's just take a moment.' Walton runs his fingers along his brow. 'We don't know what this so-called information is yet. And even if it's something big, it doesn't necessarily mean anything. I mean, this is the suspect's mother we're talking about. She could be coming up with any old story in an attempt to clear his name.'

Stefani purses her lips, forcing herself to remain composed. She doesn't understand why Walton is so desperate to pin this murder on Daniel, why he's so averse to exploring any other possibilities.

'Sir, we already know Mark is capable of lashing out. And there are plenty of witnesses to confirm he frequents the pub a fair bit. We need to establish if this is regular behaviour. If it is, there is a very real chance that he could have hurt Hannah in a rage.'

Walton leans back in his chair. 'So, what are you suggesting, that he's our mystery older man too? That he was sleeping with his own stepdaughter?'

Stefani grimaces. 'Stranger things have happened, unfortunately. He was only with Cynthia for a year before they got married. It's not like he's watched Hannah grow up from a kid.'

'And what do you think, Davies?'

Davies blinks, as if surprised to have been called on. He glances between Stefani and Walton. 'I think it's an avenue worth exploring.'

Walton exhales loudly and shrugs. 'OK. Let's see what Alex Forrester has to say for herself, and if we think there may be something to it, we can bring him in.'

'Thank you, sir.' Stefani nods gratefully at him and leaves his office. Davies follows and she gives him a look that says, *God, I hope this hunch pays off.* He returns the same look. There is a lot riding on this. They have to start getting some good luck at some point, surely?

No sooner has she sat down at her desk than her phone starts to ring. She frowns at the caller ID.

'It's Alex Forrester,' she says. Davies raises his eyebrows.

Eyeing Walton to make sure he's still safely in his office and out of earshot, she picks up the phone and presses it to her ear. 'DS Warner.'

'Hi.' Alex's voice sounds on the other end of the line, throaty and nervous. 'It's Alex. Alex Forrester. I . . .'

There is a pause, but Stefani can just about hear Alex's shaky breathing. Eventually, Alex continues.

'I'm not coming into the station. I don't have any information to share.'

An uneasy sensation settles into the pit of Stefani's stomach. 'I don't understand . . . ?'

'I was lying when I said I had something on Mark,' Alex says quickly. 'I'm sorry, I thought it might prompt you to look at other suspects. I thought you might release Daniel sooner. It was rash and thoughtless, and as soon as I hung up I realised how wrong it was.'

There is a long, long silence. Alex's words stretch out between them, a thick blanket hanging in the air. Davies is watching Stefani, brows knitted together, as if he can tell from Stefani's expression that something is wrong.

'Mrs Forrester,' Stefani ventures carefully. 'You do realise what you're saying right now, don't you? Perverting the course of justice is a serious crime.'

Another silence, and Stefani wishes she could see Alex's face, to watch for any tells in her expression. Something isn't right here.

'I know. I'm sorry.'

'I want you to think really carefully about this.' She bunches her free hand into a fist, the frustration seeping out of her. 'If you're being intimidated or pressured to drop this, we can help you.'

'I'm not,' Alex cuts in sharply. 'Please, forget I said anything.'

The line goes dead.

'Damn.' Stefani slumps in her chair.

'Do I want to know?' Davies asks.

'Check Mark's alibi again,' she says. 'See if anyone witnessed him in the area the night Hannah disappeared. I have a feeling he's guilty of a lot more than making a few empty threats.'

Luke gives Stefani a sympathetic smile as she opens the door. The stress of the case must be pretty evident on her face, and she looks just about as tired as she feels. She had desperately wanted to stay on at the station and do some more digging on Mark, but there was no way she'd be able to explain that to Cassie. Besides, she's been looking forward to tonight for weeks, and though Cassie would try to make out otherwise, she thinks she's been looking forward to it too.

'Thank you,' she says as Luke hands her an overnight bag.

'No problem. How are you doing?'

'Fine, thank you.' She turns to her daughter. 'Hey, Cass! Ready for our sleepover?'

They have an awkward hug, resentment still lingering from Cassie from their run-in at the football game, and Luke clears his throat. 'Don't forget, Cass, you need to leave fifteen minutes earlier than usual in the morning to get to football practice on time.'

Luke kisses her on the cheek, then heads off, leaving Stefani with the pressure of this evening weighing heavy on her shoulders. Cassie looks at her, sullen but expectant.

'Fancy ordering in?' Stefani says.

'Whatever.' Cassie shrugs, though Stefani can see she's softening.

They opt for a Wagamama takeaway, and the last of the chilly atmosphere evaporates as Stefani attempts to eat with chopsticks and Cassie mocks her, like she always does. They watch a Marvel film – Cassie's pick – and indulge in sharing Ben & Jerry's straight out of the pot while snuggled up on the sofa under a fuzzy blanket. By the time the movie is over, the sky is inky black outside, and Stefani feels a stab of regret that the evening has gone so quickly. Spending quality time with her daughter has been a welcome distraction, but more than that, something she's desperately needed without even being aware of it.

Cassie senses it too. 'I wish I could stay tomorrow night as well,' she says, peering up at Stefani through her long lashes. Stefani squeezes her closer.

'Your dad will want you home tomorrow after practice. But maybe I could have a chat with him, see if we can do this more often?'

Cassie nods, a grin spreading over her face. She looks so grown up these days, but occasionally, when she gets excited, hints of her child-self sneak through. Biting her lip, she reaches a hand into her overnight bag and pulls out a spiral-bound book made up of brown recycled paper. Her fingers brush over the cover.

'What's that?'

'It's a scrapbook.' She flips open the cover to reveal the first page, decorated with Polaroid-style photos and stickers.

Stefani leans in, her breath hitching. The pictures are of Cassie and Hannah.

'I thought it would be a nice thing to do for Cynthia,' Cassie says, 'I had so many photos of Hannah on my phone. It seemed a shame to think her mum would never see them.'

A wave of pride washes over Stefani and she blinks away a few tears. 'That's a lovely thought,' she says, her voice cracking.

As she looks at the photos, she can't believe she never knew how close Cassie was to Hannah. There are selfies from their school prom, the two girls looking twice their age with glamorous make-up and long, slinky dresses. There are action shots from a day at the bowling alley, with Hannah cast in a pink glow by the neon lights, arms stretched high above her head as she celebrates a strike. There's a silly photo taken in the school playground, where the two of them seem to be showing off the fact they've swapped one sock each.

Stefani glances at her daughter as they flick through the pages. 'How are you coping with all this?'

Cassie shrugs. 'I'm OK,' she says, her aloof exterior holding steadfast, and then, 'I miss her a lot.'

Another thought settles over Stefani, burrowing itself deep into her brain. Her chest tightens. She needs to ask Cassie about the photos she found on her desktop. They're likely nothing, but if they do mean something, if they can throw any more light on the case, it would be wrong for Stefani not to at least pursue them with her daughter.

'Cass, I need to ask you something,' she says, glancing down at her. An ache of guilt fills her at the thought of spoiling an otherwise perfect evening. She wishes with all her heart that she wasn't involved.

Cassie peers up at her. 'What's up?'

She takes a long, slow breath. 'This morning, I borrowed your laptop.'

'My laptop? Why?'

'Mine died and your dad said you wouldn't mind me sending a few emails. Anyway, I, er . . .' She takes a moment to choose her words, praying that this won't make Cassie hate her. 'I found a folder with pictures in it. Pictures of Hannah.'

She pauses, allowing what she's said to sink in, watching for any kind of reaction in her daughter. Cassie frowns. Stefani can see her words ticking over in her head. Then the realisation hits and her eyes widen.

'You don't understand,' she whispers, a muscle tensing in her jaw.

'You're right. I don't. So help me to understand.'

Cassie's cheeks redden. She gets to her feet suddenly, taking Stefani by surprise, and begins to pace the living room.

'Why did you have to look on there?' she shouts abruptly. 'Are you investigating me now, is that it? Am I just another suspect in your case?'

'Of course not!' Stefani is on her feet now too. She steps over to Cassie and places a hand on each of her shoulders. 'I haven't mentioned them to anyone. But I need you to tell me the truth. Why do you have all those photos of Hannah on your computer?'

Cassie blinks at her, her eyes glazing. 'Because . . .' She falters, tries to look away, but Stefani squeezes her shoulders gently to bring her focus back.

'Because what?'

'Because I was in love with her, OK?'

Endless seconds tick by. Cassie's face creases as she tries to hold back the tears, but she can't. Her hands fly to her face and she sobs into them, her cries muffled against her fingers.

'I tried to tell her how I felt and she was so mean to me. She said we couldn't be friends anymore. She even deleted all the pictures of us together. Then she started spending all her time with Daniel and pretending like I didn't even exist. I got jealous and . . .'

She cries some more, gulping for air between weeps, and Stefani pulls her towards her chest.

'I don't understand,' she says. 'What about Ethan?'

Cassie scoffs. 'He actually wants to spend time with me. He just . . . makes me feel wanted, I guess.' She buries her face into Stefani's shoulder. 'I don't know why I took all those photos. I was so hurt by the way she shut me out. I guess I became a bit obsessed.'

Stefani's stomach twists, knowing full well how this looks. Hannah rejected Cassie in such a cruel way that she ended up effectively stalking her. If ever they needed another suspect besides Daniel in this case, they've sure as heck got one now.

After a while, Cassie pulls away and looks up at Stefani, her face puffy with red splotches. 'Are you going to show the photos to the people at your work?'

Stefani stares back at her daughter, her head aching, her chest hollow. She doesn't know what to say or do. The question she really needs to ask – *Did you have anything to do with Hannah's death?* – sits like thick tar on her tongue. She just can't bring herself to say it.

'No,' she says eventually. 'We'll keep this between us.'

Relief flooding her face, Cassie nuzzles back into Stefani's chest and wraps her arms around her waist, a non-verbal message that she still needs her mum. Stefani doesn't say anything, just stands and holds her.

CHAPTER THIRTY-FIVE

ALEX

Ten Days After the Murder

I'm still clutching the phone in my hand even though I hung up the call to Stefani hours ago. Jase and I have sat here in silence ever since. The images of me carrying Hannah's body out of the farmhouse replay in my mind over and over. Even though I know it's me in the video and that night is burned into my memory like someone's taken a branding iron to my brain, it seems like a completely different person. Thinking about it now, I can't believe I did something so stupid. So reckless.

I stare blankly ahead at nothing in particular. 'He's going to get away with it, isn't he?'

'He?'

'Mark. He's going to get away with killing Hannah.'

Jase leans forward, a thoughtful expression on his face. 'How do we know it was Mark? Surely anyone with access to the farm could have got hold of security footage?'

'There's something else I haven't told you.' I take his hand, intertwining our fingers. Now that he knows what I did, I'm overcome with the need to feel close to him, as if I'll fall to pieces if I'm not holding on tightly to him. 'Hannah was cheating on Daniel. I found a receipt for this seedy little hotel, and when I went there, they said they'd seen her kissing a man who looked like Mark in the lobby. It's him, he sent me this video. I told Cynthia I was going to the police about the hotel. She must have told him.'

Jase shakes his head, puffing out his cheeks as he exhales. 'Jesus Christ.'

'Yeah.' And then it's like a dam has broken; tears bursting from my eyes and soaking my cheeks, my jeans. 'And now, because of what I did, he's going to get away with it and our son is going to go to prison.'

Jase pulls me towards him as I sob and I cling to his shirt, my body trembling against his. He strokes my hair and cradles me as if I'm a scared child.

'No,' he says after a moment. 'Daniel's not going to go to prison. I won't let that happen.'

I sit up, wiping my face and snivelling. 'What can we do? Everything I have on Mark is circumstantial. I haven't got any real proof. And if I go to the police he'll release the video. They'll think I killed her.'

Jase shakes his head and lets out a heavy sigh. 'I wish there was something I could do to make all this go away,' he says, looking down at me, his face filled with remorse. 'I'm supposed to protect you both.'

He's looking at me, waiting for me to reassure him that it's not his fault, but my mind is elsewhere.

'Alex?' he says. 'What is it?'

'I think it's about time we went back to the farm.'

The following day drags. We've had to wait for our chance, and by the time we arrive at the farm, my fingers are twitching from anticipation. The farmhouse is empty. We knew it would be. Cynthia has always been a regular churchgoer, anyway, but since losing Hannah that seems to have increased. The only posts that appear on her Facebook feed these days are updates from the church: tea and coffee evenings, fundraising events, Bible-study groups and the like. Right now, they'll be sitting in the pews for the evening service, singing their hymns and bowing their heads to pray. This is our window of opportunity.

My only concern is running into Steve or Erin – I don't think I'd be able to convince Steve to let me in a second time – but, as predicted, they're out on the fields. From the entrance gate, still adorned with now wilting flowers, I can see the silhouette of the tractors gliding up and down the horizon, too far away for them to notice any unexpected visitors.

'We should split up,' Jase says, keeping his voice low as if he's worried they'll be able to hear us even from this distance. 'You check out the farmhouse, I'll see if there's anything else in Daniel's room.'

I frown. 'I've already searched Daniel's room. That's how I found the receipt.'

'But you weren't looking for evidence against Mark then, were you? You might have missed something.' He can clearly sense my reluctance to venture away from him, because he squeezes my hand and says, 'This is our last chance to search the farm. It'll be too risky to come back after this. We need to be thorough.'

Though my head is screaming at me to stay as close to him as possible, I nod and he lets go of my hand. He climbs back into our truck and drives down the dirt path towards our home, and I am alone.

I move quickly and quietly, avoiding the front door with its secret security camera and instead heading for the cellar. There's a broken window down there that they've been meaning to get fixed for years. It got picked up in the police search as a potential entry point for intruders, but, as far as I know, that theory was quickly dismissed in favour of pinning the blame on my son.

I have to smash the remaining glass with my elbow in order to fit through the gap. The noise of it shatters the quiet of the fields and I wince, praying the sound is lost to the wind. I listen for a moment. No one is coming. Using the sleeves of my jumper to protect my hands from the shards still attached to the frame, I haul myself up and through the window. This is the most active I've been for over a week and my muscles stage a protest as I climb. Once through, I turn back to inspect the mess I've made. I sweep up the glass, which looks more like tiny fragments of ice, and hide it behind one of the old cardboard boxes that never gets moved. I don't think they'll notice.

My first stop is Cynthia and Mark's bedroom. This is the one room of the house I've never been in, and an odd shiver runs down my spine as I push open the door. I shouldn't be here, the sense of it is overwhelming, but I have to. I'm well aware the police will have already searched the house from top to bottom, but they don't know Mark and Hannah like I do. They could glance over something they consider to be totally irrelevant, but to someone who knows the family, it could be key. There is also the distinct possibility that he's got sloppy as time has gone on, assuming that my poor boy would take the fall for his actions.

I'm not even sure what I'm looking for; perhaps a note from Hannah to him, something to prove he was the one at the hotel with her that night. Looking for evidence of an affair isn't exactly my forte, but there has to be something, some moment where they didn't quite cover their tracks. I search through the wardrobes, rifling through Mark's pockets. Then in the washing basket, checking all the unwashed clothes. I crouch to check under the bed, feel about under the mattress. I ransack the drawers in the dresser, checking underneath each one in case there's anything taped under there. I run my fingers along the top of the mirror, the wardrobe, the doorway, coming away with nothing but dust. When I don't find anything, I make my way to Hannah's room.

My breath catches in my throat as I open the door. The room hasn't been touched. It's been left dormant and stagnant, Hannah's memory preserved. It looks every inch a typical teenage girl's room: Polaroid pictures strung up on the wall with fairy lights, a selection of Colleen Hoover novels propped up on a shelf, a fluffy faux-fur rug on the floor, her clothes folded on the bed ready to be worn. But even though I've seen this room before, it doesn't look real. It's like a picture in an estate agent's brochure. A shrine perpetually waiting for its inhabitant to return, even though the reality is that she's never coming back.

Chewing back the lump in my throat, I take a tentative step into the bedroom and conduct the exact same search, but still my efforts prove fruitless. Beginning to lose hope, I move on to the bathroom. I catch sight of my reflection in the mirror and stare at it, at my bedraggled face. The stress has got to me. Deep circles sit underneath my eyes and my cheeks have hollowed. The pit in my stomach deepens and fills with self-doubt. What if I can't save Daniel? What if in destroying the evidence at the crime scene I've as good as sealed his fate? I may as well have put the handcuffs on him and sentenced him to murder myself. What kind of mother am I if I can't even protect my own son? The one job I'm supposed to do.

Before I can get too wrapped up in my regret, a sound coming from downstairs makes me shrink back into the bathroom and push the door to. Holding my breath, I press my ear to the wood of it. Someone is in the house. Footsteps echo through the old building, quick then slow, uneven, as if they're stumbling around. They travel to the kitchen, where they are accompanied by the clattering of cupboards. A bead of sweat forms at my hairline and tickles my skin as it rolls, my hands growing clammy.

I edge out of the bathroom and peer down to the hallway from the landing. I can't see anyone, but the sound of movement is still coming from the kitchen. Holding my breath as if the very sound of it might give me away, I creep down the stairs, trying desperately to remember which ones creak. My mouth grows dry and my heart beats faster with every step. Once I near the bottom, I peek around the bannister to the kitchen. It's Mark. He's sitting at one of the breakfast bar stools, head drooped back and an open bottle of Budweiser clutched in his hand. He's drunk again. Did he just leave Cynthia at church to go drinking? Or was he never even with her? Perhaps my allegations have caused a rift in their marriage after all. Perhaps Cynthia has actually listened to me and told him he needs to get out.

I seize my opportunity and sneak past, rounding the corner in the hall until I'm back in the cellar. Then I'm hauling myself up, clambering through the smashed window and dropping down onto the damp ground, relief washing over me. I pull out my phone and call Jase. From here, I can just about see our truck parked up outside our barn house. It's a wonder Mark didn't see it when he arrived home.

Jase isn't answering. The robotic voicemail service sounds and I shove the phone back into my pocket, before breaking into a run down the dirt path. We need to leave. We can't be here. If we're spotted, I'm screwed. I run as hard and as fast as I can until my legs and my lungs burn. The telltale beginnings of a cramp are working their way up my calf but I push myself forward. The path seems to stretch out before me. When I finally reach our front door, I practically topple through it, crashing into our open-plan living space.

'Jase, we need to . . .' The words are snatched from my mouth.

I blink a few times as I process the sight before me. Jase is in the kitchen, standing on one of our dining-room chairs, one hand up on the top of the spice cabinet. In his other hand is a mobile phone. One that I've never seen before.

'What's that?' I say.

His eyes are wide with shock at my sudden entrance. He looks between me and the phone, then back again.

'I don't know. I just found it.'

He gives me a small smile, just one corner of his mouth turning up, and scrapes a hand through his hair. A red tinge is creeping along the skin on his neck. He looks nervous.

I take a step forward and hold out my hand. 'Let me see.'

Jase immediately jerks the phone back. 'It's got a passcode on it. You won't be able to get into it. I've been trying. We'll have to have a look when we get back to our room. What were you going to say when you came in?'

My eyes narrow as I take in his shifty posture, his refusal to meet my gaze, his repetitive swallowing.

'What made you look on top of our kitchen cupboards?' I ask. It's not exactly an obvious place to search for evidence of an affair. Unless, of course, he knew to look there.

He opens his mouth to respond, but no words come out. He can't explain himself. This isn't a phone he just happens to have found, I realise. It's his. But why would he need a secret phone? And why would he lie to me about it?

And then all the dots connect in my head, and I can't believe I didn't see it sooner. The receptionist's words echo in my head. '*He was tall, dark hair . . . I reckon he was in his late thirties, maybe early forties.*' My immediate reaction was to think of Mark. But, of course, that description could easily fit another resident of this farm. One I would never have even thought to suspect.

'Mark wasn't the one sleeping with Hannah, was he?' I say eventually. 'It was you.'

CHAPTER THIRTY-SIX

STEFANI

Eleven Days After The Murder

'Right.' Walton bustles over to Stefani's desk not five minutes after she's arrived, his face flushed as if he's just run a mile. 'Warner, Davies, start getting the paperwork together. We're going to charge Daniel Forrester.'

'Wait, what?' Stefani jumps up from her seat, but Walton has already turned his back on her and is starting to retreat into his office. She follows, brows furrowed. 'Has new evidence come to light?'

'No, but we have enough.' He doesn't make eye contact with her, just shuffles a few piles of paperwork around on his desk. 'The kid disappeared the night she was murdered and stayed in hiding for over a week. Not to mention Hannah was cheating on him. It's obvious. And, of course, there's his . . . anger issues.'

Stefani lowers her eyebrows. 'We can't discriminate based on a pre-existing brain injury. You know that.'

'Of course not. But, let's be honest, all the dots line up. And if he's innocent, why isn't he telling us everything? Why keep up the "no comment" act unless he's guilty? It's the boyfriend, Warner. It's always the boyfriend.'

Stefani closes her eyes against the headache pulsing behind them. 'Sir, all our evidence is circumstantial. If we charge him, we'll be laughed out of the courtroom. His attorney would have a field day.'

'Commissioner reckons we've got a strong enough case for a conviction and I'm not about to argue with him. We need this case closed.'

In sync, they both check the clock on the wall. They have just under two hours until they legally cannot hold Daniel any longer. The press have been slowly gathering outside like vultures circling their prey, poised and ready to release their story about the incompetency of the police force. It isn't Walton who wants Daniel charged to save face. This has come from further up.

'Sir,' Stefani says by way of agreement.

Walton nods at her as she spins around and exits his office. But she has no intention of starting on the paperwork.

'I'll be back in a bit,' she says to Davies as she snatches up her jacket and strides out of the room. She can hear Davies calling her, questioning where she's going, but she ignores him. Her gut is telling her that Daniel is innocent, and she'll be damned if she's going to sit back and watch while an innocent kid is convicted of murder.

Stefani bounces nervously on the balls of her feet as she waits on the doorstep of Dr Eriksen's office. The building is plain and unassuming, nestled amongst a row of charity shops and fast food restaurants. The only clue as to the building's purpose is a silver plaque on the wall above the entry keypad, which reads 'Dr M. Eriksen – Cognitive Behavioural Therapist'.

Taking a deep breath, she presses the buzzer again. She didn't call ahead; perhaps he isn't even in. She's about to try calling the number on his website when the clink of locks being opened sounds from inside.

Dr Eriksen is a small man with a kind face, probably in his early sixties. He squints at Stefani through round, thin-rimmed glasses.

'Do you have an appointment?' he asks, and Stefani clears her throat.

'Sorry, no. I'm DS Stefani Warner.' She flashes him her ID. 'I'm investigating the murder of Hannah Carmichael. Can I come in?'

His forehead wrinkles and he rubs his jaw. 'I'm not able to discuss the particulars of my sessions with Daniel Forrester, if that's what you're here for. Patient–doctor confidentiality.'

Stefani nods and offers him her friendliest smile. She had been expecting him to say that. 'I understand that, but I'm hoping you'll be able to answer a few questions without compromising your ethics.'

He shuffles in his spot while he deliberates, and Stefani holds her breath. If he doesn't speak to her, she's not sure what her next move is. Finally, he stands to one side and holds the door open. 'Very well.'

His office is exactly what Stefani had expected: warm neutral tones on the walls, three plush armchairs centred in the room all facing each other, a few potted plants in the corners. The artwork on the walls is enough to bring a little colour to the place without injecting any real personality. It is comfortable and inviting, yet professional.

Dr Eriksen gestures at one of the armchairs. 'Would you like a tea or coffee?'

'No, thank you,' she says as she sits, sinking into the foam cushion.

'So...' Dr Eriksen sits opposite her, and she is met with the distinct sense of being analysed, like she's another of his patients. 'What can I do for you, DS Warner?'

She clears her throat. 'How long have you been treating Daniel Forrester?'

'Four years. I first saw him while he was recovering from his brain injury in hospital.'

'What kind of symptoms do you normally see in someone with a brain injury similar to Daniel's?'

She's hoping that by asking him general questions rather than specifically asking about Daniel, he might be able to share more. She doesn't need to know what the two of them speak about in their sessions, she just needs a better understanding of Daniel. Dr Eriksen gives her a small smile, as if he knows exactly what she's trying to do, but proceeds to sit back in his chair, hands crossed on his lap.

'Do you know much about the brain, DS Warner?'

She frowns, slightly taken aback by having the questioning turned onto her. 'It stores all of our knowledge, our memories?' She says it like a question. She's unsure what kind of answer he's looking for.

'It controls everything,' Dr Eriksen says. 'The tiniest twitch of your muscles, every emotion you feel, even the simple act of breathing. Now, the frontal lobe, which is what was injured during Daniel's attack, is considered our behaviour and emotional control centre. It's what gives us our personalities. When it's damaged, you can suffer from neurobehavioural consequences that can impact the way in which you behave. We call it disinhibition.'

Stefani nods, leaning forward. 'And that's what Daniel suffers from?'

'Yes. Think of it as losing your filter. You know, when you think something but know it's not appropriate to say out loud, that's your filter stopping you. But in a frontal lobe injury, that filter can get cracked and allow things to slip through.'

Stefani thinks back to their interview with Daniel, how he called her pretty and laughed when Walton read him his rights.

'Does it just affect what you say or . . . can it affect your actions too?'

'It affects all sorts of things. Impulsively spending money, divulging personal information too freely, being overly familiar with others, laughing at inappropriate times . . . aggression. It can get the person into a lot of trouble in a social context.'

There is a heavy, loaded pause as Stefani pictures how Hannah might have been killed, how her dead body was dragged into the pig barn.

Dr Eriksen must have known what she was thinking, because he adjusts his glasses and says, 'When it comes to situations like these, it's easy to blame someone who suffers from disinhibition. They become an easy target. But cognitive behavioural therapy, which is what we practise here, is often very effective. It allows the person to redirect and change unhelpful thoughts and behaviours. Daniel has never missed an appointment and the progress he's made in the last four years is really quite admirable. In fact, his love for camping was born out of our sessions. It's his way of recognising feelings like anger and giving himself the space to process them.'

Stefani nods thoughtfully as she absorbs this information. 'Just one more question, Dr Eriksen, if you don't mind.'

'Go ahead.'

'Do you think Daniel could have killed Hannah?'

He takes a moment to consider her question, then smiles. 'No, DS Warner. I do not believe he is capable of killing anyone.'

The cold air hits Stefani as she leaves the comfort of Dr Eriksen's office, thanking him for his time. She hasn't come away from this conversation with any tangible evidence, but what she has come away with is a renewed sense of purpose. She's not alone in believing Daniel's innocence. She just needs to find proof.

It's as this thought crosses her mind that she spots a police car parking up across the road, and her stomach flips. DCI Walton gets out and slams the door with such force, it's a wonder it doesn't fall off its hinges. He marches towards her, face stony.

'Sir, what are you doing here?' She's trying to sound breezy, feigning the confidence that usually wins Walton over and causes him to forget why he's annoyed with her, but she can see from his eyes that it's different this time.

'I had Davies tail you and it's a bloody good job I did!'

Stefani's eyes flick over to Davies, who has also clambered out of the car and is now shuffling awkwardly beside Walton. He mouths the word 'sorry' to her.

'I can explain,' she says.

'No, don't bother. You're off the case.'

Stefani flinches, her throat constricting. 'What?'

'You heard me. You disobeyed my orders for the last time. You're done.'

CHAPTER THIRTY-SEVEN

ALEX

Eleven Days After the Murder

'It *was* you, wasn't it?' I repeat, every ounce of anger I feel compressed into those five words. Blood rushes in my ears. My mother's words ring in my head. '*I get a bad vibe from him. He's not the commitment type.*'

'Alex, I can explain . . .' Jase says eventually, but no explanation comes. His mouth gapes open, as if he's lost the ability to talk. I place one hand on the door frame to steady myself, concentrating on not passing out. Black spots are dancing across my vision. A sob erupts from my mouth, along with the taste of bile.

'It just happened, a stupid mistake . . . and I tried to stop it. I was going to tell her it was over, I swear. I really tried, but . . .' He trails off, pathetically.

I stare at him. Everything slots into place. He's been different for weeks, months maybe. I'd put it down to work stress, but all the time . . . And now, he's been standing back, knowing full well that it was him, not Mark, who was Hannah's older man. He's betrayed me, and his son.

Suddenly, rage consumes me and I charge at him, a guttural scream tearing from my throat. My fists impact with his ribs, sending him toppling off the chair, the phone bouncing and skidding across the wooden floor. I punch him again and again, wishing I could rip his skin off. He grabs hold of my wrists and holds them rigid. I writhe under his grasp, but he's stronger than me.

'You have every right to hate me!' he shouts, giving me a little shake. 'But you need to calm down! If Steve or Erin hears us—'

'Calm down?' My head is spinning. If he wasn't holding my wrists right now, I fear my knees would buckle underneath me. 'You watched her grow up! It's sick!'

'I'm not proud of it, OK? Trust me, I haven't been able to sleep. It's been tearing me up inside.'

'Oh, well, poor you!' I twist, snapping my arms away from him, and he finally lets go. For the first time, I thank God Daniel is still at the police station and not here to see this.

Daniel.

'Daniel was smashing up his room,' I say. 'He'd argued with Hannah that night. Called her a bitch. Did he know?'

Jase swallows. 'He found out, yes.'

'Oh my God!' My voice comes out a screech. 'That's why you didn't want him to come home! Because you were scared he'd drop you in your disgusting little secret!'

'All right!' Jase is shouting now, his attempt at remaining calm cracking. 'I know what I did was wrong. But I just needed some time. I needed him to give me a chance to figure out how to fix my mistakes.'

I glare at him in disgust, snot streaming down my top lip, hair stuck to the sweat on my forehead. Jase and Hannah. Hannah and Jase. It doesn't make sense. We've always been good, strong. Yes, the romance has dwindled a little over the years, as you'd expect from a marriage that's gone through something as traumatic as we did, but we were still happy as far as I knew.

And then another thought hits me like a lightning bolt, punching me in the gut. If Jase was sleeping with Hannah, could he have . . . ? Oh God, no.

'You weren't really at work the night Hannah died, were you?'

His face pales, and that's all the response I need. My body snaps into action. I stumble backwards, distancing myself from him, suddenly terrified of my own husband, before pulling my phone from my pocket.

'Alex, what are you doing?'

'Calling the police!' I nearly drop it as I fumble to unlock it.

'No, don't! I didn't kill her. That wasn't me.'

He lunges for me, making a grab for the phone, but I stumble away. My back smacks against the dining-room table. He reaches for the phone again and I lurch to the side, ducking low.

I make a beeline for the front door but feel myself being jerked back by my shirt. My hand reaches for the first thing I can find – the letter sorter – and I fling it upward towards Jase's head. He grunts as the corner juts into his cheek and he stumbles back, knocked off balance. I take my chance and lunge forward.

'Alex!'

I can hear him scrambling after me as I sprint through the front door, can sense him behind me, but I don't turn to look.

Just keep going. Get out of here while you still can.

I'm so close to the truck, but his firm hand grabs my arm. Suddenly, my legs aren't supporting me anymore. I fall forwards, my hands grasping at air. A sharp, searing pain shoots along my temple as my face impacts with a rock, followed by a wave of dizziness. My head swims, mouth filling with saliva as the farm blurs before me.

'Shit!' Jase crouches beside me and I want to push him away, but my arms aren't responding. 'Why did you make me do that, Alex? Why?'

I press my hand to my head. It's wet, sticky. A deep gash stretches across my eyebrow. Blinking, I try to focus. The rock is pointing up, it's knife-like edge tinged with my blood. Beside me, Jase is gripping his hair, panicked, and it's then I realise what he's doing.

He's trying to figure out whether to kill me or not.

He doesn't want to, I don't think. I'm guessing he didn't want to kill Hannah either. It will have been similar to this, a moment of hot-headedness that got out of hand.

My hands reach around me, hoping to grab on to something, *anything*, that I can use to protect myself. But there is nothing. The world spins. Jase's hands are on me, fingers digging into the tops of my shoulders. I try to fight him off. I squirm and kick, claw at his arm, drag my nails across his skin.

'Stop fighting!' he bellows as he pulls me up off the ground and bundles me into the back of the truck. As a trickle of blood drips down the bridge of my nose and into the corner of my eye, my thoughts instantly switch to Daniel. How could Jase do this to our son?

I look up one more time, into the eyes of the man I love, the adulterer and the murderer, before he slams the door on me.

CHAPTER THIRTY-EIGHT

HANNAH

The Day of the Murder – 9.55 p.m.

Daniel's face is etched with concern, his eyebrows knitted together.

'Hey,' I say. 'You finished work early.' I'm trying to sound breezy, but the dampness of my cheeks and the red rims of my eyes give me away easily.

'It was quiet, so they sent me home. What's wrong?'

I had been so sure as I'd sent the text to Jase that I was ready to tell everyone, to get it all out into the open, but now I'm face to face with Daniel, the words are trapped in my throat. The wind whistles around me and it's as if it's whispering to me, telling me what an awful person I am. My eyes pan to the farmhouse. I'm not sure that's the best place to talk, especially not with Alex still there.

'Can we chat at yours?' I say.

He wraps his arm around my shoulder as we walk to keep me warm. I don't want him to. His kindness is making me feel sick with guilt, but I can't bring myself to tell him to stop. I clench my fists tighter with each step, running hypotheticals through my head, all the different ways this conversation could play out.

By the time we reach Daniel's house, the tension in the air could be cut with a knife. He's been good, hasn't pressed me to tell him what's wrong, but it's meant we've been locked in awkward silence. He unlocks the front door and I shuffle inside, my breath growing shallow. I've been rehearsing what I'm going to say, but now, faced with his expectant expression, my mind is blank.

'Han, you're worrying me,' he says. 'You know you can tell me anything.'

Not this, I think. How can I? How can I tell him that I've been cheating on him? That I've been cheating on him with his own dad. That I'm pregnant with his dad's baby. I can't. The gravity of what I've done, how selfish I've been, is hitting me properly for the first time. I've been so wrapped up in my fantasy romance that I've not allowed myself to really think about how wrong it was, but now I am.

'I . . . I need to tell you . . .'

Before I can say anything else, the sound of a motor draws my attention to the window. Headlights have pulled up outside. Jase.

When he bursts through the door, his face is bright red and his chest is heaving. Daniel's eyes flick between us.

'What's going on?'

I look at Jase, wondering if he's finally going to man up and admit it. But he's not. I can see it in his eyes. He's trying to think of an excuse, some way to wheedle his way out of this. Just like that, my anger is reignited, seeping through my body. The words tumble out of me at force.

'We have something to tell you, Daniel,' I say before my head stops me. 'We should have told you a long time ago.'

Daniel looks so innocent, so confused, when he turns to Jase. 'Dad?'

I wait, holding my breath.

'I don't know what she's talking about,' Jase says.

I jerk as though he's slapped me. 'You cowardly son of a bitch!'

'Hannah, please . . .'

I look at Daniel, who still looks bewildered. But my rage overcomes the shame I feel at what I've done to him.

'What your dad is too chickenshit to tell you,' I snap, spittle flying, 'is that we're together. We've been together for months.'

The silence that follows my outburst is deafening. I immediately regret it, wish I could pluck the words back out of the air and swallow them down, but it's done. The truth is out.

Jase raises his hands and takes a tentative step towards Daniel. 'OK, son, listen to me—'

The words are snatched from his mouth as Daniel lunges at him with his fist raised. It narrowly misses Jase's face as he ducks to one side. I gasp, hands flying to my mouth. Unsteady on his feet, Jase staggers and falls to the floor with such force, his phone and wallet go shooting out of his pocket and skid along the polished floor. Daniel looks down at the mess and frowns. For a moment, I wonder what he's staring at, and then I realise. He bends down and picks up Jase's wallet, and the receipt from the hotel that's poking out from it.

'All those times,' he mutters under his breath, more to himself than to us. 'All those times you said you were working late, and you were fucking my girlfriend in a seedy hotel.'

It all happens so quick. One minute Daniel is staring at the receipt, wide-eyed and shell-shocked, the next he is charging at Jase again, pouncing on him and wrapping his hands around his father's throat.

'You bastard!' he bellows. 'You *fucking bastard*!'

The two of them crash into the wall, Daniel attacking Jase like a rabid dog, Jase desperately shielding his face from the incoming swipes.

'Stop it!' I scream, but they don't hear me.

I don't know what to do. He's going to kill him. I have to do something.

'Please!' This time I throw myself between them, one hand pressed on each man's chest, but I do so just as Jase goes to take a strike back at Daniel. His fist impacts with my stomach and I stumble backwards, clutching my abdomen, the wind knocked out of me. But, to my surprise, I don't feel pain. I feel nothing. I'm numb. Perhaps I'm dying. I hope I'm dying.

***

POLICE RELEASE MAIN SUSPECT IN HANNAH CARMICHAEL CASE

West Mercia Police issued a short statement today to confirm that nineteen-year-old Daniel Forrester, who was considered the chief suspect in the murder of Hannah Carmichael, has been released without charge. The suspect was arrested on Friday 28 April after a six-day search for him.

A spokesman for West Mercia Police confirmed that Daniel Forrester is to be 'released under strict bail conditions'.

The victim, named locally as Hannah Carmichael, was pronounced dead at her home in Ledbury after human remains were found. Police are continuing to appeal to the public for any information or dashcam footage regarding the night of Wednesday 19 April, and ask that members of the public remain vigilant at all times until the killer is caught.

@mama799: What the hell?! They're letting him back out on the streets?? #JusticeForHannah

@zobobo: Lock up your daughters, peeps! What is the world coming to?

@news_junkiee: Only a matter of time until there's another murder headline . . . #LockThePsychoUp

CHAPTER THIRTY-NINE

STEFANI

Eleven Days After the Murder

When Stefani wakes, it takes a moment for her to realise where she is. Her left side is burning hot, pins and needles plaguing her fingers, and her neck twinges as she lifts her head. Cassie is fast asleep slumped against her, a puddle of drool soaking into Stefani's jumper. Since Stefani promised to keep the photos between them, Cassie's been warmer towards her. Almost like the rift between them is starting to be filled in and patched up. She was meant to be back with Luke tonight, but after he found out Stefani had been placed on 'temporary leave', as Walton liked to call it, he asked if she wanted to keep her for another night, with the proviso that she made sure she showered and had her bags packed ready for school tomorrow. She cried loud, ugly tears of gratitude down the phone at him, which she'll probably be embarrassed about next time she sees him. They decided to binge-watch the *Twilight* films and had, apparently, fallen asleep on the sofa midway through the first *Breaking Dawn*.

Now, Stefani fumbles around for her phone and squints as the screen lights up. It's nearly 11 p.m. Luke would have a fit if he knew Cassie wasn't in bed on a school night.

'Cass?' she whispers. Cassie mumbles something in her sleep and nuzzles deeper into the warmth of Stefani's chest. Stefani tries again, giving her a little shake. 'Cass, we've got to get you to bed.'

'Huh?' Cassie sits up slowly, her head lolling to the side, eyes blinking heavily.

'Come on, you.' Stefani shuffles and slides out from underneath her, then holds out her hand and leads her bleary-eyed daughter to the spare room. She wishes Cassie was still small enough that she could carry her to bed. Cassie barely wakes up as she drags her feet across the floor and buries herself under the duvet. Stefani takes the opportunity to tuck her in, giving her a soft kiss on the forehead.

Shutting the door behind her, she retreats from the bedroom and stands aimlessly for a moment in the middle of the living room, her brain simultaneously distracted and unstimulated. She's not used to not working. She's unsure of what to do with herself. She should probably just go to bed, but her little catnap on the sofa was enough to charge her brain to the point where she just knows she'll end up lying awake staring at the ceiling.

In an utterly unlike-her move, she heads over to the kitchenette and rummages about in the cupboards for a wine glass and a bottle of Merlot. She'd never normally drink on a Sunday because of work the following morning, but she supposes that's not something she needs to worry about for the time being. Work has been her entire focus for the past eleven years. It's what drove her and Luke apart. It's what allowed him to become the primary custodian due to his ability to work from home versus her ever-changing shift pattern. She gave up so much for her career, and now she has to wonder if it was worth it.

She sits down with her glass of wine and stews. She's not sad about being kicked off the case, she's angry. She wants to scream. Walton's words ring in her ears. *'You're going soft on the Forresters. You're not emotionally equipped to handle this case.'* What a load of bullshit. The only reason she's been removed from this case is because she wasn't about to sit back and watch as the senior commissioner shot for a hasty conviction to save face with the media. A cowardly move. She stiffens, feeling pissed off all over again.

Surprising even herself, she curls her hand into a fist and punches the coffee table. The wine glass totters, then falls, the burgundy liquid spilling out over the mahogany and creeping towards her closed laptop.

'Shit!' she says as she rushes to grab the kitchen roll from the windowsill. She lays a few sheets across the wine and watches them soak it up. That would have been the perfect end to a terrible day; ruining her company-issued laptop by spilling alcohol all over it. Walton would really love her for that.

She dumps the now red wad of kitchen roll into the bin and pulls off a couple of fresh sheets to get the last few drips. But as she wipes it up, her hand slackens, then stops. Something stirs in the cobwebbed corner of her brain. Her eyes roam to the laptop and she stares at it for a moment, before picking it up and sitting on the sofa with it propped open on her knees. It takes an age to turn on. She just about managed to bring it back to life after its crash yesterday, which she has determined was due to her refusal to ever clear space on the thing, but it's still struggling.

Finally, it powers up and she navigates to her emails. She finds the one she sent to herself with the password-protected folder containing Cassie's secret photos of Hannah. She types the password into the field and the thumbnails flash up, all seventy-seven of them. Double-clicking into the first picture to bring it up full screen, she scans the scene. Hannah is sitting on the little brick wall outside the school, deep in a phone conversation, completely oblivious that her photo is being taken.

Stefani swallows hard and eyes the bedroom door to make sure Cassie isn't reappearing. Nerves playing at her insides, she clicks through all the photos once, seeing nothing of particular importance. She's not even sure why she felt the need to look at them again in the first place. She already did a quick browse to see if they contained any evidence when she first found them. But something is telling her to look closer.

Tucking her hair behind her ear, she goes through them again, this time at a slower pace, scrutinising each one carefully. She stops on the eighth picture, her finger hovering over the mouse. This picture shows Hannah on a street a couple of towns over – Stefani recognises the Nisa and that crummy hotel in the background – and at a guess she'd say Cassie had positioned herself behind one of the trees in the park to snap it, based on the angle. Hannah is almost looking directly at the camera, but she's not. She's waving at someone over to the right, though the person isn't visible. Not clearly, anyway.

Stefani's eyes drift back to the Nisa, to the window behind Hannah. There's someone there, reflected in the glass, waving back at her. Stefani's pulse quickens. She zooms in, the reflection pixelating slightly as a result, but there's no doubt about it.

The words escape her mouth in a husky whisper. 'Jase Forrester?'

'Cassie! Cassie!' She shakes Cassie's shoulders, jolting her out of sleep.

Cassie rubs her eyes with the back of her hand. 'What?'

'I'm so sorry to wake you up, darling, but I need you to look at something for me.'

Stefani places the laptop on Cassie's bed and lifts the lid. The room lights up in a blue glow. Cassie's face contorts and she pulls the duvet up over her eyes.

'Jesus, Mum, are you trying to blind me?'

'I'm so sorry,' she says again. She feels like a terrible enough mother as it is, waking Cassie up at nearly midnight, and even worse for having gone through the photos, again, and while she was asleep and unaware, but this is too important to let guilt stand in the way. She pulls up the photo again and angles the screen towards Cassie. 'Do you remember taking this photo?'

Cassie peeps out from behind the duvet, then recoils. 'Why are you looking at those again?'

'Please, darling, just answer the question. Do you remember taking it?'

She squints, shaking her head slightly. 'Um, I'm not sure. Actually, yeah, I think I do. Why?'

'What was Hannah doing? Was she meeting someone?'

'I think . . . I'm not really sure. It was months ago.'

'Please try to remember. She's waving at someone in the photo, yes? Did you see who she was waving at?'

Cassie sits herself up, rubbing her eyes again, and looks closer at the photo. She traces her finger over the fuzzy reflection in the Nisa window.

'Oh, yeah,' she says after a while. 'She was meeting Daniel's dad. I thought it was a bit weird at the time but just assumed Dan would be meeting them too.'

A sinking feeling settles in Stefani's gut. 'Did you see where they went?'

'Not really. I panicked that she'd see me spying, so I left. They seemed to head towards that gross hotel,' — she jabs her finger at the screen — 'but it's not the sort of place Hannah would normally go, so they probably didn't.'

Stefani stares at the hotel. *I'll bet they did*, she thinks.

As if reading her mind, Cassie's eyes widen. 'Do you . . . do you think he was Hannah's older boyfriend?'

She can't speak for the moment. She's too focused on thinking over Jase's alibi and searching for potential gaps. The realisation of where she is and who she's with hits her like a lightning bolt and she slams the lid of her laptop down.

'Don't worry. You get yourself back to sleep. I shouldn't have woken you.'

It looks as if Cassie is about to protest, but before she can, Stefani stands and leaves the room, closing the door firmly behind her.

Her mind races. She pulls out her phone and dials Walton's direct number. It rings and rings, grating through her, and she worries he's not going to answer, but finally the ringing is replaced by a gruff, sleepy voice.

'This better be good,' Walton says. She's obviously woken him up.

'Sorry, sir, it's about Jase Forrester.'

Before she can say any more, Walton huffs. 'If you've heard from him, tell him to answer his damned phone. Daniel reached his maximum time in custody and we were going to let him go for now but he was refusing to leave without his mum.'

Stefani's blood runs cold. 'She didn't show up to collect him?'

'No. You'd have thought with the fuss she made about him staying in, she'd have been waiting outside for him. Mental-health procedures state we can't make him leave without a responsible adult even though he's over eighteen, so apparently we're turning into a sodding B and B.' He coughs loudly into the phone, clearly not bothering to cover his mouth. 'Anyway, I thought I told you to leave off this case.'

'I know,' Stefani says. 'And I'm sorry to disobey you again, sir. But there's something I think you should know. I think Alex may be in danger.'

CHAPTER FORTY

ALEX

Eleven Days After the Murder

The dark silhouette of trees whips past the window as Jase drives. The sight of him makes my stomach roil. I try to focus on steadying my breathing, even though chills are slinking down my spine as images of Hannah's lifeless body invade my thoughts; her wide, terrified eyes, all that blood. She must have been so frightened when she saw it coming. If Jase did that to her, what's he planning to do to me? Having the farm nestled amongst acres of fields and meadows and wild woodland makes getting rid of me easy. Perhaps he's planning on driving me out to the pond and dumping me there, like I considered doing with Hannah. Bile sours my mouth at the thought. I still can't comprehend that it was Jase, my Jase, who did this.

Focus, Alex, I repeat the mantra in my head. I will not let him get the better of me. I can get out of this.

Slowly and methodically, I look around the car for my options. I could jump up and strangle him, take him by surprise. But then he'd end up crashing the truck and we could both die. I could wait until he pulls over, pretend I've passed out from the blow to my head until he tries to get me out of the car and then attack him and run for my life. But I have no idea where he's taking me. We could be headed to the middle of nowhere, and even if I did escape, I'd pass out from exhaustion before I even made it back to a main road. If I'm going to make a break for it, it has to be now, before we get too deep into the countryside.

I take a slow, measured breath.

Get ready. Get ready. Go!

I lurch forward, the abrupt movement making my head spin, but I don't let it slow me down. I scrabble for the handle and throw the door open with the little strength I have left. Wind rushes into the car.

'What the fuck?' Jase whips around and grabs at my collar, yanking me back. The car swerves. I'm flung against the back of his seat. The tyres screech against the road as he turns the wheel sharply, using the pressure of it to slam the door shut again. I wince at the sound of the central locking activating. 'What the hell do you think you're doing? Are you crazy?'

'Let me out!' I lean through the centre console and start pummelling my fists against his arms, his shoulders, his head. The car skids again as I reach across him and make a grab for the lock control. He forces my hand back. Pain shoots across my wrist, making me howl.

'Alex! You need to calm down! You're going to end up making me crash!'

I shrink back, nursing my wrist, and glare at him. 'What are you going to do to me?'

'What?'

'Where the fuck are you taking me?' I screech, all the emotions of the day merging into one and spilling out of me.

'Jesus, you really think I'm going to hurt you?'

'You really think I'm going to trust you after what you did to Hannah?' I retaliate.

'I didn't do anything to her,' he says.

The truck descends into hostile silence. Jase's hands tighten around the steering wheel.

'I know you're angry, and I understand why,' he says after a while, and I want to laugh. It's almost comical. 'But if you'll give me just a chance to actually talk about this. Please, Alex.'

But I don't want to talk about it. I don't want to hear a word he has to say about Hannah. I don't know if I'm more furious about what he did to her or the fact he tried to get our son to keep it a secret and ended up making him the prime suspect in the process.

'Unlock the doors.' My voice is grave and low, threatening. I say it again and again, growing louder each time, 'Unlock the doors.

Unlock the doors! UNLOCK THE DOORS!' until I'm screaming at him. I've lost my mind. I'm like a feral beast, shrieking and beating his flesh. If I can distract him enough, he'll have no choice but to stop and then I can make a run for it.

'All right!' he yells over my shrieks. 'I'm pulling over!'

The truck slows, then stops, and the locks pop up. I open the door and scramble out, my legs buckling underneath me. I whip around, readying myself to scream as loud as I can for help. It's only once my feet are on tarmac that I take a moment to see where I am. I blink, confused. We're at the hospital.

'You need to get that cut on your head checked out,' Jase calls to me through the wound-down window.

I shake my head, unsure of what to say, but I'm not going to stick around long enough for him to change his mind. I take a few tentative steps backwards, inching away from him, and then I'm running, sprinting towards the hospital entrance.

CHAPTER FORTY-ONE

STEFANI

Eleven Days After the Murder

Stefani pats a nervous tune on her thighs as Davies blue-lights to the hospital, followed by two other police cars, one of which Walton is driving. From calling him to tell him about the photo to now, everything has been a frantic rush. What if she's figured this all out too late? What if Alex is his next victim, lying dead somewhere, and if Stefani had only been a little quicker she could have saved her?

Luckily, it didn't take the team at the station long to run the number plate of the Forresters' truck. They spotted him rolling into Hereford County Hospital at just gone 11.45 p.m., with Alex being very much alive, and according to their updates on the radio, he's still there. Despite the speed at which Davies is powering down the road, Stefani still wishes they could go faster.

Luke wasn't best pleased when she phoned him and asked him to sit in with Cassie while she accompanied Davies in the car, but he agreed nonetheless. Cassie is technically old enough that Stefani could have left her home alone, but this case has made her reluctant to risk it. She'll need to pay him back somehow for being so patient with her these last few weeks. Even though she knows Cassie had fallen back to sleep before she left and has no idea she's gone, pinpricks of guilt still stab at her that she's here dealing with the Carmichael case instead of at home with her daughter. But this is it now.

It's just gone midnight when they arrive at the hospital, and, sure enough, the truck is still parked up. As they swarm, Jase's face is illuminated by the police car headlights. He looks momentarily shocked, his eyes wide and dazzled by the brightness, but that shock quickly filters down into resignation. That's the face of a guilty man if ever she saw one. He knows the game is up.

She doesn't even need to tell him to get out of the vehicle. He's already out, hands raised, by the time they dash over to him. Walton pulls his arms back and cuffs him.

'Jase Forrester, I am arresting you on suspicion of the murder of Hannah Carmichael. You do not have to say anything, but it may harm your defence if you do not mention when questioned something which you later rely on in court. Anything you do say may be given in evidence.'

'I didn't do it,' he says. 'You've got the wrong guy.' But even as the words leave his mouth, he doesn't struggle or fight. He looks a beaten man, nothing left to give, as his head is lowered and he's guided into the police car. Stefani watches him, disgust and hatred swelling inside her. Once he's in and the door has been slammed on him, Walton steps over to her.

'Those pictures,' he says, and Stefani feels her face burn.

'I know,' she says before he can continue. 'I should have said something the second I found them. It was unprofessional and I fully understand if you have to fire me.' Even as the words leave her lips her stomach turns, the thought of actually getting fired making her light-headed, but she knew there would be repercussions for her actions.

'You massively delayed the resolution of this case, Warner.' Walton crosses his arms, his brow narrowed. 'If he had killed Alex, it would have been on your shoulders.'

She swallows and looks down at her shoes. 'I know.'

There's a silence while she waits for the inevitable, but then Walton's tone switches.

'I suppose,' he says, 'that the senior commissioner doesn't *have* to know how long you knew about them.'

Stefani's eyes flick up at him.

The corner of his mouth turns up, just a little. 'We'll keep it between us,' he says. 'But if anything like this happens again . . .'

Stefani isn't sure what to say. Her mouth just hangs open in shock.

'This is the part where you thank me, Warner.'

'Oh! Sorry. Thank you, sir, so much.'

He sighs. 'And I'm sorry, too,' he says, and she furrows her brow.

'What for?'

'For not trusting you. You said we should focus on finding the older man. I should have listened.'

She flushes, knowing full well this won't be the last time they have a conversation like this. He'll never change. He'll always think his way is right. When the next case comes along, she'll exert far too much energy trying to prove that she knows what she's talking about, and when she's proven right he'll come along with his tail between his legs and apologise again. But that's OK. She's used to him now. And he's used to her.

As Walton drives off with Jase in the back, Stefani draws in a deep breath and closes her eyes. This case has drained her. Kept her up at night. And now, it looks like the end is in sight.

Stefani watches Jase carefully. He's hunched over the table, wringing his hands, his face pale.

'Mr Forrester. Can you tell us about the evening of nineteenth of April,' she says, sensing the anticipation bleeding from Walton sat next to her. 'When you were with Hannah Carmichael?'

He shifts in his chair.

'I met up with Hannah at the Rose Hotel just after 8.15 p.m.,' he says. 'We went there every few weeks. It was out of the way, so there was less risk we'd get spotted.'

'So when your colleague said you were with him in the time between your meeting finishing and you getting called back into work . . .'

'He was covering for me. He's known I've been having an affair for a while and he's always covered for me if I've needed him to. He's a good mate.'

Stefani quirks an eyebrow. She supposes they have different definitions of what a 'good mate' is. They'll need to speak to him too, of course – lying to the police is a serious business – but, for now, their priority is sitting in front of them.

'You were sexually involved with Hannah, correct?'

He nods. 'Yes. It was a mistake I regret very much now. But we were having a relationship.'

Stefani keeps her tone level. 'Did you argue that night? You and Hannah.'

He looks up, and for a second she thinks he is going to deny it, but he nods.

'Yes. Hannah wanted me to end my marriage, and I wasn't . . . well, in hindsight, I didn't want to, because I love my wife, but I told Hannah it wasn't the right time.'

'I see.' Stefani's lip practically curls. 'So, this caused a row?'

He hesitates. 'It was partly why we argued. But that night Hannah also told me she was pregnant and that it was mine.' He pauses, dropping his gaze away from Stefani, as if he can't bear to make eye contact. 'And I told her she should get an abortion.'

Stefani and Walton exchange a glance. Her skin crawls. There are very few people in the world she could say she hates, but right now Jase is one of them. He wipes his face with his sleeve, dampness coming away. *Good*, Stefani thinks. *You should cry. You should feel guilty.*

'What happened then?'

'She was very upset, and she left. She went home, back to the farm. I tried calling her, but she wasn't answering. So I rushed back to our house, and that's when I found her with Daniel.'

Stefani leans back. 'Did Daniel know about your affair?'

'He found out that night. Hannah told him,' says Jase. 'It was a mess.'

'Finding out his father was sleeping with his girlfriend. That must have been terrible for Daniel.'

Jase has the decency to look ashamed at least.

'Yeah. He went for me, quite rightly, and then . . .' His eyes are glazed over, as if he's replaying the scene in his head.

'Go on,' Stefani prompts.

'She tried to stop us fighting and I accidentally lashed out at her. She sort of . . . collapsed.'

Stefani's breath hitches. Is this how Hannah died? Perhaps when she landed she hit her head and Jase and Daniel decided to get rid of her body. Accidental killing is more common than intentional murder.

'I didn't kill her.' Jase's voice is steady and he looks Stefani straight in the eyes, which throws her. It's not often the guilty make such direct eye contact with their accuser, unless they're a sociopath, of course.

'Go on,' she tells him.

Jase slumps back in his chair. 'She was OK, not hurt, just shaken up and still very upset. She then went back to her parents' house and that's the last time I saw her. I swear.'

Stefani shakes her head, frustrated. Not guilty. That's how this is going to go down? She was convinced she was getting a confession out of him. It was all going so smoothly.

'So what did you do after she left?'

'I tried to calm Daniel down. He was ranting and raving about telling his mum and I convinced him to keep it a secret.'

'How did you do that?'

'I told him it would hurt her too much. Daniel would do anything to protect Alex. I knew if I made him see how much it would destroy her to find out the truth, he'd keep his mouth shut. I suggested he go camping to cool off so she didn't suspect anything. He eventually agreed, for her sake, and then I got a message from the hospital. I was on call that night and I had to go back in. It wasn't until the next morning that I found out Hannah was missing.'

Stefani nods slowly. All the pieces add up. Why Daniel disappeared that night, why he was totally unreachable, why he refused to reveal who Hannah's secret lover was when they questioned him. It all makes sense. But Jase isn't telling the whole truth. He says he never saw Hannah again that night, but someone killed her. And if there's one thing she knows about Jase Forrester, it's that he's a liar, and he's manipulative.

It's always a little awkward walking through a hospital in police uniform. Stefani feels as though all eyes are on her as she makes her way past one of the waiting rooms. They're wondering which patient is a criminal, and whether they should be concerned or not. She purposefully doesn't make eye contact, instead focusing on the blue signs above the doorways that indicate which ward she's approaching.

Alex is the only patient on her ward. She's sitting propped up by pillows, staring out of the window next to her with a far-off look in her eyes, a sort of trance. There is a thick dressing strapped to her forehead, and a red tinge is starting to creep through the fibres. She doesn't even notice as Stefani draws near, so she gives a little cough to alert her of her presence. Alex's eyes snap towards her, suddenly on high alert.

'DS Warner,' she says, softening. 'How did you know I was here?'

Stefani hesitates, wondering just how ready Alex is to receive this news. She braces herself before delivering it all in one breath. 'New evidence has come to light implicating your husband. We ran his plates and apprehended him in the car park about two hours ago.'

Alex barely reacts. She gives her a slight nod, then returns her eyes to the window, the far-off expression reappearing on to her face.

'This doesn't surprise you?'

She doesn't respond. The doctor who treated Alex briefed Stefani before she came here, explained how Mrs Forrester presented herself with a deep gash to the forehead caused by impact with a rock during an altercation with her husband. Based on her reaction, Stefani assumes she must have found something out.

'How are you feeling?' she asks.

Alex shrugs. 'Fine. It looks worse than it is. They're only keeping me in for observation.'

'We'll need to take a full statement once you're feeling up to it.'

'OK.'

The ward falls silent apart from the repetitive beeping of hospital machines. Alex presses her palm in between her eyes and drags it down across her cheek.

'I just don't get it,' she says finally.

Stefani shuffles awkwardly in her spot. She's not sure if she's talking about Jase being an adulterer or a murderer. 'People are capable of all sorts of things, even if we think we know them.'

Alex nods thoughtfully. 'The affair I can get my head around, just about. But . . .' She pauses to tighten her fists around the cotton blanket that's draped over her legs. 'If Jase is a murderer, why am I sat in a hospital bed right now and not in a shallow grave?'

@mama799: So . . . wait . . . the boyfriend didn't do it? #JusticeForHannah

@itsmeg175: OMG the guy they've arrested is a doctor at the County Hospital. I totally recognise him!!

@carocarobear: It's horrible living so close. It could have been any one of us you know?

@vegan_lover: I highly doubt he killed her for the sake of it. He obviously knew her #JusticeForHannah

@simonLpaul: Bet he was shagging her. Guarantee it.

@zobobo: #Iwould

CHAPTER FORTY-TWO

ALEX

Twelve Days After the Murder

'Excuse me?' I poke my head over the receptionist's desk and offer up my warmest smile. 'I'm really sorry to bother you, but is there any update on my discharge forms?'

I hate hospitals. I vividly remember waiting for Daniel's discharge that night four years ago. At 10 a.m. we were told he was good to go and just needed his forms, but seven hours later we were still pacing, desperate to get home. I haven't been waiting quite so long today, but it feels like an eternity. Because this time I know my boy is waiting for me. I'm so desperate to see him, I can practically hear his voice in my head.

'I believe they're just finishing them now, Mrs Forrester,' the woman behind the desk says, and I cringe at her use of my last name. I suppose I'll have to talk to a lawyer and get divorce proceedings underway. Part of me doesn't want to just yet. I feel like I should take some time to process everything and recover from our ordeal before I deal with the stress of all that. But the other half of me is sickened by the very thought of being legally married to that man. I want to cleanse myself of him in every way I can. My skin is red raw from the amount I've scrubbed myself in the hospital shower, and I still feel dirty.

'OK, do you know how long it'll take?'

'Should only be another ten minutes or so. The doctor has just finished her lunch break.'

I have to bite my lip to stop myself from asking if it would have really hurt her to sign the papers quickly before she went on her lunch break.

Wait.

Daniel's voice. It's not in my head.

I spin around so quickly, I get a head rush, black spots dancing across my vision, as I try to zone in on his voice. He's there, walking down the hallway, arm in arm with my mother, towards me. My feet trip over themselves in my desperation to get to him and we collide into each other, squeezing as if it were a competition to see who could squeeze the hardest, and he drops to his knees and I drop with him. So, so much has happened since we last saw each other. We cradle each other in a heap on the floor. My shoulder is damp from where he is sobbing quietly into my shoulder. I run my hand through his hair and whisper, 'I'm here, I'm here,' and this is how we stay, holding each other against the world, until neither of us has any tears left to shed.

I don't know how long we're like this for. Long enough that by the time we stagger back to our feet my discharge papers are ready. I blink at Mum through the tears.

'Thank you for bringing him,' I say.

She smiles back at me. 'I knew how much you needed each other.' I'm surprised Daniel even remembers her, but in this moment I am bizarrely, eternally grateful to have her here.

I take my discharge forms and the three of us make our way through the labyrinth of sterile hallways. Daniel's hand grips on to mine, a welcome contrast to the way he would ordinarily stiffen at my touch.

'Are you OK, darling?'

I wince as the words leave my mouth. I don't want to baby him – I know he won't like it – but after everything we've been through, I can't help myself. Twice now I've come so close to losing him, and I never want that to happen again.

'Yeah, I guess.' He slows just as we're nearing the main entrance and I glance at Mum.

'I'll be paying for the parking,' she says, shuffling over to the ticket machine.

I return my gaze to Daniel. He slides his foot along the floor, searching for words, his head bowed.

'I just want you to know I'm sorry... for not telling you about Dad.'

My throat tightens, a lump of betrayal lodging itself against my vocal cords, but I swallow it down.

'I wish you had told me,' I say, my voice cracking. 'But it wasn't your fault. Your dad should never have asked you to keep his secret.'

When Daniel looks up at me, his eyes are glossed with tears. 'I never thought he'd do what he did. If I had—'

'None of it is your fault,' I stop him, and dry his cheeks with my sleeve. 'Come on, let's get home. We've all had a long day and we need to try to get some sleep.'

He shakes his head. 'I can't. Every time I close my eyes, I see Hannah and Dad.'

Me too, I think.

Mum returns with the paid ticket. 'Are we ready to go?'

'I don't know if I can go back there,' Daniel says, his voice quivering.

My lips press together. 'Darling, we just need to pick up some bits from the farm. We can find an alternative living solution in the morning.'

'If you want,' Mum says, 'Daniel could stay with me at the B and B? Give you a chance to sort what you need? There are two beds in my room.'

My eyes flick between her and Daniel, who is nodding hopefully at me. The thought of separating from him again, let alone allowing him to go with my mother of all people, feels completely wrong. But I can see it in his face. I can't make him go back there.

'OK,' I say eventually. 'But I'll be there first thing in the morning and then we can figure out what we're going to do. OK?'

He nods again and, though dread is once again tugging at my insides, we make our way through the glass doors.

The crowd waiting outside is twice the size of the group that hounded Jase and I outside the police station. The familiar flashing of cameras starts up the second we step foot over the threshold, and for a moment I can't see any way through.

'All right, all right, back up,' a voice booms over the commotion. Two security guards are pushing the mob back, parting them Moses-like. We don't hesitate in making a beeline for the car park, shielding our faces as best we can. The questions fire at us thick and fast.

'Alex! Did you know your husband was a murderer? When did you find out he was sleeping with Hannah?'

'Alex! How do you feel knowing your husband tried to let your son take the fall?'

'Daniel! Have you seen your father at all?'

'Alex! Did your husband put you in hospital?'

'Who do you believe, Alex? Your husband, or your son?'

'Yeah, hasn't Daniel got form for violent behaviour? He's a psycho. They probably planned it together! He should never have been released!'

This last comment meets my ears half a second before the chaos ensues. The first egg just misses us. The second hits Daniel hard on his temple, causing him to shrink down and cower towards me. The security guards shout for backup and continue trying to push people back, but they're fighting a losing battle.

'Lock the psycho up!' the protesters amongst the press cry. It's all I can do not to storm at them and rip their boards out of their disgusting hands and smash them across the heads with them.

'Get in the car,' Mum says, and for the second time today I'm grateful she's with us. She holds the door open as I usher Daniel into the back seat and crawl in next to him.

When I look around our living room now, it's not the same room. Where I'd once loved the vast open space, had been comforted by the glow of the fireplace, had enjoyed the sleek modern design, now all I see are the ghosts of everything that's happened. We can't stay on this farm. Not now. I never thought I'd want to leave. I figured I'd be just like Cynthia's mum, Peggy, clinging on to it until old age came for me. But now it's as if the life, the memories, the good times we've had here have been ripped out of the very soil, replaced by dead weeds.

I'm folding the washing, attempting to trick myself into believing that everything is normal. It's laughable really. You only have to look around, to hear the absence of Jase watching the football on the TV or of Hannah laughing and joking with Daniel, to know that nothing will ever be normal again.

My eyes drift to the lights flashing on in the farmhouse. It's starting to get dark again. I don't know where the day has disappeared to. By the time we'd fought through the crowds at the hospital and I'd said a tearful goodbye to Daniel at the B and B, it was already four o'clock, and I spent a good three hours attempting to get some shut-eye on the sofa before giving up and busying myself with the washing instead. Last night at the hospital I had a wonderful painkiller-induced slumber, but here it's different. I can't even look at the bed Jase and I shared, and even if I could I know any sleep would be plagued by nightmares.

Once I've finished the load of washing, I place T-shirts and jeans into the suitcase I'm preparing for Daniel, trying to pretend I'm packing for us to go on holiday. Maybe we should do just that. Get Mum to drop us at the airport and fly away somewhere warm and exotic. I lower the suitcase lid and lean on it for a moment, wondering what to do with myself now. My fingers itch to start cleaning, to scrub the house from top to bottom and rid it of any lingering trace of my husband, but I'm so tired. I can't face attempting to sleep again, and even my cross-stitch seems tainted now. I'll need to start a new one to match our new life, though God knows what that will look like.

The lights in the farmhouse are still on. They must be struggling to sleep too. I haven't seen them since Jase was arrested. Stefani was the one who spoke to them and arranged for me to return home. My heart aches for the friendship that I feel as though I've lost with Cynthia. I always thought if anything ever happened between me and Jase I'd have her to fall back on. We would have wine-infused nights at swanky bars to dull the hurt. We'd raise our glasses and declare that we don't need a stupid man in our lives to make us happy. We'd be each other's rock.

On autopilot, I find myself grabbing a Merlot from the cupboard and heading outside. It's been drizzling with rain. The air is fresh and carries with it the crisp scent of water on earth. I clamber into our truck. The engine is disconcertingly loud in contrast to the quiet of the night.

Someone in the farmhouse must have heard me coming because as I approach the curtains in the upstairs bedroom ripple, as if someone is peeking around them. It's chilly this evening, but I am sweating. I wipe my clammy hands on my jeans before knocking.

Before long, the sound of the chain being slid across comes from inside, and when the door opens I am face to face with Cynthia for the first time since we met up in the café. I give her a timid smile as I hold up the bottle.

'Peace offering?' I say.

'You've got a nerve,' she replies, her hand gripping the door.

'Please . . . I didn't know, Cynthia. About Jase. I had no idea.'

She stares at me, thinking. Eventually, she takes her hand off the door.

'You'd better come in, I suppose,' she says, quickly checking to make sure there are no journalists lurking. The coast is clear.

Glowing sparks dance into the breeze, a snowstorm of orange embers amidst the white of the stars in the sky. One of the best things about living in the countryside is the lack of light pollution. Most nights are starry nights. I realise, as I reach my hands out towards the flames and allow the warmth to spread through my fingertips, that the last time we did this was the night I found Hannah. A chill creeps over my skin at the thought.

Cynthia sips her wine, taking her time to swish it around her mouth before swallowing it. I don't think either of us knows what to say. We don't want to talk about what's happened and yet it's as if that's all there is, a five-hundred-pound gorilla sitting between us that neither of us wants to acknowledge.

When I can't take the awkwardness any longer, I say, 'Where's Mark tonight?'

Cynthia's lips curl and I immediately regret my choice of subject. 'Probably at the pub. I barely see him anymore. He's been going there a lot since . . .' She trails off and we fall back into uncomfortable silence.

I take a swig of my drink, wishing I'd brought something stronger.

'I'm sorry,' she says after a moment, staring deep into the flames. 'For accusing Daniel.'

I stiffen, heat spreading up my neck. I'm suddenly too flustered sitting this close to the firepit. I need to shuffle my seat back but I don't want Cynthia to think I'm being rude.

'It's OK, you have nothing to apologise for,' I say honestly, because what else can I say? How can I judge Cynthia for jumping to Daniel as the prime suspect when I did exactly the same? 'It's me who should be apologising. If I'd known what Jase was doing . . .'

I pause, wondering what I actually would have done if I'd found out about his affair before it was too late. Perhaps if I had and had made him leave the farm, Hannah would still be alive. It's sickening how little I knew him. I had no inkling that he was cheating or that he was capable of such violence, and I would never have pegged him as someone who would try to blackmail and scare our son into hiding his secret. Or me, for that matter. He sent me that text and the note, warning me to stop digging, although clearly he hasn't followed through with giving the video to the police or I'd be in handcuffs right now.

As this thought churns in my head, my eye is drawn to the door. It's a classic farmhouse door: dark oak with black iron hinges and surrounded by a stone porch. Two metal lanterns serve as the exterior lights. I assume, from the angle at which the footage was shot, that the security camera is hidden behind the one on the right. But I can't even see it sitting this close. How would Jase have known there was a camera there?

Cynthia must see me staring at the light, because she says, 'Are you OK? You look as though you've seen a ghost.'

'When did you get the CCTV camera installed?'

Cynthia goes completely still. 'What?'

'The camera behind the light up there. When did you get it?'

'Oh, um . . . I . . . I'm not sure.'

I don't know if it's the firelight distorting things, but it looks as if the colour has completely drained from her face. She's refusing to meet my eye.

Puzzle pieces start slotting together in my mind; a sudden, hideous moment of comprehension. My heart is beating so fast, I can feel it in my throat as realisation slithers down my spine.

'Jase didn't send me that letter, did he?'

Cynthia lets out a forced half-laugh. Her hands are trembling, her wedding ring tapping against the glass as she grips on to it. 'What letter?'

And that's all the confirmation I need. Jase wasn't threatening me at all. Cynthia was.

CHAPTER FORTY-THREE

STEFANI

Twelve Days After the Murder

Stefani is lying awake on top of her made bed, picking at her fingernails. She was instructed to go home and get some sleep, since she's been clocking in so many extra hours lately and now that Jase is in custody, there's no need for her to be at the station until the morning when questioning resumes. But she's past the point of sleep. Her brain won't switch off. It just keeps running through everything like a movie strip on loop.

Jase is still maintaining that he didn't kill Hannah. His story makes sense: how he followed Hannah home and got into an argument with Daniel, how he told Daniel to go camping, right up until the bit where he says he was called into work and never saw Hannah again. His phone records confirm that someone from the hospital did indeed call him, and that the call was answered, and the CCTV at the hospital confirms he did turn up to work and stayed there until 3 a.m. But even though his story does all check out, there's no saying he didn't kill Hannah, get rid of her body and *then* go into work so that he had an alibi. He's obviously a man of low morality to have slept with Hannah in the first place. It's not a far stretch to think he could be a murderer. But there's one thing that's bothering Stefani. It's what Alex said at the hospital. If she had found out he was the killer, why didn't he kill her too to stop himself from getting caught? Maybe murdering his teenage lover was doable but his wife of twenty-three years was a step too far?

Frustration building, Stefani sits up and grabs her phone. Davies is still working; they're going to swap in the morning. She calls his mobile as opposed to the station, and he picks up after the second ring.

'What are you still doing up?' he says.

'I need you to do me a favour. Can you send everything we have on the suspects' alibis from the night Hannah died to my laptop?'

Davies' sigh rattles down the phone. 'Stef, give it a rest will you. We've got him. It's only a matter of time until he cracks under pressure.'

'Please. You know I wouldn't ask unless I had real reason to.'

More sighs and huffs, before Davies finally says, 'Fine. But Walton won't like it.'

Stefani bites down the urge to say that she doesn't care what Walton thinks, and thanks him. She moves to her work-issued laptop and watches her inbox eagerly, refreshing every couple of seconds. After what feels like an eternity, an email pops up from Davies. It has attachments of each key suspect's alibi; files that Stefani has looked at countless times already. But the last time she pored over them was before Jase was arrested. Maybe, with what she knows now, she'll spot something she previously missed.

She starts by going over Jase's alibi one more time, but there's no way to prove what he did between leaving the house after the argument with Hannah and Daniel and heading back into work. That one's a dead end. She moves swiftly on to Mark's. Again, there is CCTV evidence of him at the hotel he stated he was staying at for his business trip. There is that gap still where he left the hotel that night and they lose him on the street cameras, but he was only gone for three hours. Stefani checks on Google maps how long it would take for him to get home and back, and the journey totals two hours and forty-five minutes. That would only leave him fifteen minutes to kill Hannah and dispose of her body, which seems unlikely. There is also the lack of motive, now that they've ascertained that Jase was the mystery lover. Stefani dismisses him as another dead end.

Alex's alibi is the most difficult to confirm. She was at the farm the whole night, so they've only got Cynthia's recollection of the evening and Alex's word to go on. Could she have found out about the affair and killed Hannah in a fit of rage? Perhaps she left the firepit earlier than Cynthia remembers, and she overheard the argument between

Jase, Hannah and Daniel? Of course, the whole reason Daniel went camping was so that he didn't spill the beans to his mother, but who's to say she didn't already know? Stefani highlights Alex's name as a definite possibility.

Daniel has been released now, but that's not to say he's no longer a suspect. He could equally have killed Hannah in a rage after finding out she was cheating on him with his dad. They've confirmed that he left work early that night, which coincides with his and Jase's recollection of the argument. But between Alex being with Cynthia and Jase getting called into the hospital, there are definite gaps where he could have quite easily killed Hannah. Stefani still feels in her gut that he's innocent, but gut instinct won't be enough for Walton. She highlights his name also.

Finally, she moves over to Cynthia and Bradley's alibis, which sort of coincide with each other. According to Cynthia, straight after Alex left the firepit, she drove to pick up Bradley from a club in town, and, as far as she knew, Hannah was with friends. Clearly, she didn't have the best grasp on her daughter's social life since Hannah managed to travel to a seedy hotel, sleep with a man old enough to be her father and get into an argument with him and her boyfriend when she got home without Cynthia even realising she'd returned. There is CCTV footage that shows Cynthia pulling up to the club at 12.10 a.m., so that checks out, but something feels off.

She returns to Google maps and types in the address of the club. Her eyes narrow as she stares at the numbers on the screen, adding it all up in her head. The timings don't quite work. Cynthia said she left to pick him up immediately after Alex left, which they've both confirmed was around 10.45 p.m. But it only takes forty minutes to drive from the farm to the club, which would have her arriving at around 11.25 p.m. That's a whole forty-five minutes off. So what was Cynthia doing in the time between Alex storming off and leaving to pick up Bradley? And why would she lie about her movements that night?

Stefani massages her temples as her head spins. There's no motive there. Why would Cynthia want to kill her own daughter? Unless of course . . .

Theories flash through her mind. It could have been an accident. Perhaps she found out that Hannah was pregnant, that her Oxbridge-bound high-achieving daughter wasn't quite as perfect as she wanted her to be. Maybe they got into a fight and Cynthia unintentionally killed her, then tried to cover it up. It's definitely possible. Could Stefani be onto something, or is her tired, overworked brain piecing together something that isn't even there?

And then another thought occurs to Stefani, one which sends her blood running cold. Alex and Daniel have returned to the farm. If Cynthia really did kill Hannah, they could be in danger. She pulls out her phone and dials Alex's number. It rings and rings and rings, and then finally goes to voicemail. It's late; she could very well be asleep. But Stefani's internal alarm is ringing, screeching at her, telling her something is wrong. She tries again and still it goes to voicemail.

CHAPTER FORTY-FOUR

ALEX

Twelve Days After the Murder

My phone buzzes in my pocket, but I'm frozen to the spot, unable to move. All I can do is stare at Cynthia as she flounders for something to say, some way to explain the threatening note. How could I have been so stupid? I'd been so sure that Mark was the one blackmailing me that I never even for a second considered Cynthia.

My mouth is dry and sticky. I'm completely out of my depth. I don't know what to say to my best friend of nearly thirty years right now. But I can't let her see how rattled I am.

'Don't bother trying to think of a lie,' I say, forcing my voice to sound calm and measured, projecting a confidence that I most definitely do not feel.

'Why would I lie to you? You're my oldest friend.'

She doesn't even realise it, but she's made a mistake. I've known her long enough to know when she's hiding something. Cynthia is the type of person to take a false accusation terribly. She should be ranting, defensive, incredulous right now. Instead, she's trying to match my level of calm. It's obvious it's an act.

'*You* sent me that note telling me to stop digging. *You* threatened me with the video. You'd have only done that if . . .' I can't bring myself to say it, but what other explanation is there?

Part of me is hoping if I say it out loud she'll snap out of it and call me a bitch for even suggesting such a thing and come out with some perfectly logical explanation for all of this. But I don't need to say it. Cynthia's facade has slipped. She falters, a sob escaping her lips, then crumples, her faux-baffled expression collapsing. A strangulated choking sound escapes from deep inside her throat.

'I killed her!' She buries her face in her hands. 'I didn't mean to! But when she told me she was pregnant . . . I just lost it and . . . it was an accident.'

'A fatal accident.' I watch her as she sobs, still in disbelief that she's actually admitted it. Her cries mix with the wind whistling across the field around us, picking up leaves and swirling them through the air as if it's playing a game with them. They drift over to the pig barn and I flinch. I've purposefully avoided looking at that cursed building every time I've returned to the farm since that night. To look at the pig barn is to remember what I did. Such a heinous act, one I'll never forgive myself for. But I did it for my son. I did what any mother would do, didn't I?

My gaze drifts back to Cynthia, whose tear-stained face is now watching me expectantly. She's probably waiting for me to call the police.

I did what any mother would do.

The phrase repeats in my head on a loop. I shake my head slowly.

And then I say, 'I don't believe you. You couldn't kill Hannah, Cynthia. You couldn't do that.'

Cynthia twitches, looks bewildered at my U-turn. 'I just admitted that I did. You know I sent you the camera footage.'

'Yes, you told me to stop digging,' I say, clenching my hands together. 'Which is exactly what I would have done if Daniel had been the killer. I was willing to do what I did, to clean up the crime scene and get rid of poor Hannah's body to protect him. Just like you're willing to take the fall to protect Bradley.'

CHAPTER FORTY-FIVE

HANNAH

The Day of the Murder – 10.20 p.m.

My breath mists the air as I trudge home. I place my hand back on my stomach, tears sploshing down my cheeks. I don't know who I was kidding thinking I could raise this kid. I can't even protect him or her while they're inside me. Jase tried to insist on taking me to get checked out at the hospital after he hit me – not his hospital mind; God forbid his colleagues find out about his dirty little secret – but I didn't want him anywhere near me. Now I'm regretting the decision to turn him down but am too proud to go back and ask him for a lift. I'll see how I feel tomorrow and go and get checked out if I'm still sore. I still need to figure out what to do.

I give our house a wide berth as I approach, so as not to accidentally get spotted by Mum. The last thing I need is to run into her now. There'd be no hiding that something is wrong, and if she found out about the pregnancy, that would be the decision made for me. I'd be on my way to the abortion clinic before I could even draw a breath to argue. No, I need to figure this out for myself.

An odd sense of déjà vu washes over me as I sneak back through the kitchen door. When I left just under three hours ago, everything was perfect. My fantasy life with Jase and our baby was tangible, reachable. Now I'm totally lost. How can things change so much in such a short amount of time?

It's still early, but I can't think of anything I want to do more than curl up in my bed. I'm feeling tender and nauseous. Whether it's from everything that's happened or from the pregnancy, I'm not sure. But

I do know that I want to sleep it off. I plod up the stairs and cross the hallway to my room.

'You're home late.'

Bradley's voice makes me jump and I spin around. He's leaning against the door frame of his bedroom, arms crossed, mouth pulled into one of his cocky smirks. His pupils are tiny. I grimace. Mum and Mark are so bloody naive to have not figured out Bradley's coke habit yet. They didn't even question when he suddenly started strutting around in expensive trainers and splurging on AirPods. His crappy little Co-op job isn't exactly a big earner. It doesn't take a genius to figure out he's dealing as well now.

I'm disgusted to call him my brother.

I roll my eyes. 'Sorry, I didn't realise I had to keep you updated on my whereabouts.'

He doesn't say anything, just gives me this horrid grin.

'I'm going to bed,' I say, turning away from him.

'I found your test.'

I stop. Nailed to the floor by a creeping dread, I can't move.

'You what?'

'Your pregnancy test? Found it stuffed in the bin. Naughty, naughty.'

I curse myself for putting it in there instead of taking it with me. I got so flustered with Bradley banging on the door, I didn't even think. I don't know what to do. I'm too tired for this. I feel as though I'm trapped in some godawful nightmare. Bradley is standing opposite me as if he were squaring up to someone, ready to fight.

'What do you want?' I say quietly.

His mouth twists up at the sides. Not quite a smile, more a sneer. 'Oh, I don't know. Maybe I should let Mum know that Little Miss Perfect isn't quite so perfect after all.' His words come out harsh and bitter, spittle flying each time he says the word 'perfect'.

Panic starts to rise in my core.

'Maybe,' he continues, starting to move towards the stairs, 'she'll stop getting on my fucking back constantly. Maybe she'll stop asking me why I'm such a fucking disappointment. Why I'm not as fucking successful as my fucking sister!'

'Please . . .' I run after him, bile rising in my mouth. My feet trip over themselves as I follow him down the stairs. When we reach the bottom, I grab his shoulder, willing him to stop soldiering towards the firepit. 'Bradley! Please, I'm begging you not to say anything. I'm sorry, OK? I'm sorry that she makes you feel like that, but it's not my fault!'

'Nothing ever is, is it, sis?' He rounds on me, eyes fiery. There's no talking him down when he's like this. Our relationship is strained at the best of times. When he's high, it's downright warlike – who will beat the other down first?

'No! It's not my fault!' I screech at him, all the anger and hurt from this evening bursting out of me in an avalanche. 'If you tell Mum about the test, I'll tell her what you've been doing. Your little moneymaking venture will be over!' I yank one of his sleeves up, revealing a maze of inflamed track marks and puncture wounds along his arm.

He pushes me away and storms into the living room, but I'm not done. I've had enough of people pushing me around today. This was the final straw. Bradley has unwittingly unleashed an enraged, resentful beast. I charge after him and throw myself in front of him, getting right up in his face.

'Maybe if you got your shit together and stopped with all this, Mum would actually be proud to call you her son!'

He moves so quickly, I don't even have time to register what he's doing. There's a crashing sound, then a shrill ringing, and I feel a sharp, burning pain on the side of my head. My body has gone unresponsive. None of my limbs are working, neither is my mouth. Even my eyes don't seem to be functioning. All I can see is white. And then I realise why. I'm lying on the floor, staring at the ceiling. Why am I lying on the floor?

The white turns to black as I blink, but it takes longer than usual to open my eyes again, more effort. What the hell is wrong with me? Why is it so hard to keep my eyes open? When I do eventually force them open, I can see Bradley hovering over me, his hands in his hair. He's saying something; his mouth is moving, but I can't hear properly. Everything is muffled as if I'm buried under my duvet. I wish I was buried under my duvet. I'm so bloody cold and tired. I want to go to bed.

I try to say Bradley's name. I need him to help me, to go and get Mum or call an ambulance. But nothing leaves my mouth. There's something in his hand. I squint at it, wishing the room would stop spinning enough for me to figure out what's going on. It's grandma's vase, the blue and white one Mum displays so proudly on the coffee table. But it's broken. The bottom seems to have come away, leaving a sharp, jagged edge, and it's covered in blood. Why is it covered in blood?

My gaze moves to Bradley's face. He's got a bizarre look in his eyes and it sends a flash of fear through me. I twist away from him, try to drag myself along the floor, but it's like every limb has run out of battery. He kneels down beside me as he watches me struggle. And then I realise what he's doing. What he's already done.

'Please . . .' I don't even know if the word has actually left my mouth or if I'm imagining things, but it doesn't matter. His hands find their way to my neck. His fingers dig in and there's an explosion of pain in my tendons.

Then everything is swirling. And slow. And black.

CHAPTER FORTY-SIX

ALEX

Twelve Days After the Murder

'I had to. I had no choice,' Cynthia finally says, her entire body trembling despite her proximity to the fire.

Nodding, I keep my voice as non-threatening as possible. 'Tell me what happened.'

She hesitates, then stands up and starts pacing wildly, her shadow dancing against the farmhouse brick. 'After you stormed off that night I went inside and . . .' She grimaces, clearly picturing the scene. 'And there she was. Just lying there. My little girl. And he was just standing over her, staring at her as if she was just asleep. He hadn't tried to call me or anything.'

She drags her fingernails down her face, leaving angry red marks which glisten under her tears, as the words pour out of her in a steady stream. 'I didn't know what to do. I went to call an ambulance . . . but Bradley grabbed the phone from me. He told me Hannah was already dead . . . and that I had to help him. He begged me. Got down on his knees and begged me to help him. And I . . . I couldn't lose both my children in one night.'

She falls to her knees now, digging her fingers into the bare earth below her as if she wishes it would swallow her up. I want to run to her and wrap her in my arms, but I'm paralysed. All I can do is watch her break down in front of me.

'I drove him to the club so that he'd have an alibi,' she continues. 'As far as anyone would know, he wasn't home all evening. I was going to bring him home and call the police. We were going to make it look like a forced entry, like a burglary gone wrong. But by the time we got back—'

'I'd already cleaned up the crime scene.'

She nods slowly. 'We looked at the security camera to try to figure out what had happened. If I'd known you'd get involved, I would never have—'

'Of course I was going to be involved!' I shout, surprising both of us. 'It doesn't take a genius to figure out my boy would be the prime suspect! Did you even think of that while you were busy saving your son? Or was it planned . . . because Daniel was an easy target?'

'No . . .' Her face creases and she buries it in her hands. 'I just acted on impulse. Nothing was planned. I'm so sorry, Alex!'

I exhale heavily, suddenly feeling very vulnerable. I need to call the police. I need someone here with me. I stand, moving at a snail's pace, and take a few wary steps away from the fire. Cynthia's eyes shoot up.

'Where are you going?'

I swallow, feel around in my pocket for my phone. It's there, a solid block of security, but I know if Cynthia were to go for me, I wouldn't be able to unlock it quick enough to call for help. I don't *think* she would hurt me, but I can't be sure. Again, I have to ask myself what I would be willing to do for Daniel.

'You can't leave,' Cynthia says, the sorrow and remorse in her face replaced by fierce determination. 'You can't tell anyone. Hannah's gone. Please, Alex. Mark has been drinking himself into oblivion. Bradley is all I have left.'

'Cynthia, I can't let Jase take the fall for murder.'

'Why not? After everything he did? He cheated on you with my eighteen-year-old daughter! Doesn't that make you want him to suffer?'

My breath hitches in my throat. The image of Jase and Hannah together is seared into my brain. I shake my head, willing it to evaporate. Part of me, a large part, wants to see him go down. But I've done too many awful things. If I ever want to have any hope of sleeping again, I just can't.

'Oh, he will suffer,' I say. 'He's going to lose everything. His family, his home, probably his career once they find out what he did. But he is not a murderer. It wouldn't be right.'

'If you leave I'll send the footage to the police! You'll go to prison. Maybe both of you will. It's not a far stretch to say you helped to cover up what your husband did. Who will look after Daniel then, with both of you locked up?'

I suck in a breath through my teeth at this manipulation. Cynthia knows the way to get me to do what she wants is to use Daniel. Again, I bite down on my fury, though, I need to keep a clear head. I straighten myself and look into her eyes.

'It's time to stop running,' I tell her coldly. 'We both need to own up to our mistakes.'

The colour drains from her face as she realises her ploy didn't work, that I've called her bluff, that she can't hold the footage over me anymore. Ignoring the pain of my oldest friend's betrayal, I turn my back on her and start making my way to my truck. I'll go straight to the police station, turn myself in before she can. I'll tell them everything; how I found Hannah, how I thought Daniel had killed her, how I got rid of the body, right up to everything I've found out about Cynthia and Bradley. If I'm to go to prison, so be it.

But before I can take another step, something hard impacts with the back of my head. There's hot, searing pain. Then blackness. An impenetrable darkness that consumes me.

CHAPTER FORTY-SEVEN

STEFANI

Twelve Days After the Murder

The engine roars as Stefani thunders down the road. Her body is flooded with adrenaline. She jabs at her phone in the Bluetooth holder, instructing it to call Alex again, but just like the previous five attempts, it rings a few times before going to voicemail.

'Fuck!' she cries out in frustration, swerving to avoid a rabbit in the road. Her body shakes with adrenaline as she steadies her car. When she first tried to call Alex, she had reasoned with herself that she might just be asleep, but with every failed attempt, the sense of dread has deepened. Something's wrong. She just knows it.

Her stomach flips as her phone starts to vibrate against the holder and she scrambles to answer the call while keeping her eyes on the road.

'Alex?'

'No, it's me.' Walton's voice crackles out of the speaker. 'Are you driving?'

Stefani's shoulders sag. 'Yes. I know you told me to wait—'

'I didn't just tell you to wait, DS Warner. I gave you a direct order! You are not permitted to go anywhere near that farm on your own.'

Even through the phone, Stefani can sense his anger, but she doesn't care.

'Is backup on its way?'

'Stefani, you need to come back to the station right now. Just because there are gaps in Cynthia's alibi, that doesn't prove anything. Let's talk this out here, and then if we still think it's necessary, I can send a team over to the farm.'

'Sir, with all due respect, by then it could be too late.'

Walton continues to rant down the phone, but Stefani is no longer listening. She's arrived. Slowing her car to a crawl, she hangs up on her boss. She'll pay for this later, no doubt.

Nothing on the farm looks out of place as far as she can see. There's no sign of anyone out and about, which isn't strictly surprising given the late hour, but there are lights on in both the farmhouse and Alex's house right on the other side of the field. There's another light too, in the barn halfway between the two homes. Loud screeching is echoing out from the breeze-block structure. It's the pigs. The times she's been here, she remembers the pigs squealing when someone entered their barn, restless, as if anticipating being fed. A chill, hundreds of tiny ants creep over her as she realises that's the sound they probably made when Hannah's cold dead body was thrown into the pen.

Someone is in there. Why would anyone be in there at this time of night?

She pulls up next to the gate and switches off the engine. Ideally, she'd want to stay in her car and drive up to the barn, but if she's right and Cynthia has attacked Alex, she has to be careful. If Alex is still alive, it would only take Cynthia hearing the engine of a car for her to panic and do something . . . stupid. She has to approach on foot.

She doesn't walk on the path for fear of getting spotted. Instead, she clambers over the stile and into the first field. Cuttings of wheat or some other type of grain – Stefani doesn't know much about farming – crunch underfoot. The pig barn doesn't look that far away, but now that she's making her way towards it, trying not to trip on the ridges of dried ploughed earth, it dawns on her just how far it is. It's not long before she's sweating, her shirt clinging to her skin.

'Help!' The scream that comes from the barn could easily be mistaken for a gust of wind whistling through the trees. It's almost ghostlike. But Stefani is sure now. It has to be Alex.

Finally, she's close enough to the barn that she can just about see through the doorway. Someone is in there. She can see their shadow moving across the wall, pacing. She readjusts her position slightly, trying to get a better vantage point, praying they won't be able to hear her heart battering against her ribcage. A sharp gasp escapes her throat as she spots someone else, huddled in a ball on the ground. It is Alex. She's tied up, her wrists and ankles bound by cable ties, her hair matted with blood.

Stefani pulls out her phone, rushing to turn the brightness down on her screen so as not to highlight her presence, and taps out a message to Walton.

I was right. Get backup here NOW!

'You don't want to do this,' Alex is saying. 'If you kill me, they'll know it was you. You know that, right?'

Stefani still can't see the pacing figure. They're hidden behind one of the walls and she can't get any closer without risking getting spotted. But she doesn't need to see who it is.

'Will you just shut up for a second and let me think!' the figure shouts.

It's not Cynthia at all. It's Bradley.

CHAPTER FORTY-EIGHT

ALEX

Twelve Days After the Murder

Bradley is still gripping the rifle tight, as if it's an extension of his arm. This is a working farm. I've been around guns most of my life. But never have they instilled so much fear in me.

'You made me do this,' Bradley says, not directing his words to me but to the air around him, as if he is merely thinking out loud. 'I gave you the chance. Mum and I told you to stop digging. Why wouldn't you stop?'

I tense. There's desperation in his voice, and desperation is dangerous, unpredictable. The only way I'm going to get out of this is to pander to him.

'I'm sorry, OK? You're right. I should have left it alone. But I still can.' I take a breath. 'If you let me go now, I won't say anything. I promise.'

'You're lying!' He's in my face now, the sudden movement causing me to shrink back against the barn wall.

'I'm not! As long as Daniel is safe, I'll stay quiet. Jase can go down for Hannah's murder. They'll never find anything tying you to it. I got rid of all the evidence!'

He hesitates, thoughts visibly ticking over in his head. Every muscle in my body is rigid, burning as I wait for his response.

His lips curl at the edges. 'No. I don't believe you. You won't be able to live with it. You're weak, just like my mum.'

As he says this, my eyes dart around the barn. Cynthia is nowhere to be seen. What happened after Bradley knocked me out? Did she just go back to the farmhouse, leaving her son to deal with me? Or did she try to help me?

'Where is she?'

His grip tightens on the gun, knuckles turning white. 'You're a mum, Alex,' he says. 'What are mums supposed to do for their kids?'

I shake my head, unsure of the reaction he wants.

'I asked you a question!'

Flinching, I search for something to say. The noise of the pigs is too loud. I can't think straight.

'Anything. They're supposed to do anything for their kids.'

'Yeah.' He nods, looking down at the dusty concrete beneath his feet. 'See? Why couldn't I have had a mum like you? You'd have done anything for Daniel. Anything to protect him.'

'Bradley, what did you do to your mum?'

I'm not sure if he's even heard me. He carries on, unyielding.

'She tried to stop me from tying you up. Said you were right and that we needed to stop running. She was going to turn me in, the fucking bitch!' He scrunches his free hand into a fist. 'She never cared about me. Not like she did Hannah. I was always her disappointment, the mistake she wished she'd never made. I'm so sick of her never putting me first. I thought after Hannah was gone things would be different, but they've got worse! It's as if . . . as if she hates me.'

As he rants, a flicker of movement catches the corner of my eye. I lean forward ever so slightly, praying that he doesn't notice. My eyes narrow to focus on the crack of the outside field that I can see from where I'm sitting.

Stefani.

My heart thunders as I sit back up straight. Stefani is here. The police are coming. I just need to keep him talking for a little bit longer. I need to get him to calm down, to see reason, before he snaps altogether.

CHAPTER FORTY-NINE

STEFANI

Twelve Days After the Murder

'Your mum did try to protect you though, Bradley,' Alex says carefully. 'She knew what you'd done and she didn't say anything.'

He lets out a mirthless laugh. 'She only agreed to drive me to the club and give me an alibi because she couldn't bear the shame of everyone knowing her screw-up of a kid is a murderer. It was never about keeping me safe. It was about keeping up appearances.'

'But she tried to blackmail me to stop digging. She wouldn't have gone that far just for the sake of appearances.'

'You really think that was her idea?' Finally, he steps into Stefani's view. She eyes the rifle in his hand, wondering just how many seconds it would take her to reach him if she sprinted. 'When we got home and found Hannah's body gone, it was me who remembered to check the security camera. Me who told her to keep the footage in case we needed leverage against you. She was going to turn herself in the second she realised you were involved! Not to mention when the police started questioning her precious husband. It's been like dealing with a fucking teenager. Like I said, she's weak.'

He used the present tense. Does that mean Cynthia is still alive?

'Bradley, listen to me. If you kill us both, the police will definitely know it was you,' Alex says.

'No.' He shakes his head wildly, as if trying to convince himself what he's saying is true. 'It could have been Mark. He's probably pissed out of his brain at the pub right now. He could have killed you both in a drunken rage. Or it could have been Daniel.'

Alex's face clouds at the mention of Daniel, but it's clear she knows not to retort. Bradley is volatile, a fuse ready to blow. Stefani knows she should wait for the backup to arrive, but she's not sure how much more time she's got. At any second he could turn the gun on Alex, and the likelihood of that happening only increases the longer this goes on.

'Think this through, Bradley,' Alex says. 'It's not going to work.'

'Shut up! SHUT UP! Let me fucking think!'

He throws his hands up to his ears, inadvertently dropping the rifle as he does so. Stefani doesn't hesitate. She launches herself forward, bursting into the barn. Bradley is momentarily caught off guard. His eyes flash as Stefani makes a grab for the rifle. She's almost too quick for him, but he gets there just at the same moment. They both scrabble on their knees for the gun. Her nails scrape against the concrete as Bradley yanks her back. He grabs a handful of her hair and she howls. Twisting back, she clamps her mouth around his forearm, sinking her teeth into his skin. A metallic taste seeps onto her tongue.

He falls back. 'Bitch!' he cries as he nurses his bloody arm.

Stefani grabs the rifle and swings it round, pointing the barrel directly at his head. He stares up at her, paralysed. For one long, agonising moment, neither of them speak.

'You can't kill me,' he says finally, his words puncturing the silence. 'You're a police officer.'

Stefani smirks. 'You're right.'

She pulls the barrel sideways, then swings. The cold metal impacts with his head and he collapses to the floor.

CHAPTER FIFTY

ALEX

Twelve Days After the Murder

I suck in a sharp breath as Bradley falls to the floor. Stefani stares at him for a moment, then drops the rifle and hurries over to me. She pulls out a Leatherman from her pocket and cuts the cable ties. Relief washes over me as my wrists are freed. I wince, eyes watering. Raw, angry lines stretch across my skin.

'Come on, let's get out of here before he comes to,' Stefani says, holding out her hand to help me up. I grip on to her as if I'll float away if she lets go, while she grips onto the rifle with the same intensity.

My ears ring as we step over the threshold of the pig barn. I never want to return to this building for as long as I live.

A laboured, helpless wail carries across the wind and we spin around in unison. Our eyes rake over the murky black of the solitary landscape, focusing on the gun shed in the next field over.

'Cynthia . . .' I whisper.

Stefani's gaze darts between the shed and the barn. Bradley is still lying motionless on the floor, but how long he'll stay there, we've no idea.

'Backup is coming,' she says, a cloud of condensation puffing out in front of her face. 'We should wait for them.'

The cry sounds again. It's not a human sound. It's tortured and anguished. Despite everything, I have to help her.

'If he wakes up before they arrive he'll kill her. We can't leave her.'

Stefani grimaces, looking longingly back at her car, then nods. 'OK, let's go.'

It's quicker to cross the field than to round all the way to the dirt path. A more direct route. But the hay in this field has yet to be cut. It's tall, up to our waists, making it impossible to keep an eye out for burrowing holes. Stefani trips after a few paces, and no sooner have I helped her back up than my foot plunges down into one too. The shed twists in front of me as I fall and I grit my teeth as my ankle twists. There is a sickening snapping sound and pain erupts behind my kneecap.

'Are you OK?' Stefani says as she offers me her elbow to grip on to so that I can pull myself back to standing. I nod silently, biting back the tears, and we hobble on, with me leaning on Stefani for support.

We finally make it to the shed. Cynthia's cries are still carrying over the wind, but now that there's just a thin wall of brick between us I can hear the grief in them. Grief for Hannah and for Bradley. As a mother, I know that love doesn't just stop for your child, however they behave.

I round to the front of the shed and go to pull open the door, but am met with the clunk of locks.

'Shit . . .' I whisper, worried Bradley will hear me, even from this distance. 'He's locked the door.'

Stefani bangs her fist against the wood. 'Cynthia? Can you hear us?'

The sobbing ceases, then Cynthia whimpers, 'Yes. My leg. He hit it with the rifle. I think it's broken.'

I look back at the barn, terrified I'm going to see Bradley sprinting towards us, but there's still no sign of him.

'How long until your backup arrives?' I say.

Stefani checks her phone. 'I . . . I'm not sure . . .'

'What's the matter?'

'The message,' she says, anxiously. 'I messaged for backup, but it didn't send.'

'The signal is really bad out here,' I say, my shoulders dropping. The flicker of hope I'd felt when I spotted Stefani outside the barn snuffed out.

Stefani leans against the wall of the shed while I wrack my brains for something to do. I glance over to our home and wish Daniel had come with me after all. If he was with us, he'd have heard mine and Cynthia's cries for help.

'Help me knock the door down.' I take a few steps back and plant my feet to the ground, knees bent. Stefani hesitates, but does the same. 'Move out the way of the door if you can, Cynthia!'

There is a rustling as she drags herself away. 'OK!' she calls from inside.

'Ready?' I say, bracing myself. 'After three. One, two, three!'

We both run full force, crashing our shoulders against the wood of the door. Fire shoots up my arm and into my neck as I stagger backwards. The door remains steady, unyielding.

'This isn't going to work,' Stefani pants, rubbing her shoulder.

I glance at the gun in Stefani's hand. 'What if you shoot the lock?'

She shakes her head. 'That only works in movies. We're more likely to hurt ourselves with flying shrapnel than get the lock open.'

'Well, we can't just leave her.' The wobble in my voice betrays me, letting out the panic I've been trying to smother.

Stefani thinks for a moment, then looks back at the barn. She takes a deep breath.

'Stay here,' she says. 'I'm going to go and get the key.'

CHAPTER FIFTY-ONE

STEFANI

Twelve Days After the Murder

Stefani doesn't want to go back. Every instinct in her body is screaming at her not to return to that godforsaken pig barn. But she became a police officer for a reason, to help others, and so she trudges on. She settles into a rhythm, stepping over the earth ridges, trying to remember where the holes are that they fell down before. Just a little bit further. She'll get there, recover the key, free Cynthia and then they'll all drive away from this farm. Just a little bit further.

Finally, she reaches the stile and clambers over it, nearing the barn. The pigs are still screeching. Angry that they've not been fed. She peers back at the gun shed, but it's too dark. Even with the moonlight beaming down, casting a ghostlike glow over the fields, she can't see Alex anymore. She tightens her grip on the rifle, the heaviness of it in her palm the only thing keeping her going.

Bradley is still lying on his back on the straw-covered concrete, exactly where she had left him. His chest is rising and falling, but apart from that he is still. She swallows hard as she edges towards him, closer and closer, and crouches beside him. Her hand trembles as she gently reaches for his jacket pocket and slides her hand inside. There's nothing in there. She tries in the other pocket. This time, her fingers brush against a packet of chewing gum and what feels like a used tissue. She shudders and retracts her hand. Where is the key? Her heart skips as she lifts one side of his jacket, exposing his T-shirt underneath. There's an inside pocket. It's zipped.

Stefani's mouth fills with saliva and for a moment she thinks she might vomit, but she gulps it down, gripping on to the zip and sliding it down. She keeps her eyes fixed on Bradley's face, watching for any twitch, any sign that he might be waking up. Her fingers reach into the silky lining of the inside pocket and loop around something hard and cold. She's got it.

CHAPTER FIFTY-TWO

ALEX

Twelve Days After the Murder

I can't see Stefani. I have no way of knowing if she's managed to find the key or if she's even safe. All I can do is stand here, leaning up against the door, feeling utterly helpless. I tilt my head to the side as I listen to Cynthia's whimpers. She's stopped howling now she knows help is coming, but the hurt and the heartbreak hasn't ceased.

'Cynth?' I say, tracing the hinges of the door with my fingers. They're ice cold.

'Mmm?'

'I'm sorry for what I did to Hannah.'

Tears prick at my eyes as the words leave my mouth, and a heaviness settles into my gut, as if I've swallowed cement. I've realised, as I've stood here waiting for Stefani to return, that it's not just me who has been living with this horrendous secret. Cynthia has too. She's known all along what happened to her daughter, and she hasn't been allowed to even attempt to come to terms with it. She was wrong to give Bradley an alibi. Everyone will know that. The law will see it that way, as will the papers and the people who read them. But can I really judge her for that decision? Has she been punished enough? Have I?

A rustling sounds and I squint, peering across the wheat field. A figure is wading towards me through the stems, but the light in the barn behind them has plunged them into a silhouette. I can't tell who it is. My muscles tense as I watch the figure get closer, wishing Stefani had left the rifle with me. I'm ready. If it's Bradley, I can make a run for it.

Finally, the figure is close enough that I can just about make out their features in the moonlight. It's Stefani. She holds her hand up triumphantly, though I can't see what she's holding.

'I've got it!' she calls.

Dizzying relief flushes through me, my limbs shaking as they relax. This is nearly over. Just a few more steps and Stefani will be here with the key.

And then I see it. Another dark figure, directly behind Stefani. Terror trickles down my spine.

'Stefani! Behind you!'

But it's too late. Bradley launches at her, throwing his arm around her throat. My brain doesn't get a chance to process what's happening. Stefani thrashes and flails as Bradley tightens on her throat, cutting off her airway. She attempts to reach up and prise his arm away, but her efforts are futile. He's caught her at an awkward angle. She can't get any leverage. Her boots are skidding across the dirt.

'Bradley! Stop!' I shriek as I stumble towards them, my attempt to reach them hindered by my twisted ankle, but he doesn't let up.

'Get . . . Cynthia . . .' Stefani gurgles. Then, with one swift motion, she launches her arm up and a small shadow flies through the air. I just about see the glint of moonlight on metal before it plummets back to earth. The key.

I fall to my knees where I think it landed, desperately feeling around the soil. Sharp rocks and dead stalks of wheat stab into my palms. A frustrated scream bubbles in my throat, but just before it escapes my mouth, my wedding ring clinks against something round and cold. I snatch the key ring up and haul myself back to standing, just in time to see Stefani's eyes rolling back into her head. She stops fighting, stops flailing and goes limp.

I was too slow.

Bradley hurls her to one side and her body disappears amongst the crops, landing with a stomach-turning thud. I feel as though I've been punched in the gut. I can't breathe. Can't think.

He tilts his head, bends down to inspect her body, and I take the opportunity. I twist on my heel and limp back to the shed, force myself through the razor-sharp pain that's shooting up and down my leg, and shove the key into the lock.

Cynthia practically falls through the door as it swings open and we collapse in a tangle of limbs on the hard ground. I grip on to her and she on to me as we pull ourselves up, both with our pathetic injured legs. We don't dare to look to see how close Bradley is. We just move, staggering in the opposite direction, towards my house.

I hear it a second before I feel it. The gunshot ripping through the air. Then I'm swallowed up in a world of red-hot agony.

CHAPTER FIFTY-THREE

ALEX
Twelve Days After the Murder

The explosion of pain is unlike anything I've felt before. I hunch down, back arched, and let out a strangulated wail as I cradle my hand. Blood is streaming from the congealed mess where my index finger should be. My vision turns hazy, misting at the edges. It's too much to bear.

Hands, Cynthia's hands, slide under my armpits and pull me forward. I can't even focus on where we're going or what we're doing. All I can think about is the pain.

Another shot rumbles through the night, sending birds flapping, terrified, out of the nearby trees, and we duck and somehow it misses us.

We walk faster. Each step is agony. My chest is heaving with the effort of breathing. Saliva sprays out of my mouth, sweat drips off my hair, as we drag ourselves towards my house. The truck parked up outside is like a beacon. The only thing I can see. I scramble about in my pocket for my key fob and press down to unlock the doors. Cynthia hobbles into the back while I throw myself into the driver's seat. I jam the key into the ignition and turn it with my good hand, while the bloodied remains of my other hand lie limp in my lap. The engine judders, then dies.

'Fuck!' I try again. 'Come on, come on, COME ON!'

It sputters a few more times, then finally rumbles to life. Cynthia knocks the gearstick into first for me. I'm just about to release the clutch when Bradley springs out of the wheat field, onto the dirt track. Now that he's standing in the glow of the headlights, his face is properly visible, and I see it in his eyes. Wild. Barbaric.

He points the rifle at the windscreen. I follow the aim of the barrel with my eyes and it plays out like a movie in my head. The bullet puncturing through the glass as if it were nothing more than a flimsy piece of paper, then burrowing itself into my skull, blood spraying everywhere, the life leaving me in a fraction of a second. Daniel would have to identify my body. I'd never see him again. Never be able to hold him again. Suddenly I'm filled with renewed focus. I will not let Bradley tear me away from my son.

My foot stamps down on the accelerator. The engine roars, screaming in protest. I release the clutch and dust kicks up around us as the wheels spin. Bradley doesn't have time to respond. The truck powers forward, Cynthia screams behind me, and then it's as if the only sound in the world is Bradley's bones breaking as the bonnet smacks against his waist and he is dragged under.

@itsmeg175: Oh how I wish this trial would be livestreamed. What I'd give to be a fly on the wall! #JusticeForHannah

@carocarobear: I hope both of them get life. It's what they deserve!

@vegan_lover: You have got to ask yourself what you'd have done in that situation though. Mother's instincts and all that.

@simonLpaul: @vegan_lover Mother's instincts my arse. None of it should ever have happened #JusticeForHannah

@itsmeg175: Do people really believe the boyfriend had nothing to do with it??

@vegan_lover: @itsmeg175 The two mothers gave a full confession. What more do you want?

@carocarobear: Tbh even if the boyfriend didn't do it I still reckon he should be locked up somewhere . . .

CHAPTER FIFTY-FOUR

ALEX

Four Years After the Murder

My heels click along the pavement as I walk. I glance down at my watch. I'm running a couple of minutes early, but that doesn't bother me. I'd rather have a few extra minutes to psych myself up. Already my face is burning, the thought of what I'm about to do making me feel sick. It's been so long since I talked about what happened, and I'm not sure I'm ready to go there again just yet.

My hands are sweating in my gloves, but I don't want to take them off. In prison, nobody batted an eye at my four fingers. Most of the women I interacted with had scars of some description. But in the two weeks since I was released, I still haven't got used to the looks I get when I'm walking down the street. I have an appointment to see someone about a prosthetic finger next week, but I haven't decided if I'm actually going to go yet.

I approach the café we've agreed to meet at and take a second to hover outside. I never felt particularly comfortable in busy cities before, but I'm even less so after my time inside. I suppose I understand Daniel's reasons for moving to London. It's a world away from where everything happened, and he's desperate to forget. To move on. He's been good enough to take me into his rented flat while I figure out what I'm going to do with my freedom, so I can't complain too much about the noise and the feeling of never being able to slow down.

My eyes fix on a table through the window of the café and my breath hitches. She's already here, even earlier than me. She catches me staring and straightens herself, waving enthusiastically.

The bell above the door rings as I step inside and I immediately want to shrink down to the size of an ant. Even now, four years on, I hate the feeling of attention being drawn to me, the sensation that people are watching me. Did that person look up because they recognised me from the news? Do they know what I did? I'm just imagining things, of course. No one is really looking at me. They're all locked deep into their private conversations. The only person looking at me is Stefani.

'Hi.' I force a smile as I pull out the chair opposite her and take a seat.

'Hey, I got here a little early, so I took the liberty of ordering a bite to eat.'

She pushes a plate towards me with two pain au chocolats, warm, with the chocolate oozing out of the sides. The buttery scent makes my stomach growl, but I'm feeling too nauseous to eat.

'Thank you. I think I need a coffee first though,' I say, and head over to the counter to order a couple of lattes.

When I return, cups in hand, I'm met with one of those awkward silences where neither one of us is sure who should speak first. While I search for something to say, I take a sip of my coffee, not even caring that it's burning my lips, and try not to look at the darkening around Stefani's neck. The scar left from our ordeal.

It was a miracle she survived, honestly. It was very hit-and-miss for a long time. She was in intensive care in a medically induced coma for weeks while they tried to ascertain whether the lack of oxygen had damaged her brain. Those few weeks were pure hell for me. The thought of someone else suffering with brain damage because of me was more than I could bear. But she pulled through against all odds, and she got in touch just days after my release. I'm still not sure exactly why she wanted to see me. I suppose we all need some kind of closure.

'How have you been?' I say eventually.

'Good. I've been good. I'm still a police officer but have chosen to work more behind the desk. I'm still helping people but . . .' She trails off, then lets out a small laugh. 'I think I've seen enough action to last me a lifetime.'

I smile. 'Yes, I don't blame you.'

'Besides, the hours are far more flexible. I'm able to see Cassie a lot more, which is good.'

'That's great. How is she?'

Stefani smiles, that look that only a mother can give when thinking about their child. 'She's doing well. She's graduating from uni this year, got her BA in photography, and she's going to stay with me for the summer. It's going to be the longest I've had her for . . . well, since Luke and I divorced.'

'Stefani, that's . . . that's really wonderful. I'm happy for you.'

Several beats pass.

'What about you?' she prompts. 'Any plans for life on the outside?'

I bite down on my lip. 'I'm not sure yet. I can't go back to farming, but that's all I've ever known. You'd have thought four years in prison would have given me enough time to figure it out, but apparently not.'

I run my finger along the rim of my cup, thinking back to the moment I was sentenced. Stefani's testimony did help, as did Cynthia's. The court was able to prove that Bradley murdered Hannah, and that my killing him was an act of self-defence. But there was no way I was going to get away with what I did to Hannah's body. I was charged with unlawful burial, and Cynthia and I were both charged with perverting the course of justice. Cynthia still has two years left on her clock. If I'm totally honest with myself, I wish I'd been given longer. I don't feel like I deserve to be thinking about what my life will look like from here on out when Hannah can't.

'Daniel's done really well for himself,' I say, giving myself a little shake. 'He's training to be a social worker now. And he's got a lovely girlfriend. They're expecting a baby at the end of the year.'

'Oh, Alex. That's wonderful news.'

I nod, feeling my chest swell with pride. I still can't believe I'm going to be a gran. I thought it would make me feel old, but I can't wait. Even without the farm, at least this baby will give me some purpose. Of course, it does mean I can't sleep on his sofa bed forever, and I won't want to be too far away, so it looks like I'll have to get used to busy, crowded, concrete London.

'So,' I say, taking another sip of my coffee. It's cooled down a little now and I relax into the warm liquid trickling down my throat. 'Why do I sense that you asked me here for more than a catch-up?'

Stefani blushes and picks at one of the pastries, bits of yellow flaking off onto the plate. 'Well, as I said, I've moved to more of a desk job. And part of my role is to ensure our police units are working efficiently and to the best of our ability. I coordinate various training seminars and conferences, and they're attended by police officers from across the country.'

I nod, though inwardly I've no idea what any of this has to do with me. She stops picking at the pastry and sits back in her chair.

'The conference I've been working on has been a bit of a passion project of mine. It's been in development for over a year, and I've really had to fight to get it into circulation. There were a lot of questions about whether we needed it or not, but it's finally been accepted and will begin in two months.'

'What is it?'

'Protecting the Welfare of Vulnerable People in Police Custody. We're going to be re-evaluating all processes when it comes to holding, questioning and interrogating suspects who are considered vulnerable. This could be Black and minority ethnic groups, those with learning difficulties, those with mental health conditions or . . .' She pauses, but I already know what she's going to say.

'Those with brain damage,' I finish for her.

'Yes. I spoke to someone once who said it was all too easy to blame people like your son for crimes they didn't commit and his words have never left my head. I want to try to ensure that's not the case.'

My eyes are inadvertently filling with tears. I want to jump up and wrap my arms around her. It takes everything in me to keep my composure.

Stefani looks at me intently. 'I'd like you to be a speaker at the conference. They need to hear from someone other than another police officer. Someone who has been affected by these issues.'

I gape at her. 'You want me to speak in front of a crowd of police officers?'

'I know it sounds intimidating. But you'll have plenty of time to practise, and of course it would be paid.'

I shake my head, the very thought of it causing sweat to prickle on the back of my neck. 'I'm really sorry, Stefani, but I don't think I can.'

Stefani nods, the disappointment clear as day on her face. Before she can say anything, her phone starts to ring. I politely look away and focus on nibbling at the pain au chocolat while she answers it. When she hangs up, a pained look crosses her face.

'I'm so sorry. I'm going to have to shoot off.' She rummages about in her handbag and pulls out a card, sliding it across the table. 'My number's on there. Just promise me you'll have a think about it.'

I take the card and flip it over in my hands a few times.

'I'll think about it,' I say. 'It was lovely seeing you.'

'You too. Give my best to Daniel.'

Hauling her bag onto her shoulder, she gives a friendly wave to the girl behind the coffee counter and leaves. I look down at the card again, pressing my lips together.

I was asked so many times while I was in prison what I wanted to do when I got out. We had group sessions where my fellow inmates made all sorts of plans. A handful wanted to do some form of charity work as a way of recompense for their sins. A few wanted to go back to education, and lots wanted to continue with passions they'd discovered during their time inside. But I was never sure what to say when it came to my turn.

I know what Daniel would say. *'Of course you should do it, Mum. You wanted something to do, some direction in life. Why not use your free time for good?'*

I suppose I could make a difference. It's not a completely ridiculous idea.

The bell on the door rings again as a group of chattering teenage girls bundle inside, and a cool breeze follows them, brushing over my face before the door swings shut again. I have no other plans for my day. I'm free as a bird, can go in whatever direction the wind takes me.

I finish off my pastry and coffee and leave a large tip on the table. Then, clutching Stefani's card in my hand, I make my way back out onto the street. I breathe in the air around me and listen to the life buzzing around me.

    I can sense it now, for the first time since I stepped foot outside the prison. My next chapter.

ACKNOWLEDGEMENTS

It goes without saying that the characters portrayed in this book are entirely fictional. However, I do have to first and foremost extend my heartfelt thanks to 'E', for letting me talk to him for hours on end about his experience recovering from severe brain trauma. It's thanks to him that I was able to understand Daniel's character properly and really explore the stigma attached to brain damage.

Of course, I can never thank my editor, Hannah Smith, enough for deciding my writing was worth being published back in 2021. Thank you not only for believing in me, but for your endless hard work and support. Thanks also to Emily Thomas, Sandra Ferguson, Jen Porter, Marina Stavropoulou and the entire Embla Books team for being an absolute powerhouse!

I couldn't do any of this without my incredible agent Emily Glenister, who has been my rock throughout my writing career so far. Apologies for the late-night stress-emails and WhatsApp messages (I am sane – I promise!) and thank you from the bottom of my heart for championing me and my work.

Infinite thanks to my husband for keeping me grounded and giving me a boost of inspiration when I needed it. Thanks also to my mum, my dad and stepmum, my grandad, my brother and sister and all of my lovely in-laws for cheering me on.

Thank you to Lauren North for continuing to be one of my biggest supporters, and to TM Logan and Sarah Pearse for helping me to celebrate my debut.

Finally, huge thanks to William Shaw and David Fenell. I wrote the first three chapters of this novel at a writing workshop at The Bookmakers in Brighton (the brainchild of William and hosted by David) and it was the kick up the bum I needed to get this story started.

ABOUT THE AUTHOR

Becca Day lives in Surrey with her husband, two daughters and cocker spaniel. She studied acting at Guildford College and went on to start her own Murder Mystery theatre troupe. It was this move that inspired her love of crime fiction, and when she sold the company, she threw herself head first into crime writing. Her short fiction has won several prizes and *The Girl Beyond the Gate* was her first full-length novel. Aside from writing, she is also an avid reader and runs Reading Parties with fellow author William Shaw.

ABOUT EMBLA BOOKS

Embla Books is a digital-first publisher of standout commercial adult fiction. Passionate about storytelling, the team at Embla publish books that will make you 'laugh, love, look over your shoulder and lose sleep'. Launched by Bonnier Books UK in 2021, the imprint is named after the first woman from the creation myth in Norse mythology, who was carved by the gods from a tree trunk found on the seashore – an image of the kind of creative work and crafting that writers do, and a symbol of how stories shape our lives.

Find out about some of our other books and stay in touch:

Twitter, Facebook, Instagram: @emblabooks
Newsletter: https://bit.ly/emblanewsletter